THUNDERSTRUCK

by

KENDALL GRACE

Dedication

To my son and daughter. Mom loves you.

Acknowledgements

Heartfelt thanks to Shaman Robbie Houcek for her wisdom of Native American tradition and her excellent care when traditional medicine failed me. Any mistakes involving your beautiful culture are mine, although I tried to be a good student. Thank you, also, to Claiborne Farms in Paris, Kentucky. Major plot points in this book would not have been possible without the knowledge you so graciously imparted. And lastly, to the late Mr. Prospector. The story of this stud planted the seed for a book set around horse breeding. May eternity be filled with lush grass and willing fillies.

CHAPTER ONE

Jo Montgomery blinked dust from her eyes, asking herself not for the first time what in the hell she'd gone and done. She'd never been the impulsive type. But desperate times called for desperate measures, and she was nothing if not desperate.

"Where you want this, lady?"

"Um…" Jo eyed the sofa as if it were an unwelcome guest, its shiny red fabric mocking her. The movers sighed as she stalled, balancing the load precariously between the two of them. "Over by the window, I guess."

"You want the plastic off all this stuff?"

She took in the dust bunnies larger than many dogs she'd owned and shook her head. "Better leave it on. I've got some cleaning to do."

One of the men snorted, muttering something under his breath as he and the other mover lugged the sofa across the room, plopping it down in front of the large bay window, which boasted a clear view of her weed-infested front yard. Sun pushed through the grime on the windows, dappling the cushions and urging optimism she wasn't on board with yet. Somewhere between passing over the Texas border and

1

entering the western edge of Alabama, her cranberry-colored Cadillac CTS began to feel more like a sealed coffin than a luxury to toodle around in. Visions of her sister's disapproving expression as Jo had pulled out of the driveway in front of the moving van had taunted her with each passing mile.

What had she been thinking, buying this dilapidated farmhouse—sight unseen from an ad on the internet, no less—in the middle of nowhere? She hadn't been thinking clearly, that's what. A real "do-me-over", the ad had boasted. Being a licensed real estate agent, Jo knew that statement left open a large area for interpretation. Upon her arrival, she'd discovered "plow-me-over" was a more accurate description.

Still, she was a very motivated buyer. Fresh start, that's what she wanted. A new beginning, as far away from her ex and her role as a senator's wife as possible.

Jo's attention snapped to the movers as they wrestled the large Oriental rug her dad had given her when she'd graduated from college through the front door. They dropped the rolled wool on the floor, dust rushing up to encircle them. Jo coughed, clearing the air with a wave of her hand. She blinked her eyes rapidly, certain more dust would irritate her new contact lenses. Her vision was clear, though, giving her a crisp view of her investment.

Man, this place is a dump.

Renovations had seemed like just the thing to help bolster her shaky confidence. The fixer-upper tease had sold Jo on the house, if only to prove to herself she could handle something, anything, on her own. And it afforded her a chance to get lost in a project, keeping her mind far away from her past. Glancing around at the worn floorboards, the sconces hanging by their wiring and the peeling wallpaper, she realized she might have bitten off more than she could chew. As a matter of fact, the entire picture was already leaving a bad taste in her mouth.

"Excuse me."

Jo whirled at the sound of a Southern drawl echoing in the nearly empty room. A tall man was leaning against the doorjamb, a smile on his lips, a cowboy hat twirling idly atop his hand.

"You the new owner?"

Her gaze followed the movement of his wrist as he rotated the hat in slow circles. When the motion stilled, her attention darted to his face. He stepped aside as the movers pressed through the front door with a pair of floor lamps.

"Yes," Jo said, walking toward him with her hand extended. "I'm Jo Dan—" She shook her head slightly. "Montgomery. Jo Montgomery."

The corners of his eyes crinkled with his smile. "It's nice to meet you, Jo Montgomery." His hand was calloused and warm as it enveloped hers. "I'm Hawk Stephens. That's my place over there," he said, motioning to the left with a quick jerk of his head.

Jo nodded, taking in the sight of him. Dust-coated boots began the long ascent of his legs, covered in work-worn denim. His trim waist led to a broad chest and shoulders. Ebony hair reached the middle of his back, its rich hue a shocking contrast to the ice-blue of his eyes.

Eyes that were dancing with humor at her perusal, she realized a fraction of a second too late. Jo took an immediate interest in the hangnail on her index finger.

He strolled to a section of peeling paper, thumbing the age-tattered edge. "I'm glad someone bought this place. It's been vacant for a long time."

"The price was hard to pass on," she replied. Jo lifted her blonde hair from her neck. The prim bun she was so accustomed to wearing would be a relief right about now.

"Where're you from?" he asked, approaching her. He towered over her petite frame and she stepped back, wary of

3

the unfamiliar skittering of her heartbeat.

"Tucson." She diverted her nervous energy by focusing on the movers and pointed to the sofa as they entered the house with a coffee table.

Hawk leaned closer. "That's a long ways off." His irises were peppered with flecks of gray, as if an artistic afterthought by the Creator Himself. Jo stared into them, mesmerized by the way his pupils widened, swallowing up the little flecks in the process.

"Um, yes. Yes it is." She took another step back, wiping her palms against her denim-clad thighs.

The corners of his lips curled upward. "Why Georgia?"

Telling this tall drink of water she had foolishly bought this pile of rubble simply because it got her as far away from her ex as possible while still staying in the same country didn't seem like an appropriate response. For once she was quick on her feet. "I hear the pollen is outstanding here in the spring and fall."

His smile widened, exposing straight white teeth—a stare-worthy contrast to his deeply tanned skin. "Ah, Georgia pollen. I guess you haven't lived until you've been nearly asphyxiated by Mother Nature."

Laughing, Jo nodded. "I guess not."

Hawk wandered around the room, taking in what Jo knew was painfully obvious—a sad state of disrepair. He twined his fingers together behind his back, glancing over his shoulder at her. "If you need any recommendations for contractors, I can give you a few names. Good guys who stand behind their work."

She pushed her hands into her pockets, the stiff texture of the new denim scraping her delicate skin. "Oh, thanks, but I'm planning on doing the work myself." Even as the words left her mouth, she knew how ridiculous they must sound. Hawk's left eyebrow disappeared into his hairline and he began to survey her *project* again.

Jo joined him in his regard of the carcass that slightly resembled what must have been a house of some sort at one time. He stepped over to a sconce hanging off the wall to the side of the crumbling brick fireplace, running the exposed wire between his fingers. He smiled then, a beautiful smile, she had to admit, even though she suspected it was birthed in mockery.

"Okay," Jo said, conceding to his unspoken but clear take on the situation. "I could use the name of an electrician."

Hawk rubbed his chin, twirling his hat again. "You know…" He drew out the two words. "I would almost be willing to bet the farm the plumbing in this place is nearing its golden anniversary." He winked at her.

Biting her lip, she attempted to refuse his game, as amusing for him as it was proving to be. Jo placed her hands on her hips, narrowing her eyes at him playfully. "Mr. Stephens, what makes you so sure I'm not a…a…" Good Lord. Was she flirting with him?

His strides ate up the floor as he closed the distance between them, forcing her to peer up nearly a foot to meet an expression that looked suspiciously like it was courting mischief. "A what, Miss Montgomery?"

Jo couldn't help herself. A smile broke through. And it felt good. "A…handyman. Or handywoman, as the case may be."

Hawk plopped his cowboy hat atop his gorgeous head of hair and leaned close. Very close. "So, are you?"

He smelled of leather, spice and some other scent she couldn't place, but all of it combined marked him as unmistakably male. Undeniably sexy. His question forgotten, she inhaled deeply, attempting to place the familiar scent.

Hawk tipped the brim of his hat back with a long finger. "You trying to dance your way out of this one?" He didn't smile, but humor sparkled in his eyes.

"What?" Jo asked, trying to decipher what she had missed while breathing him in like a free sample at the perfume counter.

A slow, wicked smile crawled across his lips. Reaching toward her, he tucked a stray wisp of hair behind her ear. "Why, Miss Montgomery, I do believe I've gotten you discombobulated."

Jo's mouth went dry, along with her capability to speak. Welcome to Humiliationville. Population: Jo.

Hawk ran a fingertip down the length of her nose. "I'll take it by your silence that you are *not*, in fact, a *handywoman*."

She shook her head, trying not to dwell on the fact her tongue felt as if it were firmly wedged down her throat.

"Pop by my place later and I'll give you a list of those contractors."

"A-all right," she mumbled. As she watched him walk to the door, she realized with alarming clarity her road to starting over was going to be riddled with potholes. Being married for more than a decade to a man with more passion for position than for her hadn't exactly armed her with skills to interact with the opposite sex. And Hawk? She'd never stumbled upon a man like him before—a man who could kick up chaos with a glance alone. Just what was a woman to do with all that male real estate? She wasn't too proud to admit she hadn't a clue.

Hawk paused at the door. "Oh, and welcome to the neighborhood." A wink. "Such as it is."

He disappeared across the porch, loud, creaking pops announcing each footfall he made down the steps. She added their replacement to her mental punch list.

"Where you want this, lady?"

Jo looked at the loveseat she used to sit on in her old bedroom, reading, as hours ticked by while she waited for Thomas to return home. It was the only piece of furniture

6

they'd purchased together that she had requested. Now she couldn't even remember why. The movers implored her with their impatient expressions.

"Put it on the street for garbage pickup." They stared at her blankly, their mouths falling open. "Do they have large-item garbage pickup in rural Georgia?"

They shook their heads, eyeing the expensive sofa as if it were the last drunk woman at closing time.

"Do what you want with it, just don't bring it in here." Jo turned on her heel and headed toward the kitchen to investigate the plumbing that would likely be on its last leg, if not completely crippled already. Leaning on the counter by the sink, she pulled aside the frayed gingham curtain and glanced to the neighboring property.

Hawk Stephens. If they had placed a picture of *him* with the ad for this hellhole of a house, it would have been off the market ages ago.

* * * * *

Interesting.

Hawk grinned as he walked back to his farm after leaving Jo standing in her living room, nervously scratching her neck, her cheeks passing through every shade of pink known to man. He really should have behaved himself better. But he couldn't resist teasing her. Not when she was so…adorable. The top of her head barely cleared his shoulder, her stature such that a man's instinct would be to wrap her in the protection of his arms. And when he had her there…

Hawk had been shocked by the speed of his attraction as he'd stood so close to Jo, breathing in her enticing scent. She had a shy beauty he found alluring, and when she had thrust her chin up, playfully calling him on his audacity to assume she wasn't a *handywoman*, he didn't know whether to laugh at her wit or kiss her senseless. His painfully hard state gave him the answer.

Hawk turned and looked over the tree line at the pitch of her roof with its missing shingles. A sight that, until half an hour ago, had irritated him—so much so he had planned to buy the heap and tear it down, just to improve the view from his place.

A view that wasn't so troublesome anymore.

Shaking his head, Hawk resumed his walk. Jo Montgomery. She was going to get under his skin, he could feel it. But what a lovely itch to scratch.

* * * * *

Jo frowned at the navigation display screen in the dash of her sedan. 24 Oakwood Lane in Bumfuck Egypt, Georgia, could not be found. She pushed enter again, just as one would an already illuminated button in an elevator. Just to be sure.

Nada.

Jo leaned her head against the back of the leather seat, whining into the silence. She tapped the destination option and punched in the name of the city closest to the nonexistent area where her house resided. "Yeah, you search the route," she muttered at the technology, waiting for magic to happen on the screen.

"Please proceed to the highlighted route," the car chirped. The blue line on the display looked like some uncoordinated doodle a three-year-old would scribble, with a highway indicated as its termination point.

Jo shifted her car into gear. "This should be interesting." She started down her long driveway. She was instantly consumed by a cloud of clay dust. What was it with this place? Hadn't they heard of asphalt out here in the sticks?

Ten minutes later her tires met pavement. Nothing smooth,

but pavement all the same. In another five minutes she was guiding her car into a vacant parking space in downtown Vidalia.

Jo grabbed her purse from the front seat and got out of the car, shutting the door with a bump of her hip. She glanced around the square, shielding her eyes from the midday sun with her hand. Jo perused her new stomping ground. Hardware Store. General Store. Nail salon...the corner of her lip quirked. A town just isn't a town without a nail salon. Or in most cases, fifty. Her gaze settled on a building painted a bright white with red-and-blue trim. A sign hanging over the front door creaked as the breeze pushed it gently back and forth. Whistling Dixie Café.

Jo wandered over. A cup of coffee and a dose of the local color would be a good start to her exploration.

A cowbell clamored against the glass as she entered, a half-dozen patrons turning to look at her. They eyed her with open curiosity, sipping their coffees and sodas as she made her way to a back booth. She slid into it, feeling as conspicuous as a pre-makeover Sandra Dee at a Hell's Angels rally. Coming from the life she had, Jo was accustomed to being watched. But those appraisals were different. It was more about who made the suit the senator's wife was wearing. And didn't she look so supportive of her philanthropic husband as she stood by his side at function after function?

Now things were different. No one knew who she had been, so she could only be sized up for who people *thought* she was. The fear of falling short, even in the eyes of these strangers, gnawed at her.

"What can I get you to drink, hon?" A menu was slapped down in front of her and Jo glanced up at the waitress. Her chestnut hair was pulled into a high ponytail, setting off striking features. Her eyes were a cool emerald green, her full lips a soft pink. She beamed down at Jo, her pencil poised over a small pad.

"I'll, ah, have a coffee," Jo answered, returning the smile of the woman whose name tag identified her as Kristy.

"You eating?" she asked.

Jo picked up the menu and handed it over. "No, just coffee. Thanks."

Kristy smiled, dropping her pad into the pocket of her apron.

Jo slid what she hoped was a covert glance around the diner when Kristy left, relieved that as far as the diners were concerned, she'd already become yesterday's news. She had just settled back in her seat when a mug of steaming coffee was placed in front of her and Kristy plopped onto the bench on the other side of the booth.

The waitress placed her elbows on the table, resting her chin in her hands. "Man, my feet hurt. Worked a double yesterday."

Jo nodded, grabbing a sugar packet. She stirred its contents into her mug, smiling hesitantly.

"You're new around here," Kristy observed. She leaned across the table, cupping her hand around the side of her mouth. "I saw Rod Hewitt checking you out like a prize hog at the fair when you walked in. I wouldn't make eye contact, if I were you. He's a hard one to get rid of."

Jo halted the cream halfway to her mug. Was she on hidden camera? She glanced to the left and the right before settling her attention back on Kristy. "I'm sorry?"

The waitress tilted her head to the right in two short jerks. "Rod over there. The one in the ugly plaid shirt."

Jo slid a glance to her left. They were all in ugly plaid shirts, as far as she was concerned. Her eyes traveled over each booth, widening when she landed on who must be Rod, if his wink and creepy leer were any indication.

10

"Don't look at him," Kristy chastised, grasping Jo's forearm. "Look at me."

Jo did as asked, trying her hardest not to smile at the concerned look on Kristy's face. When Rod busied himself with his meal, the waitress melted back into her seat, relief flooding her features. "Whew, that was close. Would've been a world of trouble for you."

"I'll have to take your word for it." Jo smiled as she brought the mug to her lips.

Kristy nodded enthusiastically. "So, are you visiting or are you new in town?"

"I just bought the old farmhouse on Oakwood Lane right outside of town."

"Next to the Stephens place," Kristy said, a wistful tone to her voice.

"Ah, yes. That's right."

She leaned forward, pinning Jo with a mischievous stare. "Have you seen him yet?"

"Who?" Jo asked, blowing on the hot liquid that had just scorched her tongue.

"Why, Hawk of course." Kristy raised an eyebrow.

As if I should know.

"Yes. I have. He came around this morning to introduce himself."

Kristy sighed, leaning back into the cracked vinyl seat. "He's something, right?"

If by "something" she meant he could reduce a woman to a quivering mass of idiocy, then yes, he was certainly something. "I guess he is," Jo agreed. "Do you know him well?"

Kristy twirled the end of her ponytail around her finger. "Hmmm…not as well as I'd like, if you know what I mean." She winked. "I was several years behind him in school. Now my sister, that's another story."

Jo sat up in her seat, leaning her elbows on the table. She was more than a little disturbed by the fact she was suddenly riveted by this conversation. "Really?" she asked.

"Oh yeah. I lived for the stories she'd bring home about Hawk."

Jo ran her fingertip around the rim of the mug. "So, they dated in high school?"

Kristy snorted, covering her mouth with her hand. "Hawk wasn't for dating." A gleam sparkled in her green eyes. "Hawk was for dark deeds in dark places."

Jo squirmed in her seat, her cheeks flushing. Kristy smiled as if she'd landed on Park Place with Boardwalk already tucked under her side of the Monopoly board. "The stories I could tell you," she said. "Of course, my sister does tend to embellish. But rumor had it he sure could kiss." She sighed once more, pulling the end of her ponytail through her lips. "As a matter of fact, that's a rumor still circulating by women lucky enough to spread it."

"Fascinating," Jo murmured, envisioning her new neighbor and remembering the shocking thrill she'd experienced when he'd tucked her hair behind her ear. She shook the image from her mind, her attention drifting toward the kitchen as a portly man stuck his head through the window and yelled, "Order up!"

Kristy hopped from the booth. "Well, that's me." She twirled on her toes. "Oh, I didn't get your name."

"It's Jo. Jo Montgomery."

Kristy smiled and pointed to her nametag. "I'm Kristy Poole." She tore off a check from her pad and placed it on the table. "Welcome to Vidalia, Jo."

"Thank you."

She watched Kristy as she approached the kitchen window

and then Jo rose from the booth, picking up her check and taking it to the counter. A red "Help Wanted" sign was taped to the back of the register. Jo handed her bill to the large man who approached. She reached into her purse for her wallet.

"That'll be a buck five," he said, shifting the toothpick in his mouth from one side to the other.

She pulled out what she hoped was the exact change and placed it in his outstretched hand. "Hey," she said, pulling a generous tip from her billfold and dropping the expensive leather piece back in her purse. She pointed to the sign. "Is this position still available?"

He gave her a good once-over, narrowing his eyes. "You got any experience waiting tables?"

Jo thought of the countless business dinners she had hosted for her husband during their marriage. She'd done everything—the planning, the invitations, the floral arrangements, the seating charts, the cooking. Jo wasn't worried about running short orders and filling coffee mugs. "Yes, I do. Years of it."

"Can you start on Saturday?"

A surge of joy galloped through Jo. She'd placed the first block in the stack that would become her new life. "Absolutely."

He nodded. "Be here by nine to fill out paperwork." He pointed to her. "And wear something like what you got on."

Jo glanced down at her jeans and simple t-shirt, the only ones in existence among a sea of suits and coordinating sportswear. There had to be a place where she could find more of it. From the looks of everyone, it appeared to be the town uniform. "Will do," she said. "Thank you for the opportunity. I'm Jo, by the way." She extended her hand and he shook it.

"Bobby Myers. I own this place." He pushed his shoulders back, straightening his apron.

"It's lovely," Jo praised, adjusting her purse on her shoulder. "I'll see you on Saturday."

She walked to her abandoned booth and tucked a five-dollar bill under her empty mug. She waved at Kristy as she left, the bell announcing her departure.

* * * * *

The sun was just about to slip beneath the horizon when Jo finally made her way to Hawk's place to get his recommendations for contractors. Kristy's enthusiastic confession about Hawk had occupied Jo's mind for most of the afternoon after her return from town. *Hawk is for dark deeds in dark places.* A shiver slithered across her skin, her reaction unsettling. There was something about Hawk Stephens that made her nervous—disconcertingly so.

She glanced up the long, dusty driveway leading to his home. Magnolia trees lined its edges, their ivory blossoms lending a gentle beauty to the walk. A soft whinny from the distance garnered her attention and she wandered toward the sound, craning her neck to see beyond the trees in her line of vision.

She saw the horse first, its coat so black it reflected a blue sheen in the light cast from sunset. The magnificent animal danced around his trainer, following gestured commands effortlessly. Jo stood and observed, fascinated with the respect the man and animal had for one another, their interaction an orchestration of patience and practice. The horse lowered its head, nuzzling the man's chest. The trainer stroked the animal's long neck, leaning in close to its ear.

"He talks to 'em, you know."

Jo jumped into next Tuesday, turning to face a tall, wiry man with a face like aged leather.

"I'm sorry?" she asked.

"Hawk over there," he replied, pointing to the ring. "His

14

horses. He talks to 'em and they listen. Never seen anything like it."

Her vision traced the path of his finger, her pulse accelerating at the sight of black hair falling across the man's face as he pulled the cowboy hat from his head—a face she now recognized as that of her neighbor. "Like voice commands, right?"

Placing a booted foot against a tree stump, he shook his head. "He doesn't need words. It ain't that kind of talking. He has an affinity for 'em. Understands 'em. And they take to him. He gets that from his mama. That's something those fancy degrees couldn't teach him." He smiled, extending his hand. "Name's Ray."

"Jo," she replied, taking his hand. He shook it firmly, trapping it in his grip. He gave her a smile revealing a little more gum than teeth in a couple of places.

"So, what's your story?"

She gently tugged her hand but he held fast, grinning. "M-my what?" she stammered.

"You know, your story. What's a sweet little thing like you doing out here wandering around the farm? All..." He picked up her other hand to inspect it. "Single and such."

"I, ah..."

"And a pretty thing you are too. Hair like honey and eyes like caramel. Where'd you come from?" The gappy grin once more.

Jo couldn't help but smile. "I met Hawk earlier today. I bought the monstrosity next door and he told me to stop by for the names of some contractors."

Ray brought Jo's hand to his lips and pressed a kiss to the backs of her fingers, winking. "What you need done, darlin'? I'm real handy."

"Pops," a deep voice drawled.

So taken aback by this character of a man, Jo didn't even hear Hawk approach. *Pops?* Her gaze darted between the two men.

Ray chuckled. "I know, I know. Kid got all the looks in the family. You'd never know he's mine. Looks just like his mama, that's a fact." He released a weighted sigh. "Left me with my drinking, she did."

Jo opened her mouth to speak but fell victim to stunned silence. She glanced to Hawk for help, only to find him shaking his head and battling a smile. Her attention flew back to Ray when he leaned close.

"Don't you worry none. I've been sober for five years." He rubbed his chin. "That's why my second wife left me. Said I wasn't no fun once I quit the bottle."

"Oh." What else could she possibly contribute to the conversation?

Ray placed his hand on his hip, a pensive expression crossing his features. "Now, Mary Jane, she—"

Hawk's rich laughter brought the confession to an end. "Okay, Pops. Let's not scare her off right away." He turned his regard to Jo. "Miss Montgomery, a pleasure to see you again."

As he removed his hat and his long hair fell around his face, she began to tingle. In all kinds of intriguing, long-forgotten places. "It's Jo, please."

He smiled, a crescent-shaped dimple she had overlooked earlier winked at her from the side of his mouth. "I see you've met my father."

She studied the two of them. Two pairs of eyes the exact shade of blue stared back. "Yes. He's quite…charming."

Ray slapped his thigh, throwing his head back in laughter. "Charmin'. Ain't been called that before." He glanced to his son. "Now here's a lady, Silent Hawk. Knows how to act proper-like in society. She's gonna stand out like a virgin in a whorehouse around these parts."

16

He continued to hoot in laughter. Jo plastered a smile on her face, uncertain if she was the source of his humor or ridicule. She heaved a silent breath of relief when Ray's arm draped around her shoulder. "I like you, darlin'. You're real clever."

She shrugged in modesty and cleared her throat, glancing at Hawk before looking back at his father. "You called him Silent Hawk?"

Ray nodded. "That's what his mama named him."

"I'm half Apache," Hawk offered.

Jo's tingling surged into an unnerving, steady throb of awareness. Good Lord, he was devastating. She watched him, entranced, as the wind kicked up, blowing the silk of his hair across his face. One hand was in his pocket, pulling denim tautly across his pelvis, the other held his black hat. His jeans hugged muscled legs, tapering to dust the surface of worn leather boots.

His feet shifted, drawing her attention back to his face, where she expected to see amusement at her open regard. Smoldering sapphire eyes met hers instead, infusing her with heat. Unable to draw her focus away, she continued to stare, the beat of her heart echoing loudly in her ears.

"Well, okay then. I'll just head on back and leave you two kids to your…" Ray cleared his throat. "Business."

Jo turned to Hawk's father, thankful for the interruption. "It was nice meeting you, Ray."

"You too, darlin'. Charles Kinkaid is at nine in the morning, right, Hawk?"

"Yeah, and he'll probably be early."

"Eight forty-five then. G'night, you two." Ray narrowed his eyes and shook his finger at his son. Jo glanced over her shoulder at Hawk.

"Good night, Pops," he said with a nod.

Jo turned to watch Ray disappear into the nearing darkness and then slowly turned back to Hawk, as nervous as a long-tailed cat in a room full of rocking chairs. He was going to be trouble, she sensed it. Trouble she had no idea how to handle.

He was standing directly behind her when she turned, the smell of him infiltrating her senses. Horses. That was the scent she'd struggled to place earlier. Leather, spice and…horses. Jo met his gaze, fear skittering down her spine. Her breath stilled in her lungs when he reached out, pulling at a section of hair she hadn't even realized had fallen across her face to tuck it behind her ear. Jo's heartbeat tripped all over itself from the contact.

Definitely trouble. She took a keen interest in her shoes.

"So, what can I…do you for?"

Jo's gaze shot to his. "P-pardon me?" She swallowed down what felt like a handful of cotton balls, prickly heat crawling up her neck at the curl of his full lips.

Hawk plopped his hat on the tip of the fence post behind him, resting a hand along the rail. His eyes were dancing with humor as a smile spread across his face. "Southern expression. It means what may I do for you?"

"Oh," Jo replied, driving her hands into her pockets. "Um, I dropped by for that list."

He took a step toward her, closing what little distance existed between them. She angled her neck to look at him, only to find him making a studied perusal of her face, his attention dropping to her lips. Certainly he wouldn't try to—

"Right," he said, shattering what was bordering on a delicious fantasy she was out of her mind, and out of her league, for entertaining. "The list. I checked on a couple of guys I had in mind and they're not taking any new jobs right now. I want to double-check the others before I send you on a wild-goose chase."

Jo nodded and seconds ticked by in uncomfortable silence.

Hawk's gaze never left her person, trapping her beneath his relentless stare. She bit her bottom lip, a nervous habit that drew his focus to her mouth once more. He lowered his head.

Jo sucked in a breath when he aborted his journey mere inches from her lips.

"Is there anything else I can do for you, Miss Montgomery?" He traced the line of her jaw with his fingertip, pausing at her chin before slowly running down the length of her neck. When he reached the hollow of her throat, he rested his hand against her collarbone, his thumb gently stroking her skin. Her eyes fluttered closed and she swayed toward him, his warm breath fanning her lips.

"Jo," he said, applying gentle pressure against her skin with his thumb, drawing her closer.

She jumped at the sound of his voice, taking two clumsy steps backward.

What in the hell was she doing? With a mere touch this man had her on the verge of falling into the one thing she knew she wasn't ready for. The one thing a woman like her wasn't prepared to be.

Jo tentatively looked at him, humiliation stabbing at her as if she were lounging on a bed of nails. His blue gaze smoldered as he searched her face, churning up what felt like regret in the depths of her stomach. *Rumor has it he sure can kiss...*

Hawk turned to his right, plucking his Stetson from the fence. Placing it atop his head, he turned back to face her.

"Please forgive me, Miss Montgomery."

Embarrassed, all she could do was attempt to backpedal and walk away with a smidgen of her dignity intact.

"It's all right. I'm not sure what's come over me this evening." Jo forced what she hoped was a convincing smile but feared she was as transparent as cellophane.

Hawk placed his hand on her shoulder, squeezing it gently.

"Drop by tomorrow evening if you can. I should have a list of contractors by then who would be more than happy to help you." He flashed his dazzling smile, winking. "You enjoy the rest of your night."

"I will," Jo replied, turning to walk back toward her house. Her shin struck the tree stump Ray had been resting his foot on earlier and she cursed, rubbing the knot already forming beneath her skin.

"You okay?" he called.

She glanced over her shoulder and met his humored expression. Jo was glad she could amuse him so, and twice in one day, no less. "Yes, I'm fine. Thank you."

"You be careful, now."

Jo turned to assure him she would be fine, but when she saw him standing there with his jeans hugging every bulging muscle in his legs, his white t-shirt skimming the breadth of his chest and shoulders, his long black hair falling in a heavy mass around his face, she wasn't so sure she would be. Not with him around.

An inexperienced woman like you has no business taking on a man like him. You'll humiliate yourself. No doubt about it. And then you're stuck with him right under your nose.

"Oh, shut up," she muttered to her nagging inner voice.

"What's that? I couldn't hear you," Hawk said, cupping his hand around his ear.

Heat seared her cheeks. "Oh, I said I'd be careful." She gave him a wave and started the walk back to her farmhouse, crossing her arms over her chest. His stare drilled into her back until she disappeared from his vision. Mumbling under her breath, she stepped around fallen branches and exposed tree roots. Of all the towns in Georgia, and all the fixer-uppers she had perused on the internet, Jo had to go and pick the house smack dab next to one Silent Hawk Stephens.

20

CHAPTER TWO

"Tear it up, girl."

Hawk had seen the doe every morning outside his kitchen window for the last week, grazing in his flowerbeds. She'd never come before. He would have noticed if something of such significance had occurred. A sign of a woman coming into a man's life, a woman who would desire him, lay with him.

When Hawk walked into the farmhouse and saw Jo, he knew. She was the woman the deer's presence prophesized.

What he didn't know was how gun-shy she'd be. Not unlike the animal that foretold her arrival. Timid, skittish and quick to run away.

"Oh God. Not the geraniums." Hawk rapped the glass but his visitor only stared at him, a fuchsia bud dangling from her mouth. *This* doe was more like the man he'd become—steadfast and stubborn to get his way.

There had been a time, not too long ago, when the bold overture he'd made toward Jo outside his horse ring never would have happened. He wouldn't have even considered it. In this miniscule Georgia town he was an oddity, to be sure, with his heritage and people nestled so far away to the west. Being of mixed blood in a part of the country where everyone was the

21

same had always set him apart, and not necessarily in a good way.

But then he'd found Thunder, or rather, Thunder found him—a horse so unruly no one dared to take him. But the spirited animal was easy to tame under Hawk's gentle guidance, and demonstrated his loyalty by making him a very rich man. That only served to cast Hawk in the brightest spotlight possible…the most eligible bachelor in town.

Having his pick of warm, willing bodies was never an issue after the cash rolled in. And the women's motivation? Well, he just pretended not to know their true intentions. After all, he was still the same Hawk they went to high school with, the boy who grew up working on his father's cotton farm, driving a rusted-out Chevy pickup with missing hubcaps. A boy suitable for groping sessions behind the bleachers but never as a date to the prom.

It was amazing what a few million would do.

He rinsed the coffee residue from his mug and placed it in the dishwasher, glancing out the window. The doe was just meandering off, the only evidence left of her presence the half-eaten flowers.

His attention drifted to the thick thatch of trees dividing his property from Jo's. He wondered if a buck had been making a nuisance of himself in her yard. A massive animal trampling her weeds, the presence of which she wouldn't comprehend the significance. Hawk suspected the buck had been there, and if he were a betting man, he'd go all in on this one. If his bet paid out, things would become interesting between him and Jo, and very quickly. She belonged in his bed, but she wouldn't fall into it easily. Their interlude by the horse ring made that painfully clear.

The last couple of years had brought a steady infusion of women willing to warm his sheets. The fact Jo didn't swoon at his feet intrigued him to no end, he had to admit. Of course, she didn't know about the money.

A muscle ticked in Hawk's jaw. He hated being jaded. But some part of him knew he had a hand in his own unhappiness. No one forced him to take up with all those women who only wanted him for what he could give them. He had been like a kid in a candy store, overindulging and ending up with a bellyache.

"You ready, son?"

Hawk turned at the sound of his father's voice and shook the unpleasant thoughts from his head. Grabbing his hat from the counter, he joined Ray at the back door. "All set. Let's go see if we can strike a deal to make Thunder a proud papa again."

* * * * *

Two hours later, Hawk and Ray shuffled through copies of Mr. Kincaid's contract, both satisfied with the terms they'd agreed upon. Thunder could still garner a quarter million per breed, despite his occasional show of temper. As long as the stud would cooperate, they'd continue to breed him. There was too much on the line not to.

"So, Silent Hawk. You behave last night?" Ray asked in the same tone he'd used when Hawk was a boy.

Hawk chuckled, straightening the contracts and sliding them into a manila folder. "Yes, Dad."

"Now there's a surprise. You were devourin' that poor girl with your eyes." Ray leaned a hip on the corner of the desk, crossing his arms over his chest.

Hawk yanked open a file cabinet drawer and placed the folder inside. He nudged it closed with his shoulder. "Nothing happened, Pops. Promise."

Ray smiled. "Now, I'm not tryin' to get all up in your business, son. Just remember she's our neighbor. If you go and piss her off things could get uncomfortable."

Hawk walked to his favorite leather chair in the corner and dropped into it. "And what makes you think I'm going to piss her off?"

Ray's eyebrow shot up.

Hawk held his hands up in surrender. "Fine. I deserve your analysis. But remember, I'm not the only one who's doing the using around here. You think all these women who are suddenly beating down my door are here for my heart?"

"I've got eyes, Hawk, I can see what's going on." He sighed, running a hand down his face. "What I don't want to see is a repeat of last summer. You know I don't like to call your mama and tell her such things. It makes me feel like I've failed her somehow. Again."

Hawk rested his ankle on his knee, studying the stitching of his boot. "You didn't fail her, Pops. I did." He met his father's regard. "And besides, I did what she asked. I went to the Black Hills."

"But have you made any changes in your life because of it? Doesn't seem like it to me."

Hawk rose from the chair and approached his father. "Look, Pops. You can't always see what's in a person. I haven't turned my back on my beliefs again. They'll serve me when it's time."

"I just hate to see this wealth change who you are. Change the kind of person we raised you to be. If your mama could see—"

"This wealth is what's going to make her life's mission possible, isn't it?" Hawk took a deep breath, letting it out slowly. "Don't worry. We know everything has a purpose and signs are everywhere. I have eyes in my head, and Mom taught me to use them. I'll see when I need to."

Ray nodded. "Just don't be so busy messin' around that you miss what's right in front of you."

Hawk thought of the doe. And his new neighbor. He could

24

see, all right. Very clearly.

* * * * *

Jo spent her day swimming in agitation. Not just over the sad state of her so-called home, but with the constant intrusion of Hawk in her thoughts. She could still feel the heat of his hand on her neck, the whisper of his warm breath as it feathered over her mouth before she'd stepped away from him.

The near-sleepless night she had spent replaying their brief contact and her reaction to it drove home the point that Jo was, in fact, damaged. The number her ex had pulled on her self-esteem was worse than she'd feared. Sure, he hadn't touched her those last few years. But she never thought she'd forget how to be a woman. Wasn't sex like riding a bike? After her humiliating tangle with Hawk last night, it was painfully clear she needed a set of training wheels.

Now she was only left with one question. What should she do about her predicament? If anything?

This move was meant to allow her time alone. Time to discover just who she was and what she wanted. She'd never had a chance to do that. She'd rushed into her relationship with Thomas, jumping on board with his promises of love and a life together, her father's blessing only cementing the decision. And look where that had gotten her. She was ill equipped to make smart choices. That much was clear. If she knew nothing else, she knew that. Yet here she was, wondering what to do about these unfamiliar feelings her neighbor stirred in her. And convincing herself that in order to be the woman she needed to be, she had to grow a pair. Her motivations were at odds. She was caught in a tug-of-war of her own making. She wasn't exactly off to the best start in this new life of hers.

Jo forced one foot in front of the other as she made her way to Hawk's place. When she focused on the fact she truly needed the list of contractors, rather than the simple truth she could probably obtain it without visiting the man in person, it made what she was doing so much easier.

And just what was she doing? Dancing near an inferno, was what. But sheer curiosity, paired with an overwhelming need to become anyone but who she was, won out and guided her up his long driveway. She nearly turned around twice, but that was the cowardly way of the old Jo Montgomery. Not the woman she promised herself she'd become as her car ate up the miles between Tucson and this tiny slice of Georgia.

As Jo rounded the large oak tree only yards away from the horse ring, she saw him. He was leaning over the rail, securing the gate with a chain. His jeans pulled tightly across the backs of his thighs, his t-shirt showcasing the bulge of back muscles as he looped the length of metal rings around the fence post. Warmth rushed between her thighs. At the sound of her footfalls, he turned.

"Good evening, Miss Montgomery." He tipped his hat, replacing it on his head.

She smiled in greeting. "You can call me Jo, you know."

"As you wish." Hawk dusted his hands on his jeans and walked toward her. "You settling in okay?"

Nodding, she glanced up at him when he stopped before her. "It was kind of dicey last night…lots of strange noises I could only imagine were coming from critters of some sort."

Hawk smiled. "We do have our fair share of wildlife around here. You probably heard a coyote."

Shrugging, Jo ran a hand through her hair, pushing it off her face. "Coyotes I can handle, rattlesnakes even, hailing from Arizona. But this morning when I looked out my bedroom window, there was a black bear strolling off my back porch like he owned the place."

"A bear, huh?" Hawk rubbed his chin. "That's good."

Placing her hands on her hips, Jo narrowed her eyes at his calm take on the fact there were bears more than willing to

26

move in with her. Or worse. "How in heaven's name is that good?"

"Bears represent protection and healing. It was an omen you'll be safe here."

Jo studied his matter-of-fact expression. "Really? Says who?"

"Nature, Jo. The traditions of my people. Animals possess certain powers, and their presence carries meaning."

"Hmmm," she mused. "That's interesting. There was a ginormous buck outside my kitchen window this morning. Scared me half to death." She laughed. "I hate to think what that means."

Her laughter dwindled like a dying ember at the look on his face. His eyes pierced her, their icy-blue depths taking on a stormy hue. She gasped when he reached for her, drawing her into the circle of his arms with one swift movement.

Before she could react, his mouth was on hers, the tip of his tongue coaxing her lips apart.

She groaned into the kiss, overcome with the way her body responded to his. She clung to his shoulders and he deepened the kiss, wrapping Jo in a frightening robe of confusion and lust.

Hawk pulled back abruptly, his breath staggered as he looked down at her. "Come to the house with me, Jo."

His stare was unwavering as he waited on her reply. Never before had a man looked at her in this manner. With such raw…hunger. She was wading in treacherous waters. Even if she chose to dive in, would she even know how to swim? Hawk was no Thomas. If she couldn't satisfy her husband, she couldn't possibly meet the needs of a man like Hawk.

Could she?

"Jo," he said, brushing his lips against her temple. "Will you?"

His mouth met hers again, his hands cradling her face. His kiss was gentle at first, questioning, but soon returned to the heated desperation he had ignited only moments before. Wrapping her arms around his neck, she pressed her body to his, the rigid length of his erection nudging her abdomen. Eliciting that reaction in him was like a high, encouraging her to step a little more outside herself.

Hawk's arm slid under her behind, lifting her effortlessly to straddle his waist. As she tentatively pressed the juncture of her thighs to his erection, a moan vibrated from his throat, echoing through their kiss. The contact and sound soaked her panties. His touch on her body anywhere, everywhere, was going to be her undoing.

This man would be her undoing.

Heady from his scent, his taste, his touch, she drew away to look at him. Want glazed his eyes and she was drawn into them. Into *him*. Alarm bells pealed in her ears, shattering the moment, her fear pushing the bravado she had forced into existence back to wherever it normally stayed hidden.

"You okay?" His voice was barely above a whisper.

Nodding, she closed her eyes, releasing her grip on his shoulders. Hawk placed his hands on her waist, gently lowering her until her feet touched the ground.

"I'm sorry," she said. "I never behave this way." *Ever.* "Letting a man I barely know…" Jo looked away.

Hawk tilted her chin up with the tip of a finger. "Don't apologize, Jo. Not for this. Not for what just happened between us."

"I shouldn't have—"

His mouth crushed hers, his tongue demanding entrance as it traced the crease of her lips. His kiss was intoxicating, persuasive, primitive.

Hawk ran the tip of his tongue along her bottom lip, nipping it gently with his teeth. "Come up to the house with

28

me," he murmured against her mouth.

Sighing, she met his gaze. "Hawk, there's a lot you don't know about me." *Like I've got enough baggage to fill the cargo hold of a commercial jet.*

He brushed a kiss against her forehead. "So tell me."

"How much time do you have?" she asked, her self-deprecating tone causing her to inwardly wince.

He traced her cheekbone with the tip of his finger, running it slowly down to Jo's parted lips where he caressed and teased. "Time enough."

He replaced his finger with his lips, kissing her gently. "Let me fix you dinner."

Nervous laughter bubbled in her throat. Being alone with him in his house certainly wouldn't calm the nerves ricocheting just below the surface of her skin. "Oh, you don't have to. I can—"

"Make use of your fully functional kitchen?" He smiled, raising an eyebrow.

"Well, the sink works. Kind of."

"Um-hmm. *Everything* works at my house."

With the appetizer he'd just served, *that* she didn't doubt. Hawk twined his fingers with Jo's, gently tugging her into step with him as he headed toward the two-story white house on the hill.

"Come, Miss Montgomery. Let me feed you and then you can tell me all the things you think will keep me from wanting to bury myself deep inside you."

She halted, stumbling a step forward before Hawk turned to face her. Jo's heart beat a frantic tattoo, its echo dizzying. The corners of his lips curled upward. He leaned down, his mouth brushing against her ear, eliciting a shiver along her spine.

"You up for the task, Jo? 'Cause it's going to be a hard sell."

* * * * *

Jo trembled as the click of the front door echoed through the silence and Hawk led her to what would surely result in some version of a nervous breakdown on her part. Okay, so she was being a little overdramatic. But still, if the thundering roar of her heart and the shivers her rigid muscles fought to contain were any indication, she wasn't headed anywhere her tiny comfort zone could handle. She'd followed him up here, though. Idiot that she was.

Hawk held her hand firmly in his, his thumb tracing lazy circles across the back—an attempt to comfort, no doubt. It only served to stir up the riptide churning in her stomach even more. She drew in a deep breath, letting it out slowly.

"So," he said, turning to face her. "This is our place."

Our. So Ray would be here also. She relaxed a fraction. Jo stood by his side in the foyer, her eyes roaming around the open floor plan. Beautiful hardwoods, antique pine if she wasn't mistaken, stretched endlessly in all directions, disappearing into the doorways along the circumference of the great room. The walls were a warm tobacco with cream trim. A grouping, which included a chocolate-brown leather sofa and two matching club chairs, made an inviting seating area in front of a stacked-stone fireplace.

"This is beautiful, Hawk. You and Ray must love living here."

"Well, I do. Dad prefers to live in the apartment behind the stables."

"Oh," she said and gently pulled her hand from his, her security net fading to nothing. No chance of Ray appearing and saving her if she got in over her head. Which she would.

Jo attempted to push the thought from her mind and

wandered toward the great room. Crossing her arms over her chest, she stopped to look at framed photography that stretched across the one windowless wall. She sucked in a breath when she recognized her home state—each photo more breathtaking than the previous one. She stopped in front of the largest picture—the Catalina Mountains at sunset. The jagged face of stone reflected a lavender hue in the last moments of daylight. Jo traced her fingertip across the glass, outlining the peak of the mountain.

The hairs on the back of her neck stood on end when she felt the heat of him behind her. Resting his hand on her shoulder, he leaned his head toward hers, his breath warm on her ear. "Homesick already?"

"No," she answered a little too quickly and curtly. She slid a hesitant glance to his face, quickly evading his questioning look. "Uh," she said, pointing to the picture, "this is one of the most beautiful photos of the Catalinas I've ever seen. Where'd you get it?"

"My mother took it."

Jo said a silent prayer of thanks when he didn't question her reaction to the Grand Canyon state. Hawk began to knead the tense muscles in her shoulders, his thumbs caressing her nape. She bit her lip, holding back a groan. Her nerve endings sang with awareness from each touch, her blood becoming thick goo in her veins. When his fingertips brushed her collarbone, her breath stilled and she took a half step away from him, hugging her arms to herself. His hands fell away.

"Um," Jo stammered, willing away the furious blush heating her cheeks. "Did she take all of these?"

Hawk stepped around her and braced his shoulder against the wall. He studied her for a pregnant pause, rubbing his chin. "Yeah, she's pretty talented, huh?"

"That's an understatement," Jo mused. She uncrossed her arms and clasped her hands in front of her. "Does she travel to

Arizona a lot?"

Hawk pulled his hat from his head and tossed it into the nearby chair. He raked his fingers through his hair and looked back at the photograph. "She lives there, actually."

"Oh. I guess I assumed she lived here."

Hawk pushed away from the wall. "She did up until ten years ago." Jo opened her mouth to ask another question but Hawk took her hand, gently tugging her toward the rear of the house. "Let me show you the kitchen."

"O-okay." She allowed him to lead her through the house. She was surprised at the sharp contrast of the room. Where the great room was rustic and warm, the kitchen was modern and bright. White cabinets wrapped around workspaces with earth-colored granite countertops. The appliances were stainless steel and well appointed. One could host a dinner for twenty from this kitchen, Jo observed. The only continuity in style was the massive staircase that rose from the center of the room, its balusters and railing a rich, polished wood.

"Wow," Jo said as she turned around in a circle, admiring it all for a second time. "I didn't expect this."

Hawk chuckled. "I had it remodeled a couple years ago. All the appliances used to be a nauseating avocado green."

Jo nodded, thinking of her putrid pale-yellow eyesores at home. "So, do you cook a lot?"

"Well, it's either that or haul into town to the diner every night with Ray."

"The Whistling Dixie Café?" Jo asked.

"Yeah. You've already found the throbbing metropolis of Vidalia, I see." He waggled his eyebrows.

Jo laughed. "Is that what that square was?"

"Yep."

"I found it, then." Jo smiled as she remembered the quirky waitress. "Seems like a welcoming place. I, ah, got a job there, actually."

Hawk raised an eyebrow. "Really?"

"Might as well hit the ground running. I've got to finance the resurrection of that pitiful excuse for a house next door since, sadly, I'm not a handywoman."

Hawk threw his head back and laughed. "I guess that's true." He put his arm around her shoulders and began to lead her toward the stairs. She glanced at his face hesitantly, slowing her pace.

"I'm not leading you to your death, Jo," he said, barely masking his amusement. He passed the base of the stairs and continued on to the right. Jo nearly slumped with relief when she saw the bar nestled behind the staircase. "Sit," he said, pointing to a row of barstools. He walked around the mahogany counter.

"Why don't we have a glass of wine?" Hawk retrieved an Oregon pinot noir and held it in front of her. "This okay?"

"Yes." Jo scratched her neck while Hawk uncorked the wine and poured her a glass. She took a long swallow. And then another.

"Thirsty?" he asked, smiling.

"Something like that." Jo twirled the delicate stem between her fingers and met his eyes. "Truth be told, you unnerve me."

Hawk took a sip of wine, eyeing her over the rim. He placed it on the bar top and leaned close, his palms resting on the smooth surface. "You inflame me." His attention dropped to Jo's mouth briefly before returning to her eyes. "Is that what unnerves you?"

"I guess," she whispered. She inflamed him? How she'd managed to do that when she jumped like a spider had dropped onto her lap every time he touched her, she had no idea. Her eyes widened when he smiled and slipped from behind the counter. She tracked his movement as he came toward her. He moved like a panther cornering its prey—slow and deliberate.

Hawk swiveled her chair so she was facing him, capturing her fidgeting hands in his own. He leaned close, his mouth hovering inches from hers. His breath was warm and tinged with the scent of wine as it traveled over her lips. "Tell me your dark secrets, Jo."

Nervous laughter gurgled in her throat. "You get right to the point, don't you?"

"Hmm," he said, running his hand into her hair, brushing it away from her face. "I'll go about this another way."

Slowly, he edged even closer, as if gauging the reception he would receive. Jo, too curious to pull away, only eyed him cautiously. He cradled her face in his hand and his lips began a slow trek from one corner of her mouth to the other. He moved across her jaw to ultimately rest just below her ear. She shivered at the contact.

"How much do you know about horses, Jo?" he asked, tracing the line of her collarbone with the tip of his finger.

She squirmed in her seat. Turned on and terrified. "Um, the usual things, I guess."

"What are the usual things?" Hawk asked and placed his hands at her waist. He drew her closer, his fingers disappearing under the hem of her t-shirt, their calloused texture sending goose bumps across her skin. When he skimmed her rib cage she drew in a sharp breath, her hands gripping his forearms.

"They're, um…" The gentle brush of his lips against her neck was wrecking what little concentration she managed to muster under his ministrations. "Big. Heavy." Jo could feel his smile against her skin. Hawk leaned farther, his fingertips pressing into her waist. She tried to focus and cleared her throat. "Good companions. Good investments." She sighed. "And intelligent."

"That's an impressive list," he said, drawing back to look

at her. "But they're also intuitive."

"Intuitive?"

Hawk slid his hands behind her to caress her lower back. "Yes," he whispered near her ear. "Horses can sense emotions in humans, and they react in predictable ways."

Jo melted under his touch, drugged by the sound of his voice. "How so?" she murmured.

"A horse can sense grief or illness." He brushed his lips against hers. "Joy or trepidation." His fingertips slipped lower, grazing the skin just above her jeans. "Their behavior reflects what they sense." Jo placed her hands on his shoulders, her body awakening under the gentle guidance of his voice and touch.

"Horses can sense need. And fear." He drew her even closer, until she was practically out of her seat. "I have a connection with my horses, Jo. I can sense things in them as well."

"I know," she said as she tentatively slid her hands down his muscled back, her fingertips exploring every ripple and dip. Hawk nuzzled her neck, nipping the sensitive flesh. "I, ah, saw you before. It looked like a dance."

Hawk brought his hands to her face, drawing her lips to his. His kiss was hot and insistent, his tongue demanding entrance. He groaned as his mouth moved over hers, his breathing uneven. "I sense things in you as well, Jo," he murmured against her lips.

"What?" she whispered.

Hawk leaned over her, bracing his palms on the back of her barstool. "I know you need something, but you're afraid to tell me why you shouldn't take it."

Jo searched his face. "I...I'm not sure what you're talking about."

His eyes were turbulent as he stared down at her. He ran

35

the backs of his fingers across her cheek. "I'm asking you to let me give you what you need." As he leaned closer, his erection pressed against her inner thigh. "Because I'm dying with want for it."

Jo's pulse skyrocketed, and she wasn't sure if she was more excited or scared. This was a moment she knew would eventually come about in her new life as a single woman. She just hadn't counted on it being so soon—or so abruptly brought about. When she had imagined it, in those initial days after her divorce, she'd no idea how she would ultimately react, or what she would be capable of doing. Now she knew.

Not much.

She eased back from his embrace, taking what little room he offered her. "Hawk, I..." She what? How could she explain how much he terrified her? How she couldn't even begin to understand why he would desire her, the prim, near-sexless ex-wife of a stuffy senator? She shook her head slightly. "I'm not what you want. Trust me."

He leaned back, narrowing his eyes as he studied her. "What makes you so sure about that?"

Jo gently pressed her palms against his chest, rising from her seat as he moved back. She wrapped her arms around herself. "I just know. Okay?"

"Jo, you—"

"I told you there was a lot you didn't know about me, remember?" Jo tucked an errant wisp of hair behind her ear.

His brow furrowed. "And remember I said I had time enough to listen?"

Jo turned from him, rubbing her hands up and down her upper arms. "I don't know, Hawk."

He walked up behind her, stilling her movement beneath his warm grasp. He rubbed his thumbs over the backs of her hands. "Clearly I've upset you. I apologize for that." He nudged her gently until she turned to face him. "I can't be sorry for wanting you, though."

She met his eyes, unsure how to reply. He placed a kiss against her forehead. "Listen," he said, running his fingers gently through her hair. "Let me fix you dinner." He held up both hands and winked. "I won't touch you, I promise."

"Hawk, it's not—"

"Scouts honor." He crossed his chest and held up his fingers. She nearly smiled at his innocent expression.

God, she was bad at this.

Jo knew she had to get out of there before she made things even worse. If that were even possible. "Actually, is it okay if I take a rain check? I'm pretty tired."

Hawk paused, then nodded. "Of course. Some other time." He placed his hand at the small of her back, leading her out of the kitchen. "Let's get you home, then."

Any chance of a graceful exit disappeared with the knowledge he would be accompanying her home on what was supposed to be her chance to freak out in private. Damn Southern men and their manners. "Oh, you don't have to walk with me, really. You know it's not far."

He loomed over her, clearly aghast with her suggestion. "It's getting dark, Jo. You'll trip all over the place." He reached into a simple pewter bowl on the foyer table, extracting a set of keys. He shook them in front of her. "We'll take the truck."

"O-okay," she stammered. Well, at least the truck would be faster than walking. Less time for her to screw up in. A blessing, indeed.

Hawk pulled the front door closed, grasping her under the elbow. Good thing it'd been dry the past couple of days. The man would probably strip off his shirt and lay it over puddles for her to walk on. He led her to a large silver truck and opened the door. She eyed the distance from the ground to the cab apprehensively. Could she even lift her leg that high?

Hawk chuckled, grabbing her around the waist and plopping her effortlessly onto the black leather seat. She steadied herself and looked at him. "Thank you." He smiled and closed her door.

They drove the short distance in silence, Jo sneaking glances out of the corner of her eye at Hawk. How could any man be so genetically blessed? And how could any woman in her right mind even consider walking away from all that...that heat? Jo rolled her eyes in disgust. *In her right mind* being the operative phrase.

Gravel crackled and popped under the truck's tires as Hawk pulled up to her farmhouse to park. He cut the ignition and was at her door before she had a chance to unbuckle her seat belt and attempt to scramble to the ground herself. His hands curled around her waist once more as he lifted her from the truck. She opened her mouth to thank him for the ride, but he was already leading her to the front porch.

A pitiful light bulb dangling from a wire hung over the door, casting an almost orange hue across the porch. Hawk looked up at it, a smile on his lips. "Hmm...more of that charming original wiring, I see."

"Yeah, it appears so."

Hawk turned his regard to her, the smile slowly ebbing from his features. He brought his hand to her face, hesitating briefly before cradling her jaw against his palm. He lowered his head, pressing a lingering kiss to her lips. "Good night, Jo."

"Good night," she replied and watched him descend the popping stairs and climb into his truck. She stood on the porch as he disappeared down her long drive. Jo pulled her keys from her purse and unlocked the front door. Stepping inside, she pushed it closed and leaned against the rough wood.

So much for starting over in peace, she mused. Jo reached for the wall switch and flipped it. A loud pop emanated from the overhead fixture, followed by a brief flash of light and then complete darkness.

"Shit," she grumbled. She'd forgotten the damn list.

* * * * *

Hawk was taking the last bite of canned pasta out of the plastic container he'd nuked it in when his dad came through the back door. Ray peered over Hawk's shoulder.

"Glad I ate at the diner tonight, if that's what was on the menu here." Ray dropped his hat onto the kitchen counter. "You losing your touch in the kitchen?"

Apparently. Hawk thought of the apprehension that had radiated off Jo and dropped the container in the sink, his fork clattering against the stainless-steel basin. A frown creased his forehead. He crossed his arms and leaned his hip against the counter. "I just didn't feel like cooking."

Ray rubbed his belly. "Well, I just gorged on barbequed ribs and Brunswick stew over at the diner. It was piglicous." He grimaced as his stomach gurgled. "Bet I pay for it later, though."

Hawk smiled. "You always do. My canned dinner won't seem like such an unappealing choice then."

"Yeah, probably not." He crossed to the refrigerator and took out a pitcher of iced tea. "What'd you do after you got the horses settled for the evening?"

"Jo dropped by just as I was finishing up. We got to know each other a little better."

Ray placed his glass on the counter. "In what sense?"

"Not the biblical, if that's what you're getting at, Pops."

Ray raised an eyebrow. "But not for lack of trying, if I'm guessing right."

Hawk averted his gaze, turning toward the sink to retrieve

his dirty container and place it in the dishwasher. "It's not like that," he mumbled loudly enough for Ray to hear.

"What's it like, then?"

The earnest look on Ray's face brought a smile to Hawk's lips. "Seriously, Pops. Are we doing this? Since when have you been concerned about my love life?" *Or lack thereof.*

Ray shook his finger at him. "Since I came in this house and saw that kind of look on your face and found out you'd just been in the company of our pretty new neighbor."

"And what kind of look do I have?" Hawk ran his hand down his face.

"Like Santa Claus came and brought you everything on your list but the shiny red bike, which is the only thing you really wanted."

Hawk pushed off the counter and walked toward the great room, motioning for his dad to accompany him. He sat in a club chair and pulled off his boots, letting them drop to the floor. Ray sat on the sofa, placing his tea on a slate coaster on the side table.

Hawk steepled his fingers in front of him. "There's more to it than that."

"Care to elaborate, son?"

Hawk opened his mouth to speak, but closed it again, scratching his head. He crossed one ankle over his knee and rested his forearms against his leg. "Okay, here's the thing. I feel drawn to Jo. It's like nothing I've experienced before."

Ray narrowed his eyes. "Like the kind of draw people like your mama base decisions on?"

"That kind exactly." Hawk shook his head. "You know that doe that's been making a menace of herself in the yard?"

"Yeah."

"Well, it seems as though Jo has a buck doing her weeding for her."

Ray leaned back into the sofa cushions, rubbing his chin. "Hmm. That's more than a coincidence, I'll give you that. So you want to pursue Jo, obviously. Despite the plans you have with your mother?"

Hawk nodded, collapsing into the embrace of his seat as well. "Yes, in spite of that. If it becomes an issue, I'll just jump off that bridge when I come to it. The pull I feel toward her is too strong not to."

"But there's another problem, though, isn't there?" Ray asked.

"Yeah, something's got Jo scared. Really scared." Hawk looked away, staring at a crack near the ceiling molding. Awkward didn't begin to describe this conversation. But he needed his dad's input. "I've been around enough to know when a woman is attracted to me. But..." Hawk rubbed his temples.

Ray cleared his throat and took a sip of his tea. "But?"

"*But*," Hawk said, frowning at his father. "She'll fight me at every turn. I can feel it."

Ray laughed. "I hate to say it, but it looks like you may have found the one woman who isn't going to fall at your feet."

"I'm glad I can amuse you," Hawk said sullenly.

"Nothing worth having comes easy, Silent Hawk. And easy is what all those other women have been."

Hawk winced at his tone. "So, you're saying I'm getting what's been coming to me."

Ray stood, grabbing his empty glass off the table. "Son, I don't think you have anything coming to you." He placed one hand on his hip. "Well, that's not entirely true. Maybe you have the one thing coming to you that you've always needed."

Hawk rose. "Jo."

Ray placed a hand on Hawk's shoulder and smiled. "Maybe so. Be careful with this one. You don't want to scare her off."

"Yeah, I know."

"When are you headed back to Arizona?"

"A couple of weeks." Hawk followed his father as he walked toward the kitchen. "Mom and I met with the oncologist from the Children's Hospital last trip, worked out some of the logistical issues. He also wanted to see the horses we planned to use in the program."

Ray refilled his tea, leaning against the counter. "Was he pleased with Raven's choices?"

"Yeah. Mom acquired a couple more geldings that have a lot of experience with children—that will please the therapist from the autism center as well. The other three horses are gentle, but have never been ridden by children. That will be my focus once I move out there. I'll analyze their temperament and go from there."

Ray chuckled. "Speaking of temperament, how is our resident hothead doing?"

"Well, you remember the last breeding." Hawk ran his hands through his hair. "I'm seeing streaks of temper in Thunder I'm not happy about. I've been working with him each evening, trying to reverse some of the bad habits I thought I'd rid him of long ago."

Ray crossed his arms over his chest, shaking his head. "I just pray he can get you and your mom through the next breeding season before he's out of the game."

"Tell me about it. I'd much rather have all the money up front for the first two years of operation. I don't know anything about fundraising."

"Well, you and Raven can always bring someone in with experience in that area if it comes to that."

"If it comes to that." Hawk shook his head. "Let's hope it doesn't. Raising the kind of money Thunder can bring from breeding will take much longer through other means. Any problems that arise will just have me out there that much longer."

Ray narrowed his eyes. "I know we've talked about this, but I just want to make sure you don't feel obligated to come back to work this farm. You've already—"

Hawk stopped Ray with a raised hand. "You know it's not that. This is my home. As much as I love Arizona, Georgia is where I belong. Once the ranch is established and we've got some funds built up, I'm coming back."

"All right. If you say so." Ray yawned. "I'm going to turn in."

Hawk followed his dad to the back door. "Oh, I forgot to give Jo that list of contractors. Would you mind dropping it by her place tomorrow?" He reached into a drawer near the phone and extracted a folded sheet of paper, passing it over to his father.

"You don't want to take it to her?"

"It's not a matter of wanting, Pops. I think I should give her a little space. Don't scare her, remember?"

Ray nodded. "Sounds like a smart move." His attention dropped to Hawk's hands and his fingers drumming nervously against his thigh. Ray chuckled. "Yeah, good luck with that." He opened the back door.

"Oh, and Pops?"

"Yeah?"

"Tell Jo I owe her dinner."

Ray smiled, reaching past Hawk to retrieve his hat off the counter. He placed it on his head. "Will do, son."

The door closed behind Ray and Hawk leaned against the counter, staring out the window. *Good luck indeed.*

CHAPTER THREE

"Knock, knock."

Jo looked over her shoulder from her perch atop the ladder and smiled at Ray as he entered the living room. She tugged at a piece of wallpaper she'd been struggling with and pulled the strip of paper down as she descended the steps.

"Hi, Ray."

"Hi there, darlin'." He pulled his cowboy hat from his head, clutching it in front of him. "Hawk sent me over to see if you needed any help."

Her stomach did a disturbing flip-flop at the mention of his name. She glanced around her living room, the corners of her lips curling. "Well, I don't know, Mr. Stephens. I think it looks pretty damn good in here. What do you think?"

Ray looked around the room at the mess she'd made. The wallpaper had been removed in patches, areas being abandoned when she had become frustrated with them. Ray laughed, placing his hat on the sofa, still covered in plastic.

"There's no accounting for taste, I guess," he said, approaching her. He reached into his pocket and extracted a folded sheet of paper. "Here's the list Hawk promised you."

The list. Right. What she had supposedly gone to his farm for last night. She had come home with a mental list of regrets, rather than contractors. She took the paper from him, unfolding it. She scanned the page. Hawk's handwriting was bold—all sharp angles and long lines. Just like the man.

Ray peered over the top of the paper, placing his finger by a name. "Dan Jenners. He's a poker buddy of mine. Does fine work, he does." Ray rubbed his chin. "I don't hang out with him outside of the gambling, though. Too good-looking—cuts my chances with the ladies, if you know what I mean." He winked at her.

Jo smiled as she watched him perusing the list intently. Ray was the epitome of a good old boy, and on the opposite end of the spectrum from his son. If it weren't for their matching mesmerizing eyes, she'd never believe their father-son story.

"Oh!" Ray exclaimed. Jo jumped at his sudden exuberance. "Billy Crutchett. Now here's a story for ya." His eyes danced with excitement.

"Do tell," Jo said.

"Must've been two…no, three years ago. Georgia had a hard freeze." He cut his eyes to her. "Ain't real common in these parts, you know."

The muscles twitched at the corners of her mouth in her effort not to smile, since the look on Ray's face said this story was clearly not a laughing matter. "I imagine not," she agreed and bit the inside of her cheek when Ray nodded matter-of-factly.

"So, anyway, we had ourselves a hard freeze. Billy's got a small lake in his backyard." He put his hand on her shoulder. "Now just between you and me, it's nothin' more than a big pond, but don't you tell him I said so."

"A-all right." She bit the inside of her other cheek.

"Billy, the dumbass—beggin' your pardon—drags out a folding metal chair to the center of his so-called lake. You want to know why?"

45

How could she possibly not at this point? "Of course."

"Ice fishin'. Can you believe it? In Georgia?" Ray shook his head, his hand resting on one hip. "Ain't nothin' but some scrawny carp in that water. Did I mention to you Billy weighs almost three Franklins?"

"You mean three hundred?"

Ray pointed at her. "Exactly." He eyed her expectantly.

"So…so what happened?"

"Billy hadn't even had a chance to bait his hook before the ice broke through, sending his ass south." Ray blushed. "Beggin' your pardon, Jo."

She waved her hand, dismissing the unnecessary apology. "He's okay, I guess, since he's on this list?"

Ray sighed. "Yeah, he's right as rain. His dog went to yappin' its fool head off when Billy fell through. Every neighbor within a half-mile radius came rushing over." Ray snickered. "Yes sir. Billy ain't the sharpest tool in the shed."

Jo glanced from Ray to the list and back again, raising one eyebrow.

He cleared his throat. "Fine work he does. Fine work."

She laughed then. "Okay, I'll give these guys a call. Get some quotes."

"Now don't you tell Billy I told you about his unfortunate incident. Mighty embarrassin', it is."

"What unfortunate incident?" Jo grinned at his relieved expression.

Ray ran his hand through his thinning hair. "Let me help you with these walls, darlin'. It's a fight you're going to lose, I'm afraid."

She handed him the scraper with a smile. "Go for it."

He took it from her, stepping up the ladder. "Oh. Hawk told me to tell you he owes you dinner."

Jo's blush raced clear down to her toes. "Um, okay. Tell him thank you." *Or just pass him a note in study hall, for crying out loud.* Had she handled things so poorly that his only recourse was to send messages through his father? She suspected so. Jo bit back a groan.

She plastered a sunny smile on her face. "Hey, Ray. I was just about to get some lemonade. Would you like a glass?"

Ray looked at her triumphantly as a long section of paper separated from the wall. "Sounds great, darlin'."

* * * * *

The next morning brought about Jo's first day of work. She was grateful for the distraction. A certain horse— Horse *what*? Trainer? For all that's good and holy, she hadn't the faintest idea just what Hawk did with his horses, besides read their minds. And hers too, apparently. He was so close to the mark it was frightening.

But what sort of business he ran wasn't the point. The point was he had been foremost in her thoughts for the better part of thirty-six hours. He'd even appeared in her dreams— doing wicked things that heated her skin just to think about.

In preparation for her new job, she had armed herself with an arsenal of denim and brushed cotton. Jeans, shorts, skirts, t-shirts, tank tops. Many of which she would have only considered wearing for exercise in her previous life. The life she was glad was disappearing into her past. Jo checked her appearance in the ancient mirror over her bathroom sink. She had pulled her hair into a high ponytail, just as she remembered Kristy had worn hers. Her aqua t-shirt complemented her figure more than she would have expected, the slim jeans she wore making her legs look marginally longer.

With shaking fingers, Jo placed the contact lens against her eye. "Ewww..." she squeaked, blinking until she was certain it would stay in place. She repeated the procedure on the other side. Would she ever get used to sticking her finger in her eye? She had to admit, though, ditching the glasses had been an instant improvement to her appearance. Jo skimmed on some lip gloss and gave herself a quick once-over before turning off the overhead light.

Twenty minutes later she pulled her car into an empty spot behind the diner. There was only one other car in the lot. The tag read BOBBEE. Jo glanced at her watch. Right on time. So where was everyone else? Shrugging, she slid out of her car and locked it.

When she pushed open the door of the diner, Kristy came bounding over, a huge smile on her face.

"Hiya!" she said, looping her arm through Jo's.

Jo looked around the restaurant. Bobby was there, along with two cooks.

"Hi, Kristy." She followed as Kristy tugged her toward the kitchen. "I think I may have parked in the wrong place."

"Out back, right?" she asked, bumping the swinging door open with her hip and pulling Jo through.

"Yes, but there was only one other car, so I thought maybe I was in the wrong place."

A disgusted snort came from Kristy. "My boyfriend and I have to share a car. We live twenty minutes in the opposite direction. It sucks." Her smile didn't match the complaint. "And Bobby brings the cooks in with him."

"Oh," Jo replied, waving at the two men staring at her from the prep station.

Kristy wrote Jo's name on a blank timecard, turning the "o" into a smiley face, and clocked her in. Taking Jo's hand, she dragged her back into the dining room. She leaned in close. "Bobby said you're supposed to shadow me, being your first day and all." She glanced over her shoulder at an uninterested Bobby counting money in the till. "But how hard is it, really?

You can have your own tables as soon as you'd like."

"Oh, okay."

Kristy crossed her arms over her chest, tilting her head to the side. "Hey, yo, Bobby," she said, shaking her head when he looked over. "You gonna say hi or what?"

"Hi, Jo." He returned his attention to his task.

Kristy spun on her toe to face Jo. "Ignore him," she whispered. "He's on a diet. *Again.* Ornery as a grizzly, is what he is."

"Noted." Jo followed Kristy behind the counter. She was shown how to set up, take orders, place orders and deliver orders. Like Kristy said, it wasn't too difficult.

"You settling in okay?" Kristy asked as she poured cups of coffee for herself and Jo.

Jo smirked. "Well, my house is a hellhole, but besides that, things are coming together. I got some quotes yesterday afternoon from contractors Hawk suggested."

"So how is Mr. Stephens?" Kristy asked, the corners of her smile extending beyond the sides of the mug she'd brought to her lips.

"Which one?"

Kristy narrowed her eyes playfully. "Well, I saw senior last night, so I know how *he* is."

"Hawk is, ah, fine, I guess." Jo smoothed out nonexistent wrinkles in her apron, her cheeks flaming.

"Uh-huh," Kristy said speculatively. "That's some kitchen he has, isn't it?"

"I know, right? Like out of a magazine." Jo met Kristy's eyes, which sparkled with humor. Jo instantly realized her gaffe.

"Should I ask you about his bedroom?" Kristy teased, alight with curiosity.

"Of course not," Jo answered a little too quickly. "I mean, I haven't seen it."

"That's a shame," Kristy replied with a wink. She leaned her elbows on the counter.

Jo picked up her coffee, taking a sip. "So you've been in Hawk's place, I take it?" Did that squeaky voice just come from her?

Kristy's face lit up like a Christmas tree. "Well, that was subtle." She shook her head, still smiling. "I guess I don't have to ask you if you're interested in our local celebrity."

"Celebrity?" Jo's brow furrowed.

"Well," Kristy said, playing with the end of her ponytail. "For all intents and purposes. At least around here." She peered at the clock over her shoulder. "Okay, we've got ten minutes until we open, I'll fill you in. Hawk is a horse breeder."

Well, that cleared up the mystery of his profession, but little else. Jo leaned toward Kristy. "And that's significant because…"

"This is a great story. Okay, Hawk found this horse, a real hellion apparently, whose owner was really anxious to sell. Hawk bought him and brought him back to his farm. Now this part I'm sketchy on, because it doesn't make much sense." Kristy tossed her ponytail over her shoulder.

"Go on," Jo prodded.

"Well, Hawk is supposed to have some sort of gift with animals, or something like that. Anyway, he was able to tame the horse, and one of his boarders asked if he could breed the stallion with his mare. As it turns out, Thunder sired a Derby runner. It all snowballed from there."

Jo rubbed her temples. She thought she'd read something about this at some point, probably in one of the society magazines in a Kentucky Derby feature. "Did you say the horse's name is Thunder?"

"Yep. And when you see him run, you'll understand why."

Jo nodded and took a sip of her coffee. Her attention snapped to Kristy when she abruptly stood as the cowbell clamored over the door.

"Look alive. Our first customer has arrived." She took Jo by the hand and led her into the dining room. "Oh, and by the way, the Stephenses have an annual Christmas party. That's why I've seen the kitchen."

The fact Kristy felt the need to reassure Jo was embarrassing, and the relief that washed over her when no mention of Kristy's sister came up in the explanation was more than a little troublesome. Jo sighed. It felt as though the peace she'd thought she'd find with her move was slowly being choked out of her, steering her straight toward trouble. Some sense of humor God had, throwing this man into her life at a time when she had no earthly idea how to handle him. If she could ever handle him at all.

* * * * *

A week had passed since Jo had sidestepped Hawk's advances, walking away from a seduction most women would line up around the block for. But just because she hadn't taken him up on his offer didn't mean she hadn't thought about it.

Constantly.

The nights were the worst. She would lie awake, remembering his touch, and would begin a deep spiral of disturbing reflection. Hawk had set her on edge from the first moment their eyes met, stirring a desire she hadn't experienced in a long time...if ever. What did that say about her marriage? About the last twelve years of her life? Had she wasted it, not realizing there was an alternative to the reality she had convinced herself was normal? Fine?

Pathetic.

That word is the one that haunted her, stealing her sleep. As Jo stared at the ceiling night after night and minutes turned into hours, her truth unfolded. Marrying her college boyfriend, the only man she'd ever been with, had seemed like a great idea. He was driven, successful, handsome. And she was the district attorney's daughter. It was a perfect match…for a man with aspirations to become a senator.

God, had she been stupid.

So she had sacrificed herself, her happiness, to be part of a false front. Had worried over her father's reputation and feelings, disregarding her own. And what did it get her, ultimately? A divorce and not a clue how to be the woman she knew was suffocating just beneath the surface. Hawk had given her a glimpse of what she *could* be, if she were brave enough.

Her cowardly exit a week prior had accomplished what she hadn't truly wanted—to keep Hawk at a distance. Aside from dropping by a couple of times to check on her progress, he hadn't gotten within striking distance of her. As the days passed, she was forced to admit to herself how disappointed she truly was.

She found some refuge at work, where she was busy enough to take the edge off her thoughts, and she looked forward to going. Today was no different. Jo was grateful as she pulled her sedan alongside Bobby's ancient Lincoln Town Car and cut the ignition. She grabbed the book Kristy had loaned her—a steamy novel depicting scenarios she didn't think were anatomically possible—and headed into the diner.

The early dinner crowd was already there and Kristy was buzzing around, seemingly doing ten things at once. When she saw Jo, she smiled. "Thank goodness you're here. I am *so* in the weeds."

Jo stashed her purse and Kristy's book under the counter and grabbed her apron, tying it around her waist. "What can I help you with?"

"Can you get four teas for number three and deliver the food to seven?"

"No problem."

Jo had just dropped off the club sandwiches to table seven when the cowbell clanged above the door. She glanced over her shoulder and her heartbeat surged with awareness. Hawk and his dad stood by the door. Ray was scoping out a seat, and Hawk was staring her down, his eyes like missiles locked on hers. He tipped his hat at her before removing it. Ray noticed her then and smiled, strolling over. Hawk followed behind.

Jo's mouth went bone dry. Hawk never took his eyes from her face—his intent expression the kind that could dissolve a woman's panties on contact. Her attention darted to Ray when he draped his arm around her shoulders.

"Okay, darlin'. You gotta help us out. Any of these yahoos leaving soon?" Ray glanced around at all the full booths.

Jo motioned to the left with her head. "The couple in the last booth just got their check."

"Perfect. I'm going to go hover…subtle like, of course." Ray drove his hands into his pockets and moseyed over to the corner.

Hawk didn't follow and Jo turned nervous eyes to him. "How are you, Hawk?"

"I'm fine. Busy…" He placed his hand on her upper arm. "Listen, Jo, I—"

"Order up!"

She turned to the kitchen, nodding to the cook before looking back at Hawk. "I've got to get that. Can you hold that thought?"

"Of course." He gestured toward the counter. "You go ahead."

"Thanks." On impulse, she took his hand in hers, gently squeezing. He wound their fingers together, sending pulses of electricity up her arm.

"Don't you run off, though." He released her hand and joined his father in the vacated booth.

Jo turned and nearly plowed into Kristy. "Aren't you supposed to be in the weeds?"

Kristy leaned closer, stage-whispering, "They can wait. That little exchange was much too interesting to miss."

Jo walked toward the kitchen to retrieve her order, Kristy trailing her heels like a puppy. "I'm glad I can entertain you," Jo tossed over her shoulder as she headed toward the deuce at the window.

"I'll switch tables with you, Jo, so you can wait on Hawk and Ray."

Jo placed the Caesar salad and cheese steak sandwich on the table and whirled to face Kristy. "No, don't," she pleaded, shooting a glance at the corner booth. "You're already slammed and that's your section, your tips, anyway. I'll just deliver the orders that are up until I get a table."

"Hmm," Kristy purred. "If you say so. Just don't forget I offered."

"I won't," Jo mumbled, watching Kristy approach the Stephens men. Jo flexed her fingers, still tingling from his touch, and got back to work.

An hour passed as she went about the mundane tasks of her job. It was the longest hour of her life, it seemed, as Hawk tracked her every movement. He made no show of concealing his open regard, only redirecting his attention to his father if Jo stared back at him long enough. By the time the two men rose from the table, her neck and shoulders were knotted with tension.

"Why do I do that to myself?" Ray lamented, rubbing his stomach as he and Hawk joined Jo at the counter. "Two orders of ribs this time. It's shameful, is what it is." He winked at her and walked to the register to pay.

Hawk's hand rested at the small of Jo's back. "Have you got a minute?"

Jo looked around the diner at the dwindling dinner crowd and sent Kristy a questioning look. Kristy nodded, shooing Jo with her hands.

"Yeah, it's died down. I can take a quick break."

"Excellent," he said, guiding her toward the door.

They had just gotten outside when Ray breezed past them. "I'll be right back. I've got to duck into the pharmacy right quick." He rubbed his stomach again.

Jo watched Ray retreat for as long as she could get away with before turning her attention back to Hawk. "So, what's on your mind?"

"You." He ran the tip of his finger along her cheek.

Jo forced a lump the size of Montana down her throat as she swallowed. "Oh."

He removed her hand from her throat, folding it into his. "I can't stop thinking about you, but I don't know if that's something you want or not."

Jo brought her free hand up to her neck in a nervous gesture, but then caught herself. She let her hand drop, willing her eyes to stay on Hawk's. A trill of anxious laughter escaped her. "I don't think I've ever met someone as direct as you before, Hawk."

He leveled his gaze on her. "No sense skirting an issue, I was raised to believe."

She nodded. "It's not that it's not wanted, it's just…" She looked away, biting her bottom lip. Embarrassed heat crept across her cheeks when she caught Kristy's delighted expression through the window.

Hawk glanced inside and saw their enraptured audience. He took several steps back, pulling Jo with him around the corner of the diner. "It's just what?" he asked.

"Ugh," she groaned. "Hawk, I'm so bad at this." She gently tugged her hand from his and wrapped her arms around herself. "I wish you would trust me when I tell you I'm not what you want."

Hawk took a step toward her, resting his hands against the wall on either side of her head. He leaned in close, his lips mere inches from hers. "And you feel that's your decision?" He pressed a kiss to the corner of her mouth.

"What?" she whispered.

Hawk's lips blazed a trail along her jaw, pausing just below her ear. His breath heated her skin as he spoke. "You think you should decide whether or not you're what I want." His hand slid to her lower back, drawing her closer. "Too late."

She pulled back to stare up at him. "What do you mean?"

"I already want you." He cradled her face in his hands and lowered his mouth to hers, stopping just shy of the mark. "I'd say I'll try to stay away from you, give you space. But that would be a lie. I just don't have that kind of restraint." He kissed her then, taking her mouth in a heated possession. Jo melted into the embrace and nearly lost her footing when he pulled back abruptly, placing her palm against his chest where his heart fluttered erratically.

"I want you, Jo. So much so it's making me crazy." His gaze dropped to her parted lips. "I wish you weren't afraid of me."

An off-key whistling rendition of *Yankee Doodle Dandy* drifted down the sidewalk toward them. "Great timing," Hawk muttered under his breath. He stood to his full height, adjusted his hat and took a step back from her. He traced the line of her jaw with the tip of his finger. "Trust me, Jo. Please."

"Hawk—"

"There you two are," Ray said with a smile as he turned the corner by the diner. He looked between the two of them. "I'm not interrupting anything, am I?"

"No, of course not." Jo returned his smile. "I have to get back in there, anyway."

"Don't let us keep you, darlin'." Ray clapped his hand on his son's back. "You ready, Silent Hawk?"

"Sure," he said, pulling his keys from his pocket.

"Night, Jo," Ray called as he walked toward the truck.

"Good night, Ray."

Hawk placed a kiss on her cheek, his lips lingering. "Trust me, Jo," he whispered.

The moment he turned from her, she hastily made her way back into the diner, only to be greeted by an exuberant Kristy.

"Spill," she said, pulling Jo into an empty booth.

Jo looked around at the deserted diner. "Where'd everybody go?"

"Oh, it's Sunday. We don't usually have anyone come in after the five-thirty rush. We close early." She raised her eyebrow expectantly. "So?"

Jo eyed her hesitantly, weighing her options. She glanced over Kristy's shoulder at the kitchen. "I don't know…"

Kristy bounced in her seat. "Aw, come on, Jo. You can't keep this to yourself. It's got to be too *good*." She whined out the last word.

"Well…" Jo began.

Kristy's brow furrowed. "You know you can trust me, right?" Jo opened her mouth to speak but Kristy gushed on. "I mean, I know small towns have a reputation for gossip, and Lord knows I've already laid some on you." She leaned across the table and placed her hand over Jo's. "But I *can* keep a secret. Especially for a friend."

Jo took in all she said and chewed on it. What harm could there be in confiding in Kristy? She seemed sincere enough. And besides, it wasn't as if she had anyone else to talk to. With her sister's juggling act between work and law school and her clear disapproval of Jo's relocation, Meg wasn't the best option.

Jo peered over Kristy's shoulder again, glancing into the kitchen. The cooks and Bobby were occupied with breaking down the stations. "Okay, okay. You might be disappointed, though. My dilemma probably isn't too interesting."

Kristy snorted. "Oh, right. Hawk was tracking you like a hunter when he was in here. And that look on his face…" She fanned herself, but Jo was the overheated one after Kristy's comment. "What's going on between you two?"

Jo clasped her hands in her lap and tried to decide how to go about explaining what would probably come across as a no-brainer to Kristy. She cleared her throat. "Well, see, I'm recently divorced."

Kristy leaned forward. "Really? How long were you hitched?"

"Twelve years."

"So, you're not over your ex?" She frowned.

It was Jo's turn to snort. "Hardly. There's nothing between Thomas and me anymore. I didn't realize just how much I resented him until I moved here."

Kristy sent her a questioning look but Jo waved it off.

"Anyway, Hawk is very…different than my ex. Not at all what I'm used to."

"But that should be a good thing, shouldn't it?"

Jo heaved a weighted sigh. "You'd think so."

Kristy leaned her forearms on the table. "Okay, I'm trying to follow, but I'm really not sure I see what the problem is. I mean, considering…"

Rubbing her temple, Jo nodded. "I know. Let me figure out the best way to explain." Hawk's description of the intuitiveness of a horse flashed through her memory. It wasn't exactly the same as the number her marriage had done on her, but it would suffice as a safe example.

"Okay. I once spent the weekend with a boyfriend and his family at their lake house, back when I was in high school. He had a horse. Dynamo." Jo smirked. "Big huge ass of an animal."

"And?" Kristy asked, folding her hands together.

"And," Jo continued, "I was scared of him at first sight. He knew it too. We had an instant understanding, Dynamo and I. He understood I was acting like I knew what I was doing, just to impress my boyfriend. And I understood things would not end well that day."

The corners of Kristy's lips curled up. "Go on," she prodded.

"Well, ten minutes into the ride that future bottle of glue reared up at a dog that had startled him by charging the fence. I slid off the rear of him, as pretty as you please."

Kristy cringed.

"It must have knocked me out, because I woke up to my boyfriend hovering over me, calling my name." Jo laughed without humor. "I remember looking up at Dynamo, and I swear he had a smug look on his face."

"So, you're afraid of horses—I doubt very seriously that would offend Hawk."

"No, it's nothing like that." Jo pulled the elastic band from her hair and shook out her ponytail.

"Then I'm still not following you. I can't see what the issue is."

And why would she, Jo chastised herself. Not only was she being as clear as mud, but her reasoning wouldn't make sense to someone who wasn't scarred by over a decade of wrong choices. "Well," Jo tried again. "When I agreed to ride Dynamo instead of the much safer mare I could have chosen, I was pretending to be something I wasn't. My motivation may have made sense, but when you venture into unfamiliar territory that terrifies you at first sight, you're only setting yourself up for a fall. Does that make sense?"

"So Hawk is unfamiliar territory?"

"Just slightly," Jo said, thinking of the man responsible for her sleepless nights. "He's so different from Thomas. I mean, when he touches me, I just...I wouldn't even know..." Her gaze hit her lap.

"Wait a sec," Kristy said and Jo met her eyes. "Are you saying you're afraid of getting physically involved with Hawk?"

"Among other things," Jo muttered.

"Wow." Kristy sank back into her seat. "I can see how that could scramble your brain. Hawk is potent, for lack of a better word."

"Tell me about it."

"What are you going to do? You probably couldn't avoid him if you tried."

Jo shook her head. "I don't know if I'd want to."

That drew a grin from Kristy. "I don't think I blame you."

"But," Jo added, "you know what they say about not learning from the past? Only a fool makes the same mistake twice."

Kristy stared at Jo, twirling her ponytail around her finger. A smile began to spread across her lips and soon consumed her entire expression. "You know what else they say, don't you?"

"What?" Jo asked in a defeated voice. Kristy looked too pleased with herself for anything innocuous to pass through her lips.

"I believe the saying goes something like this. Get back on the horse that threw you." She rose from the seat. "You go ahead and head out. I'll close things down."

Jo watched her walk away, speechless. Her eyes only grew wider when Kristy called over her shoulder, "Nice night for a ride, don't you think?"

CHAPTER FOUR

Jo brought her sedan to a crawl as she approached her driveway, tapping the accelerator and then abruptly punching the brake. She glared at her reflection in the rearview, her knuckles white on the steering wheel. Her eyes slammed shut as images of Hawk's face—and Kristy's in the diner—paraded through her head like a slide show. Every few frames, a flash of her old life would elbow its way in between the images—an odd contrast to the woman she could see herself becoming in the company of the new people in her life. If she allowed it.

Jo slid out a long breath, opening her eyes to focus on the road stretched before her. With a disgusted groan, she jerked the steering wheel to the right, beginning the long ascent of her driveway. Halfway up, she jabbed the brake again, grumbling under her breath.

Get back on the horse that threw you.

"Oh screw it."

Jo fought the gearshift into reverse, slipping right past it into park and getting hung up on neutral before finally engaging it properly to ease back down her driveway. Kristy's no-nonsense expression goaded her as she wheeled back onto the gravel road and veered toward the Stephens farm. Jo pulled her Cadillac alongside Hawk's truck and cut the ignition. She ignored an overwhelming urge to flee as she traveled the short distance to his front door. Her finger hovered over the doorbell, a wild mix of anticipation and fear racing through her blood.

She depressed the button and stepped back, twining her fingers together in front of her.

Her heartbeat ratcheted up a notch when the faint sound of footfalls thudding against the hardwoods became silent on the other side of the door. Jo drew a deep breath as the door creaked in its frame and was pulled open.

She was not prepared for what greeted her.

Her eyes swept the length of him, from his bare feet up the long length of his legs covered in torn, faded jeans. His hair was loose around his face, falling over a bare chest that was much broader than she'd imagined, his arms and shoulders corded with muscle. Her attention dropped to his abdomen, its defined planes of muscle disappearing beneath the denim slung low on his hips.

"Jo." His voice was velvet rich and husky, the timbre soothing. "Would you like to come in?" He gestured inside the house.

No. "Yes," she managed to squeeze out and stepped into the foyer. She stood motionless, facing away from him, rubbing her thumbs against her index fingers. The door clicked behind her and she finally willed herself to turn toward him.

He studied her face for a long moment. "You okay, Jo?"

"Yes." She forced a smile. "Absolutely." Jo wrapped her arms around herself and rolled back and forth on the balls of her feet.

Hawk rubbed his chin. "Really?"

She dropped her arms to her sides with an exasperated sigh. "No, not really. But I wouldn't want to throw you off by acting like a sane person."

Hawk laughed and reached for her, pulling Jo into his embrace. "I never know what to expect with you. Keeps me on my toes." He placed a kiss on the top of her head, letting his lips linger. "I *am* surprised to see you...so soon. I thought

63

you'd leave skid marks in your wild dash away from me after what I said earlier."

"I still might. I guess I'm what you'd call a flight risk." She joked at what wasn't very far from the truth.

"Well, I'm pretty strong. I'll keep a good grip on you." He tightened his embrace, bringing her even closer. Jo settled against him, sliding her arms around his waist. His skin was warm and soft, like silk stretched over steel. She placed her head against his chest and ran the tips of her fingers across his back. His heartbeat fluttered in her ear, accelerating with each glide of her hand.

"Don't take this the wrong way, but I have to ask what brought you here. Tonight," he murmured against her hair.

She drew her head back, looking up at him. "I've, ah, decided to trust you."

His pupils dilated as he drew in a deep breath. He placed his hands at her waist. "You have?"

Jo nodded and pressed a tentative kiss to his chest, her heart beating wildly along with his. Hawk's fingertips dug into the flesh of her waist.

"Are you sure?" His voice was rough and barely above a whisper.

She looked up at him. "Yes. I think so."

Hawk lowered his head, brushing her lips gently with his. "Jo," he whispered, sliding his hand to her nape. "Let me show you how much I want you."

His kiss consumed her, lips urgent as they moved over hers. She was assaulted with sensations she'd never experienced. A fire burning out of control, its heat licking every nerve ending in her body. A desire to become completely lost in the moment. Lost in him.

Jo returned his kiss, tangling her tongue with his. Hawk slid his hands around the curve of her ass, lifting her to straddle his waist, groaning when the contact brought her flush against his erection. He pressed hot, open-mouthed kisses down the length of her neck as he attempted to draw her even closer.

Jo tilted her pelvis, rubbing his rigid length against her. A feral moan vibrated from his chest, the very essence of its meaning driving her to step a little more outside herself. She continued to move against him, letting her head drop back to better expose the long column of her neck to his greedy mouth. His kisses stilled against her throat, hot breath fanning across her skin in ragged gasps.

"Inside you, Jo. I want to be inside you." He pulled back to look at her, his eyes a stormy mix of blues and grays. One hand snaked through her hair and dragged her mouth back to his. "Please."

"Yes," she whispered against his lips, taking his face in her hands as she kissed him. His arms wound even tighter around her as he walked into the kitchen and up the massive wooden staircase. When they reached the top, Jo saw that the space was one large room that stretched across the entire length of the house. The floor was made of the same aged pine, the walls dark wood paneling with three bay windows along the southern side.

Wired lanterns dotted the perimeter of his bedroom, casting it in a dim glow. Her eyes ventured to the rear of the room, where a king-sized bed made from what appeared to be raw, knotted wood loomed with promises of the unknown. Jo glanced up at Hawk's face and then back to the bed. He carried her there, placing her on the thick down comforter and stretching his long frame beside her.

Her heart hammered so loudly she was certain he could hear it—it was the only thing she could hear besides the absurdly loud sound of her breathing. Hawk brushed her hair off her cheek and a tremor pulsed across her skin.

"Are you cold?" he asked, pulling her against him.

She shook her head. "No. Just a little nervous, I guess." She turned her face into his chest.

"Jo." He spoke against her hair. "Baby, we don't have to do this tonight. I don't want to rush you."

She looked up at him, at his smoldering eyes, his square jaw, the wild mass of hair that fell across his face and brushed her cheek, and knew what she was about to say was the unequivocal truth. "You're not. I want to." She reached up to trace his lower lip with the tip of her finger. "I want you. It's just been a…while for me, that's all."

He cradled her jaw in his palm and kissed her, a soft, feathering caress. "Thank you for trusting me. You won't regret it."

And she believed him. But trusting herself was another matter altogether. She wasn't so certain she would be able to handle the fallout of what she was about to do. She came to Georgia to heal over a decade of hurt and self-loathing, not to throw herself right back into a situation that could easily break the fragile new beginning she was forging. But as he kissed her and his hand slid beneath her t-shirt to brush the underside of her breast, she couldn't find a reason to justify caring at the moment.

Jo sighed as his palm closed over the turgid peak of her nipple, the contact causing a rush of fluid between her thighs and delicious tremors in her womb. Hawk kissed her, the tip of his tongue teasing her lips until they parted on a moan. He eased his body over hers, placing a knee between her thighs. Her hips tilted toward him, the friction tightening the coil wound deeply inside.

"Too many clothes," he said against her ear, pulling the hem of her shirt up her abdomen. Jo shifted so he could remove it. He kissed her again as he worked on her button fly. "These need to go too."

After he had liberated her of her jeans, he sat back on his

heels and let his gaze take a heated journey down the length of her body. Jo forced herself to be motionless, even though every instinct demanded she slither beneath the fur throw draped across the bed.

"You're so beautiful." He leaned over her, pressing kisses along her collarbone and the curve of each breast. He traced his fingers across the delicate lace of her bra. "This is something," he said, brushing the tips of his fingers against the Swarovski crystals concealing the front closure of the garment. It was just one of many similar sets that had grown cobwebs in her lingerie drawer from her husband's disinterest. She had dusted them off after her move, deciding to wear them on a daily basis.

Thank God.

Hawk gazed upon the obscenely expensive scraps of fabric as if they were one of the natural wonders of the world. A slow, sensual smile crawled across his lips. "Unfortunately, they have to go too."

Jo sucked in a breath when he opened the closure with a flick of his fingers. He gave her a crooked smile. "Good guess. I figured they hid the secret door behind all the jewels."

Jo's laugh was silenced by Hawk's kiss. Her breath seized when he skimmed the thin band of lace at her hip. His fingertip slipped beneath the fabric, making a slow, deliberate journey toward the heart of her. Her hips rose toward his touch as he grazed the slick folds of her sex. Jo moaned and bit her bottom lip as Hawk slid his finger deep inside her.

The feel of Jo moving beneath his touch was unlike anything Hawk had experienced before. It was as if her body was tuned solely for him, as though her response was only something he could orchestrate. The feel of her around his finger, so tight and wet and hot, held promise of what was to come. The scent of her arousal permeated the air, her soft moans like a siren's call drawing both of them closer and closer to the place where nothing else mattered but the joining of their bodies.

"Jo," he whispered against her neck, his teeth gently nipping her skin. "You feel so good." He grazed her clit with the pad of his thumb as he moved his finger inside her channel. Her breath came in short, ragged gasps, and he knew she was close. Damn, she was responsive. He'd barely begun all he had planned for her and she was writhing beneath his touch. It was hot as hell. Leaning over her, he took a nipple into his mouth, drawing on the aroused flesh. He flicked his tongue over the peak as he moved his thumb in slow circles.

Jo's back arched as she came, his name tumbling from her lips. The sounds she made as he brought her to pleasure were his undoing. His erection strained for release against the rough denim of his jeans.

Her eyes drifted open and she looked like a cat curled up in the sun—warm and satisfied. The corners of her lips lifted as she reached for him and brought him in for a kiss so hot he thought he might cross the finish line before he even got his pants off.

"Jo," he managed between her hungry kisses. "I need you. Now."

She fumbled for the snap of his jeans and he helped her, pulling the zipper down. She tugged at the fabric, pushing it off with her feet. Jo placed her hand around his erection and he groaned, desperate to feel her slick heat wrapped all around him.

She raised her hips until the tip of his penis brushed against her sex. "Hawk," she murmured, sliding her hand down his lower back. Her lips met his throat as she urged him closer with a thigh wrapped around his hips. The feel of her beneath him, so hot and wet and ready, nearly made him lose control. It took all the restraint he could muster not to drive himself deep inside her. She shifted below him, causing his cock to inch forward. Her fingernails dug into his hips.

"Jo," he said on a rush of breath. "We've got to stop."

She froze beneath him. "What?" Her eyes were wide, a look of panic beginning to consume her features.

"No, that's not what I meant." He tried to smooth the furrow between her brows with a caress of his finger. "I just need to get a condom, baby."

"Oh," she said, her cheeks flaming. "I'm sorry."

Hawk leaned across her to open the bedside table drawer. He pulled a foil packet from a box and tore it open. "Don't apologize for making me want you so much I can't think straight."

Hawk sheathed himself and positioned his body over hers. "And I can't think straight around you. It's the damndest thing." He kissed her long and slow, easing the tip of his erection inside her. She was tiny everywhere. He bit his lip as he fought the urge to drive home. She relaxed around him, drawing him closer and closer.

"Oh, Hawk," she moaned when he had buried himself fully. She moved against him, with him, sending him on a dizzying climb to fulfillment. When her breaths became rapid and shallow, he slipped his hand between them to stroke her clit in circles as frantic as his thrusts had become. She shattered around him and he followed closely behind, throwing his head back as he shuddered from his own climax.

Hawk leaned on his forearms, careful not to crush her. His chest heaved with his breaths, his pulse rioting in his veins. The place Jo had just taken him was foreign, the experience like no other. A woman like no other. But somehow, on some level, he had already known it would be that way.

He rolled to his side, bringing her with him so they were facing each other. "Jo," he whispered against her lips. "What is your name short for?"

She averted her gaze, a pink hue tingeing her cheeks. "Um, Josephine." She shrugged one shoulder. "I always hated it growing up. So fussy."

Hawk tilted her chin with a finger so she would look at him. "I don't agree." He smiled at her. "Kiss me, Josephine." And when she touched her lips to his, he knew he'd need her like this. Again and again.

* * * * *

"Crap," Jo muttered, tripping over an exposed tree root for the third time. Even the full moon was poor illumination for her reflective walk back to her farmhouse. In the middle of the night. Despite the soft purr of her Cadillac's engine, the remote chance the motor would wake Hawk was more than she was willing to risk. She had left him sleeping, too cowardly to awaken him and announce her departure. How would she explain herself, anyway?

Thanks for the great sex, but I'm going to freak out now so it's best if I go.

She had lain next to Hawk for what felt like hours, her mind dashing in a thousand different directions. The sound of his breathing had been a soft echo in the room, a chant attempting to draw her in. Comfort. That's what it promised. Jo had expected to feel chaotic after being in Hawk's bed. She was not disappointed. But it was the root of her emotions that had her disappearing before sunrise.

Hawk was much more than a bed partner to hurl her back into the land of the sexual living. He had done that, of course, awakening long-forgotten, dormant desires she didn't know she was capable of owning. He had made her feel like a woman to be coveted, not cast aside. But it was more involved than that.

Something in the way he held her, the look in his eyes as he moved, the way he said her name, made her long for something she'd never had. It made her crave. And she wasn't ready to need those things, to put herself out there like that. And it could be all one-sided, anyway. Kristy's hints at Hawk's reputation with women shouldn't have Jo thinking their situation was unique. She could very well be just another woman to grace his sheets.

And she clearly hadn't a clue how to navigate dating and men. Just the memory of Hawk holding her off, pleading for a condom, rattled her with embarrassment. If there was one person she couldn't trust to make wise decisions, she knew it was her.

"Ugh!" Disgusted with herself, she clenched her fists at her sides as her house, such as it was, came into vision. She stormed across the yard and up the steps, trying her best not to think of all God's creatures that were lurking in the vicinity. The wood gave way on step number two and her foot disappeared into the hole it left behind.

"Shit," she spat and grabbed the railing. Pulling as hard as she could, she was none too pleased when her shoe remained securely bound in the broken boards. She wiggled her ankle and managed to pull her foot from the entrapment. "Screw it." She hobbled up the stairs, leaving half of her pair of new ballet flats in the debris.

She closed the front door behind her, shivers skipping across her skin. The picture of Hawk as he came flashed in her memory. She trembled at the thought, unease wrapping its unwelcome arms around her. She'd made quite a mess, that was for sure. She'd set a course of action that couldn't be stopped even if she wanted, because now that she'd been in his bed, she wouldn't have a fighting chance against a seduction by Silent Hawk Stephens.

* * * * *

Jo was awakened at a godforsaken hour after barely sleeping a wink by some sort of fowl—the loud, obnoxious kind. The racket reverberated throughout her bedroom and her head, providing the makings of a very fine headache. She groaned, rolling to her side and covering her head with a pillow. She could still hear the little cluckers, even through the down barrier she'd erected. Irritated, she tossed the pillow aside and threw her legs over the edge of the bed.

After showering, she made her way to the kitchen and put on a pot of coffee. As it brewed, she inventoried the work in the room, doing anything to avoid thinking about when Hawk would show up on her doorstep. And he would. She didn't deserve anything less after her juvenile behavior. Jo shook her head as she took in all the inoperable appliances. This was a job for a village, not for the solo contractor she planned to hire. Perhaps she should rethink that.

She had just started to pour a cup of coffee when a tap on the glass of the kitchen door startled her into spilling most of her caffeine. She glanced over her shoulder and her heart beat a panicked staccato. Taking deep breaths, she walked to the door and pulled it open.

Hawk's eyes locked on hers and her heart raced even faster, if that were possible. His hair was pulled back into a ponytail, emphasizing the bone structure of his face. He wore dark, pressed denim and a white dress shirt. His black boots gleamed beneath the hem of his jeans. He was…breathtaking.

He strode into the kitchen without invitation. Turning on his heel, he faced her. "You make a habit of deserting your bed partners in the middle of the night?"

She closed the door, leaning against it. "No," she replied, eyeing him like a cornered animal.

"So, it's just me?"

"It's not you, Hawk. This one's all me." She ran her hands up and down her arms, chilled even in the simmering morning heat.

He stepped toward her, stopping just out of reach. "I

thought you said you would trust me."

"I know. I did." She worried her bottom lip with her teeth. "I do." She walked past him to the counter by the stove. Leaning her palms against it, she took a deep breath.

His boots clicked along the cracked linoleum as he approached. His hand was gentle on her shoulder as he turned her to face him. She studied the tips of her shoes—and his—delaying the conversation as long as possible.

"Jo?"

She met his eyes.

"You going to tell me what had you disappearing in the dead of night?" he asked.

Jo grasped her hair at her nape. "It was just…my mind was all over the place. I'm not used to all of this." She gestured between the two of them. "I guess I just kind of freaked out."

"And that's all there is to it?" he asked speculatively.

"Not exactly," she admitted.

Hawk took her hand. "Will you tell me?"

She knew she must. She owed him at least that. "I didn't think I'd find myself in this situation so soon. I'm not prepared, I'm afraid." She squeezed his fingers. "I'm divorced, Hawk. As of six months ago. So to say I've got some baggage is putting it lightly."

He narrowed his eyes, rubbing his chin. "You said last night it had been a while since you had been with someone, so I assume you and your husband have been separated longer, right?"

Jo's stomach turned inside out. If there was one thing that could make this conversation worse, it would be discussing her ex-husband with Hawk. "Uh, yes. That's right."

"And this separation…is it complete?" He shut his eyes and a muscle ticked in his jaw. He looked at her again. "I know you're divorced. What I mean is…are things finished between the two of you, or are one of you *unsatisfied* with the arrangement?"

"Unsatisfied?"

His eyes bore into hers. "Do you still love your ex-husband? Or the other way around?"

Jo's eyes widened. "Oh God no. No, of course not. I mean, I couldn't have…I don't…" Her cheeks felt as if they were on fire. "Hawk, please tell me you don't think I would be the kind of person who would…" She turned from him.

He wrapped his arms around her, resting his head against hers. "No. I don't think that, Jo. I just have to be sure I'm not barking up the wrong tree." He turned her to face him once more. "Will you tell me about your marriage?"

She drew in a deep breath, holding it briefly before letting it seep through her lips. "What do you want to know?"

"Well, for starters, how long were you married?"

She couldn't be more uncomfortable if she were wearing panties fashioned from thorns. He deserved answers, though. "Twelve years."

"And the split…it was a mutual decision?"

That was a loaded question with a different answer depending on whom you asked. Jo was certain Thomas would have remained married to her if she would have agreed to look the other way, to be content with the trappings being a senator's wife entailed, even if their marriage left a lot to be desired. After a night in Hawk's bed, she knew just what she'd been missing.

"Yes. We just weren't right for each other. We're, ah, very different people. And as much as I'd like to pretend otherwise, my past will always follow me to some extent."

He sent her a questioning look, but when she looked away he took her hands in his, twining their fingers together.

74

"Obviously there's more to that story, but I won't press. *Now.* I do have to say, whatever it is, I really don't see how it could cause you to disappear like a thief in the night. Without a word...after what we did."

Her gaze slid from his. He was right, of course, but no amount of logic could erase her need to hide her past, to erect walls to protect herself. Walls she had put up during her marriage before she had finally had enough and went packing, her self-esteem shoved into the bottom of her suitcase. It would take more than one night of great sex to make her forget where she came from and how easily she could make the same mistakes.

"Jo?"

"I-I'm sorry. My life is a mess right now. Last night was probably a bit premature on my part."

He stared at her for a long pause. "Do you regret it?"

If she had an ounce of sense in her head she would lie. She would wait until she wasn't such a basket case before she burdened him with any more of her truths. "No," she whispered instead.

Hawk placed his hand at her nape, urging her toward him as he lowered his head. His mouth took hers, the memory of his touch bursting to life. Her blood thrummed in her veins, heat radiating between her legs. His kiss intensified quickly and he stepped closer, pressing her back against the counter, his large frame consuming her.

"What am I going to do with you, Jo?" he murmured against her lips. "You're killing me over here. But damn if you're not worth it." He plunged his tongue into her mouth, wrapping his arms tightly around her. She clung to his shoulders as his lips moved over hers. She could barely catch her breath when he finally pulled away and looked down at her with a smile.

"You're so tiny." He lifted her to sit on the counter,

pulling her snugly against his pelvis. His hands gripped her bottom, nestling his erection into the juncture of her thighs. "See what you do to me?" His mouth took hers, his tongue mimicking another act altogether. Jo wrapped her legs around his waist, groaning into the kiss.

A frustrated grumble came from Hawk. He pulled back, glancing at his watch. "Shit." He gave her a wicked smile. "As much as I'd like to lay you down on this *lovely* dated Formica countertop and have my way with you, I've got to head back to the farm." He kissed her again, snaking his arms tightly around her.

"You really have to go?" Jo asked against his lips, sliding her fingertips down his back and into the waistband of his jeans. Hawk's pained growl vibrated against her mouth.

"Yes. Pops and I have a meeting with a prospective boarder in five minutes."

Jo placed her arms around his neck, hugging him. "Okay," she said wistfully.

He drew back, planting a kiss on the tip of her nose. "Do you want me to drop your car by after my meeting?"

Fresh embarrassment swept over her. "No, I'll walk over and get it in a little bit. I have to work this morning."

Hawk rubbed his thumbs over her cheeks. "I love how you blush all the time. It's adorable."

That's one word for it. "You seem to bring it out in me."

He grinned and kissed her briefly on the lips. "Come see me later. I'm cooking for you tonight." Hawk lifted her from the counter, placing her on the floor in front of him. "Filet mignon?"

"My favorite."

"I should be done around six or so. Will that work?"

"Sounds good." Jo walked with him to the back door.

"Bye, baby." He took her face in his hands, kissed her

senseless, then disappeared through the door with a wink.

Jo closed it behind him, leaning on the doorknob. Her body screamed for his touch, almost loud enough to smother the nagging doubts echoing in her head.

* * * * *

"I'm fine, Meg. Really." Jo tucked the cell phone against her shoulder as she fished for keys inside her purse. When the cool metal brushed her fingers she extricated the keys, hooking the straps of her bag over her shoulder. She gripped the phone to her ear once more as she slid into the car. "I'm just on my way to work now."

"You're liking your job?" Meg asked across the miles.

Jo cranked the ignition, gazing up to the second floor of Hawk's house. She tingled from head to toe at the memory of what had transpired there last night. "Uh, yeah. I do." She pulled her Cadillac down Hawk's driveway. "Everyone's been very welcoming."

"I'm glad to hear it. Are your neighbors nice?"

"Yes, they're great. A horse breeder and his father live next door. They've been very helpful." Jo let go of the wheel briefly to wipe her sweaty palm against her jeans. She hated to lie to her sister, but she was probably the last person in the world Jo would consider laying it all out there for. At least right now.

"And the house?"

Jo breathed a little easier when Meg didn't pursue the neighbor subject. "The ad was very generous, let's put it that way." Jo laughed. "I'm going to have to sink a lot of my settlement cash into it, but it'll be worth it."

"That's, uh, nice."

Jo frowned. Nice? Did Meg even hear what she'd said? "Meg, what's going on? You sound like you're distracted."

"Oh, sorry. I am, actually. I've got something to tell you, and you're not going to like it."

Jo's pulse accelerated. "What is it, Meg?"

Meg sighed. Jo could envision her sister wrapping her hair tightly around her finger, the corner of her mouth twitching like it did when she was nervous. "Don't freak out, okay?"

"Oh for crying out loud. Just tell me, will you?" Jo switched the phone to her other ear.

"Well, I was at Mom and Dad's last night—Dad is helping me with a paper I have to do. You know how this class is kicking my ass—"

"Meg. For all that's good and holy. Just spit it out." Jo cringed at her tone. "Sorry, hon. Just don't beat around the bush. You're making it worse, whatever it is."

"Thomas came by."

Jo nearly dropped the phone. "What? Why?"

"He came to plead his case to Dad."

Jo glanced in the rearview and pulled her car to the shoulder. "What do you mean, plead his case?"

"He wants you back."

Hysterical laughter trickled through Jo's lips. "I seriously doubt that. What did he say?"

"He confessed everything to Dad. Told him about the affair—about you agreeing to keep the reasons behind the split out of the press."

"Why?" Jo thrust her hand into her hair, gripping it in her palm. "Why would he do that? Dad's going to think I'm the worst kind of idiot."

"He doesn't, Jo. He thinks it's, ah, admirable for you to be so selfless at a time when you didn't have to be."

Jo shook her head. "Well, you know as well as I do I didn't have Thomas' best interest at heart. I just couldn't handle the fallout in the press if the truth got out." She drew a

78

deep breath. "It just would have delayed the process even more."

"Yeah, I know, but Thomas painted you as a saint to Dad."

Why in the hell would he do that? "Did Dad regurgitate all this to you and Mom?"

"No, Thomas made his little speech in front of all of us. I couldn't believe it."

Jo rested her head against the back of the seat. "Why would he do that?"

"Honey, I have no idea."

"I guess he knows where I am." Jo grimaced.

"Yes. Public records and all."

"I really didn't think he'd care enough to look into it."

"Oh, Jo," Meg said, her voice tight. "I haven't even told you the worst part."

"How can it get any worse?" Jo pushed her sunglasses on top of her head to rub the bridge of her nose.

"Thomas sold Dad on his intentions. He plans to get you back, and he convinced Dad it's the best thing all around."

Jo's blood began to boil. "Best for *him*, I'm sure. How could Dad possibly take his side?"

"I've never seen Thomas the way he was last night. He seemed almost desperate, I guess. He says he loves you, Jo. That he made a tragic mistake."

"And you all believe him, I'm guessing."

A long pause followed. "Mom and Dad believe he made a mistake he's deeply sorry for. And with Dad's stake in the election… Thomas was…persuasive."

Jo slammed her eyes shut. "And you, Meg?"

"I don't trust him. You know that."

Jo hit the steering wheel with her fist. "Well, this is just freakin' fantastic. I can't even get a divorce in peace."

"I'm so sorry."

Glancing at her watch, Jo saw she was cutting it close to arriving late. "Thanks, Meg." She looked over her shoulder and pulled back onto the road. "Listen, keep me updated, okay? I don't need any surprises where Thomas is concerned."

"I'll try."

Jo frowned. With Thomas' connections, he could find out anything he desired, plot anything he needed and make himself appear to be the good guy at all costs. "When should I expect to hear from Dad?"

"Soon would be my guess."

Anger was a bitter taste in Jo's mouth. "Do me a favor, Meg. I *do not* want any visitors here. If you have to tie them up, don't let Mom or Dad fly out here."

"I don't think they would come without an invitation, but I'll keep my ears open."

"Thanks." Jo pulled onto the main road that led to Vidalia. "I'm going to be late, talk to you soon?"

"Okay, hon. I'm so sorry about this."

"I know. Thanks for telling me."

Jo could hear Meg sigh again. "I feel so bad. I should come out there."

"Absolutely not. You only have nine months of school left. You're not going to waylay your plans because of my bastard ex-husband. I'm going to be fine."

"I love you, Jo. I'll try to help as much as I can from here."

"I know you will. I love you too."

"Bye, hon."

"Bye, Meg."

Jo disconnected the call, dropping the cell inside her purse with a sigh. "Well, this is just great," she muttered. She drove the last stretch to work and wheeled into her parking spot. She flung the car door open, kicked it closed and headed toward the diner. As if she didn't have enough to consider where Hawk was concerned, now she had this…complication to deal with.

Jo peered into the window as she approached the entrance to The Whistling Dixie Café. Kristy beamed at her, waving and bouncing on her toes.

"Perfect," Jo mumbled under her breath. She hadn't a clue how much, or how little, to share with Kristy. Jo suspected her coworker would be like Chinese water torture—steadily dripping with questions until Jo became frustrated and gave her the information she craved. Jo braced for the onslaught, pasting a smile on her lips and pushing the door open.

Chapter Five

Jo's shift at work had been like tiptoeing through a minefield—each step potential disaster as she fielded question after question from Kristy. In the end, Jo had admitted she'd come to the conclusion "going for a ride" may not be as wrought with peril as she'd first imagined, but didn't go into any detail, much to Kristy's disappointment.

After her disturbing conversation with her sister, ducking into a back booth and dishing about what she and Hawk had done wasn't on the top of Jo's to-do list. She hadn't a clue what was appropriate, or inappropriate for that matter, to share. She suspected a no-holes-barred approach would be Kristy's taste, but something about sharing details so intimate didn't sit well with Jo.

She had made it to the end of her shift and home, where she took a shower until the hot water ran cold, trying to wash away the unease the day had brought before going to Hawk's. As she dressed, she pushed her troublesome thoughts from her head, focusing instead on the feelings Hawk evoked in her. In light of the disturbing news she'd received this morning, the strange mix of anticipation and fear she associated with her sexy neighbor was a welcome distraction.

Jo made her way through the thatch of trees that separated their property, being careful not to trip over the fallen branches and tree stumps. As she reached the edge of the tree line, she saw him in the horse ring, doing the same dance around a horse as he had the first time she'd seen him there.

The long line of his body glided effortlessly around the animal. Graceful, limber, sexy. Jo's core began a steady pulse as her gaze slid over him. He had changed clothes from the morning but his hair was still bound, accentuating the masculine beauty of his face.

"Yah!" he yelled, running his hand down the flank of the animal. The ground vibrated beneath her feet as the horse galloped around the ring, his speed awe-inspiring. His black mane and tail streamed behind him, bringing to mind an image of Hawk atop his back, his hair carried behind on the wind, his chest bare. Her nipples tightened at the image, desire pooling within her swelling flesh.

"Halt!"

Jo was jerked out of her fantasy by the sound of his voice. The horse stood statue still as his master approached the fence. Hawk kept his eyes on her as he walked toward where she stood.

"Josephine," he said, leaning his forearms on the railing. "Come here." His smile was slow and sexy as it came to his lips.

Jo left the safety of the trees and headed into the inferno. The heat of his gaze scorched her, even from the distance between them. The closer she got, the faster her heart beat, until it was racing nearly as fast as the horse had been. By the time she reached the fence, her panties were soaked and her mouth was dry. Hawk looked down at her—a hot, smoldering expression in his eyes. A look that promised a slow, tortuous journey to ecstasy.

Placing her foot on the lowest rail, she raised her body until their eyes were level, her hands on his shoulders for balance. He cupped her face, his lips taking hers. She melted from the contact, leaning into him, the hard lines of his chest

83

brushing against her already sensitive breasts. He deepened the kiss, his tongue plunging in and out of her mouth, flooding her sex with need at the thought of him appeasing the steady throb building.

His open lips met her throat, leaving a hot, wet path in their wake as they traveled down to her collarbone. He feathered kisses along the sensitive area before moving his mouth to her breast. His teeth closed gently over the pebbled nipple through the cotton of her sundress. She held her breath as he reached through the railing and his hand ran up her thigh, brushing the silk of her panties.

He groaned long and low. "You're so wet. I can't tell you what that does to me." He caressed her through the material, rubbing the fabric in slow circles over her clitoris. Her fingernails bit into his shoulders as her head fell back. Hawk brought his lips to her neck, his other hand closing over her breast to squeeze the flesh in his palm.

"Come for me, Jo," he said against the hollow of her throat. He pushed her panties aside, running his fingers over her slick flesh. She groaned as his fingers started their circular magic against her clit, caressing her to the edge and then retreating to plunge inside her. On his third pass she tumbled over, moaning Hawk's name as she came.

He pressed kisses up her neck and along her jaw, pausing at the corner of her mouth. "You're so sensual. The way you come for me so easily." He traced the crease of her lips with his tongue. "It makes me crazy."

She held his wrists as she moved her lips beneath his, leaning into him. He drew back from the kiss, rubbing his thumbs along her cheek. "Come lie with me, Jo."

"What?" she whispered.

Hawk lifted her over the fence, pulling her into his arms. "A woman blesses a man when she lies with him, shares her body with him." He kissed her gently on the lips. "I want to take you somewhere."

Jo stared into the deep pools of his eyes, laced with desire, and knew she would follow him anywhere. She nodded. Hawk raised his hand into the air, his fingers spread apart, and his horse walked slowly toward them and stopped behind Hawk.

"Let's take a ride."

"A-a ride?" She peered behind Hawk at his horse.

He took her hand and placed it against the animal's neck. "This is Thunder. He's my prize stallion."

"Hi, Thunder," she said with a confidence she didn't feel.

The horse took one step back, shaking his head. Hawk put his hand over Jo's and stroked Thunder's neck again. "He knows you're afraid of him."

"Smart horse." She looked over her shoulder at Hawk. "I don't exactly have a great track record when it comes to riding."

"You're as safe as a kitten with me. Thunder behaves as long as I'm with him."

She turned to look at the horse that towered over her, just as his owner did. "Um…he doesn't always behave?"

Hawk laughed. "He can get as unruly as a bull being prodded in the ass with a hot poker when he wants to."

"Uh…" Jo glanced around, her eyes focusing on a stable off to the right. She prayed it contained some old, decrepit mare—a much more suitable match for her. "P-perhaps another horse would be better."

Grabbing Thunder's mane in his hand, Hawk pulled his body onto the horse's bare back. Extending his hand, he smiled a smile capable of dissolving an iceberg. "Trust me, Jo. With me on his back, Thunder will be as docile as a pony at a birthday party."

She looked up at Hawk. Way up. It would be a long fall if

his stallion chose to act more like the star of a rodeo show rather than a three-year-old's party, but oh, what she could imagine was waiting on the other side of this ride.

She let out a long breath and stepped toward Hawk, taking the hand he offered. He hauled her up and behind him as if she were weightless, and pulled her arms around his waist. "Just hang on to me. You'll be fine."

Jo held him in a death grip when Thunder began to walk, rocking them slowly with his movement. Hawk placed his hand over hers reassuringly, pressing them against his abdomen. She gradually relaxed into his back, resting her cheek against it. She savored the sensations. The motion of the horse nudging her against the man in her arms, the hard muscles of his abdomen beneath her hands, the smell so unique to Hawk filtering through her senses.

Thunder stopped and Jo lifted her head from Hawk's back, glancing around. "Are we here?"

"Yes," he replied and jumped from Thunder's back, reaching up for her. His hands circled her waist and he pulled her down to join him.

Jo could hear water but couldn't see it. Clumps of trees surrounded them, with time-worn paths winding through them. Large boulders were scattered about, evidence of past fires at their bases. Curious, she looked up at Hawk.

"Where are we, exactly?"

Hawk tethered Thunder's reins to a post and took her hand, leading her along one of the paths. "In high school we used to sneak out here at night and revel in our debauchery." He waggled his eyebrows, stepping over a fallen tree trunk and lifting her to join him. "During the winter we kept warm with bonfires and cheap beer."

"It looks like that still goes on."

Hawk shrugged, smiling. "Somebody's got to keep up with traditions."

Her eyes focused on a clearing ahead, the sound of water becoming more discernable. She looked up at Hawk, smiling at the wistful look on his face.

"Anyway," he continued, "I used to sneak off from the group with a beer or two and come sit out here by the water."

She stopped and observed his sanctuary. A creek danced over the rocks, its water winding around the base of several large boulders, each side buffered by plush grass. A weeping willow trailed branches across the large rocks, the tips teasing the surface of the water in several places. A crane who had been intent on dinner flew off, startled by their presence. In the light of sunset, Hawk's discovery defined serenity.

"Do you still come here often?" she asked.

"Every chance I get."

Jo nodded numbly, stepping away from him to walk to the creek's edge. *Every chance I get.* Not exactly the words a woman wants to hear when she's been brought to a supposedly special place to *lie* with a man.

His hands were on her shoulders, his mouth at her ear. "Alone, Jo. I come here alone."

She leaned back into him as his lips caressed her neck. He pulled her hair aside, pressing a kiss to the juncture of her neck and shoulder, sending shivers across her skin.

"I want you here. In this place." He turned her to face him. "I want to slide deep inside you, hear you call my name as you come."

Grabbing a fistful of his shirt, she pulled his mouth down to hers, desperate for the vivid picture he'd painted. His hands were everywhere at once, skimming along the skin at her upper back, cupping her breasts, tangling in her hair. Their effort to remove clothing became a frenzied endeavor.

When they had peeled away the last of their clothes, Hawk led her away from the creek, settling her back against the soft carpet of grass. He stretched his body half atop hers, his hand gliding up her inner thigh. One finger dipped into her sex and she moaned as he ran the moisture over the folds and up to her clitoris. Her eyes fluttered shut as pressure began to build in her core. She said his name on a sigh.

"Look at me, Jo." Hawk slid a second finger inside her. She opened heavy eyelids and focused on his face. His gaze was like fire on her skin, his touch exquisite. Lowering his head, he kissed her lips, her chin, the hollow of her throat. His mouth grazed her breasts, pressed a kiss against her abdomen, and then replaced his fingers.

Jo grabbed fistfuls of grass in her palms at the first stroke of his tongue against her flesh. Her thighs fell apart as his mouth moved over her, his tongue swirling against her clitoris and dipping into her slick heat. She sucked in a sharp breath as he gently nipped the protruding bud, trembling as he drove her closer and closer. He focused on this supersensitive area before caressing her with long sweeps of his tongue. When his lips closed over her clit and he gently sucked, she shattered, plowing her fingers into his hair, holding him against her as she rode out her climax.

Desperate to feel his hard length inside her, she urged him upward until his penis was within reach. She encircled it with her hand, stroking his length, his pre-come enabling her to glide effortlessly over his cock. He hissed in a breath as she increased her pace and wrapped her leg around his waist. Mindless with need, she aligned her slick sex with his erection and raised her hips.

"God, Jo."

The muscles of his back flexed and bunched under her fingertips as he held himself over her, his cock head just breaching her heated entrance. She would implode, she was sure of it, if he didn't do something to ease this desperate ache. She dug her fingernails into his skin, writhing beneath him. "Hawk, please. Inside me. Now. Right now."

His growl would have scared her if her own words had not. She didn't recognize this woman pinned beneath Hawk, putting voice to needs she'd never felt before. Begging for a man to take her. But not just any man. This man.

In one thrust, he was buried to the hilt. The feel of him inside her, skin to skin, was indescribable. She moaned as he thrust once, twice, three times before abruptly withdrawing with a curse. He reached for his jeans and withdrew a condom, a look of regret on his face as he turned back to her.

"As incredible as that felt, I want to protect you." He sheathed himself and draped over her body, positioning his erection at her opening once more. He plunged home, sliding his hands beneath her buttocks to anchor her against him. "God, you're so tight."

The sound of his voice and his words sent a fresh surge of arousal through her. She raised her hips, running her hand up his back to his ponytail. She yanked the elastic, releasing his hair. It fell across his face and shoulders, brushing her breasts.

He murmured her name as he moved, twining his fingers with hers and holding her hands by the sides of her head.

He nuzzled her neck, his breath hot against her skin. "Jo," he whispered beside her ear. "You feel so…" His breath was ragged and his fingers tightened around hers. "Perfect." He returned his mouth to hers, kissing her deeply as he thrust. She felt her release approaching and rocked her pelvis, shattering around him.

Hawk filled her to the hilt as he met his own release. As the last of the tremors left him, he released her hands, his mouth seeking hers once again. His kiss was slow, deep and drugging. The pressure of his lips softened and he moved them to her forehead. Gently sliding out of her, he turned to his side, pulling her against him. He traced the tip of his finger across her brow, down the length of her nose and across her cheek.

"Josephine," he said, his lips against her hair.

"Um-hmm?"

Hawk took a deep breath and let it out slowly. "I'm not sure what this thing is between us, but it's strong."

His tone sent her heartbeat on a rampage. It was a clear precursor to a *however*. She sat up, leaning on her palm. She watched him, waiting.

He placed her other hand on his chest above his heart. "Do you feel it? This thing between us?"

She closed her eyes, nodding. "Yes," she whispered.

Hawk sat up and took her chin in his hand. "Look at me, Josephine."

She opened her eyes hesitantly and did as he asked.

"There's something you should know, but I don't want it to jeopardize what we've started. Can you trust me?"

Jo thought she might choke on her heart, for surely it was lodged in her throat. What impossible situation was fate getting ready to hurl at her now? She studied the sincere look on his face and tried to force herself to relax. "I'll try, Hawk."

He nodded, cupping her jaw in his palm. "I have to move to Arizona in two months."

* * * * *

Jo's fingertips thrummed against the bar top in Hawk's kitchen, the nail of her index finger clicking the base of her wineglass. She observed Hawk as he rubbed olive oil into two filets and then coated the steaks in sea salt and cracked black pepper. She followed his movements as he washed his hands and placed the platter in the refrigerator.

Picking up his own glass, he joined her at the bar. He pressed a kiss to the curve of her jaw before he took a seat.

"What can I help with?" she asked, still tapping her finger. Hawk stilled the movement beneath his hand.

"Nothing. I've already cut up the vegetables. It all goes on the grill when we're ready." He studied her face and silence filled the room. Jo looked away and took a sip of wine.

"You ready to talk now?" He squeezed her fingers.

She placed her glass on the bar and turned in her seat to face him. "Okay." Hawk had honored her request to delay the conversation he'd started by the creek, at least until they got back to his house. That reprieve had clearly expired.

Jo had felt as if she'd had the wind knocked out of her by his confession—the few words he'd spoken using up what was left of her emotional energy for the day. As if Meg's phone call hadn't been enough to finish her off...now she had this to contend with. And just what was *this*, exactly? No man should be able to turn her completely inside out so easily. She'd made that promise to herself when she left Arizona. But Hawk wasn't just any man. And he had.

"Jo?" he asked and eased his stool closer to hers. "Tell me what you're thinking."

She drew a deep breath and shut her eyes. "I wish I had known." The lungful of air seeped slowly past her lips. "Before."

"Would it have made a difference?" he asked, his voice low and rough.

She slowly opened her eyes and looked at him. Her gaze slid across the beautiful angles of his face, the shocking blue of his eyes. Her regard dropped to his hand closed over hers, to long, tan fingers capable of wicked things beyond mention. She warmed at the thought, a flush washing across her skin. "Probably not," she murmured, watching his thumb as it moved slowly across the back of her hand. "So, tell me what's waiting for you in Arizona."

"My mother, Raven."

"Your mother?"

"My mother's ranch, actually." He took a healthy swallow of his wine. "She and my uncle Ryder need me and Thunder out there for an extended period of time. I'm not sure how long."

Jo nodded, allowing Hawk to turn her hand over in his lap to trace circles in her palm. "Is her ranch similar to what you and your dad have here?"

Hawk shook his head. "Not exactly. It will be a boarding facility, and we'll be breeding Thunder for as long as he'll tolerate it, but the ranch will run as a nonprofit organization providing programs for autistic and terminally ill children."

Jo fell silent. She had volunteered at the Children's Hospital countless times while she'd lived in Tucson. The magnitude of what he and his mother were undertaking was not lost on her. "Hawk, that's so... I don't even know what to say."

He brushed his fingers along her wrist, sending shivers across her skin. "My mother remarried a couple of years after she divorced my dad—a man she had known almost all her life. They had a daughter, Rayne." Hawk smiled sadly. "She was the sweetest little girl. She would light up the room, just by walking into it." He twined his fingers through Jo's. "My sister took ill when she was four. Leukemia."

Jo's heart swelled in her chest and she placed her free hand over their clasped ones. "I'm so sorry."

Hawk issued a brief nod. "Thank you." The corners of his lips turned down. "The cancer took her three years ago. I was with her when she died."

"Oh, Hawk." Jo stroked his face, her heart breaking for him.

"The only time Rayne seemed like the little girl she used to be before her illness was when she was around the horses. You remember what I told you about their intuitiveness?"

"Of course." The horses would have comforted the sick child.

"When she died, we decided to start this ranch in her memory."

Jo cupped his jaw in her free hand, grazing his cheek with her thumb. Hawk turned toward the contact, rubbing his stubble-roughened jaw against her palm.

"Soon after the land was acquired, my mom's marriage fell apart—they couldn't weather the loss of a child. I expected the project to be put off indefinitely at that point, but she pressed on." He turned his head and placed a kiss to her palm. "And then I found Thunder."

Jo recalled Kristy's story of how Hawk had made a name for himself. She took her hand from his cheek, placing it on his forearm. "So Thunder has provided the income to finance the ranch?"

Hawk let out an exaggerated sigh. "Thunder has provided some of it. It's a very large undertaking, just to get it started."

Jo put her arms around his neck, pulling him into a hug. "I'm so sorry for your loss."

He wrapped his arms around her tightly and then drew back from the embrace. "We have the ranch, though. Rayne will always be with us."

She nodded. "Why don't you tell me about Thunder? He'll be bred out in Arizona?"

"God willing." A sarcastic laugh passed through his lips. "My mother has several prospective clients lined up, but Thunder is…temperamental, for lack of a better word."

She sent him a questioning look. "How so?"

"Well, he was completely wild when I acquired him. I worked with him, and tempered his behavior. Soon after, a boarder of mine approached me about breeding Thunder with his mare—he'd seen him run and was willing to pay me ten grand." A half-smile came to his lips. "Thunder sired a Derby runner. It doesn't take too long for word to spread."

Yeah, she'd heard that part. "So, his temperament?"

"I've, ah, kind of been on borrowed time where that's concerned. So far, his nasty disposition hasn't been seen in his offspring, just his speed. And he hasn't shown any signs of rebellion during the interview process and the breeding itself."

"But he's slipping." It was more of a statement than a question.

"Yeah. All it would take is for a prospective client to see a behavior problem, and the whole deal would be off. Even the fastest horse in the world will make a terrible investment if they have temperament issues."

Jo's brow creased in concern. "How long do you think you have?"

He shrugged. "No way to know. It frustrates the hell out of me, though, being unable to control him at all times." He smiled at her. "There's never been a horse I couldn't break."

That, she didn't doubt.

She narrowed her eyes at him. "And you said Thunder was always docile around you. Just before you talked me into a ride on your prize stallion, if I recall."

He chuckled. "You were perfectly safe. I know when to not push things with him. Believe me, he lets you know."

"So what happens if Thunder doesn't cooperate?"

Hawk dropped his head back, groaning. "Fundraising. Something I know absolutely nothing about."

And she did. "Hawk, if it comes to that, there are a lot of resources available. I wouldn't let that stress you at this point."

"I hope you're right. That would just be one more thing on my plate. I'm going to have my hands full already working with the horses that will be in the program with the children."

Yes. He would be very busy. All the way across the country. Jo did her best to push the hurt away. The rational side of her understood she was fortunate to have discovered this now, before she had the opportunity to become even more tangled in Hawk's life. The other part of her understood with great clarity she couldn't be more ensnarled in him if she had managed to crawl inside his chest and make his breaths her own. A reality she'd do best to get a handle on before she made a huge mistake.

She tried to withdraw her hand from his but he held fast. "Jo, I know the timing is awful. But this doesn't have to mean goodbye."

His eyes bore into hers and her heart sank. She couldn't see how it could be anything other than goodbye. He was going to the one place she had run from in desperation, a place trying to draw her back, if her ex-husband and parents had anything to say about it. And giving herself mind, body and soul to someone so soon after her divorce could prove to be an exercise in ignorance. No. Jo had been very foolish indeed in the past. She couldn't risk making that grave an error again.

"Hawk," she said, squeezing his fingers. "We don't have to decide anything tonight."

He brought her hand to his lips and pressed a kiss to her fingers. "Okay. But we *will* talk, Josephine." He rose from the stool, helping her from hers when she went to follow him. "Let me fix our dinner."

* * * * *

They ate in near silence. Hawk eyed Jo over the rim of his wineglass, trying his hardest to get a good read on her. It was as if she had completely shut down after their conversation, had lost the ability to even have that skittish air about her that he'd grown accustomed to. And when he'd told her it needn't be goodbye, her eyes had shuttered, as if she were drawing the blinds on his suggestion. He didn't like it one bit.

She looked up at him and a brief smile came to her lips.

"This was delicious."

"I'm glad you liked it."

He rose from the table and collected their plates, depositing them in the sink. He walked to her and drew her from the seat into his arms, where he wrapped her tightly in his embrace. Her hair smelled of some flower, jasmine perhaps, and he drew in the scent, rubbing his cheek against the top of her head.

"Will you stay with me tonight, Josephine?" he murmured against her hair, knowing true uncertainty for the first time in as long as he could remember. Nothing could get him what he needed—not his looks, not his reputation. Certainly not his money. He had found her. The woman his meditations in the Black Hills had prophesized. The one who could love him for who he truly was, not for who he'd become. A woman impervious to the attributes that drew others to him like addicts to heroin. The woman he always knew he would fight for. He just never would have believed he would have to fight *against* her.

She lowered her head, resting her cheek on his chest. "I don't think tonight. You, ah, gave me a lot to consider." She looked up at him, her eyes unreadable. "I'd prefer to be alone, have a chance to think things over. You understand?"

"Of course." He held her face in his hands and pressed a gentle kiss against her lips. "I understand." He took her hand. "Let me drive you home."

"Actually, would you mind if I borrowed your truck? I'll drop it by first thing in the morning."

Hawk searched her face. Jo was worrying her bottom lip with her teeth, her face a mask of conflicted concentration. She needed space, and as much as it pained him, he would let her go. Tonight. "Sure, darlin'. I believe the seat will move up far enough for you to reach the pedals."

His joke was lost on her, he assumed, because she

mumbled an affirmative then trailed silently behind him outside to his truck.

After Hawk hoisted her into the cab and helped her adjust the seat, he watched her drive away. He ran his hands down his face then returned to the house, locking the front door before he strode into the kitchen. He lifted the cordless phone from the cradle and punched in the numbers.

"Hey, Mom."

"Hawk!" His mother's delighted tone traveled across the distance, instantly soothing him. "This is a nice surprise. How is everything going? You still planning on coming out in a few days to help me with that meeting?"

"Yes, of course. The new gelding will be there by then, right?"

"I dropped off the check at the Perkins farm this morning, and they're bringing him over tomorrow."

Hawk rubbed the bridge of his nose. "Good. That's good."

"You okay, son?"

"That depends." Hawk kneaded a tense muscle in his shoulder. "If by okay you mean I've been hurtled into a situation I have no idea how to handle, then yes. I'm great."

Raven chuckled softly. "What have you done now, Silent Hawk?"

He ran his hand through his hair. "Well, I've found what I sought proof of last summer, when Dad sent me to you like a petulant child."

Hawk could envision his mother's face—she would appear jubilant without the burden of forcing concern to furrow her brow for his benefit. "And the lady is not amenable to your charms?"

"It's not quite that dire," he replied. "She's been hurt, so she's fighting me. And with this move…"

"Right," Raven said. "Does she know how strongly you feel?"

Hawk sighed. "With Jo, I run the risk of scaring her beyond reparation. I don't even know where to go from here."

"Okay, Hawk. Don't get ahead of yourself. Do you believe?" She paused. "I mean, truly believe? In all I've taught you, in all you know?"

"I want to."

"It's not a matter of wanting, it's a matter of doing. Do you believe she's the one?"

Hawk leaned his head back, staring at the ceiling. "Yes."

"Then you do what you must. No one promised this would be easy. If it were, she wouldn't be the one you've been searching for."

Hawk shuffled his boot against the hardwood, tapping the metal tip against the cabinet. "I know. I just don't want to make a mistake. Hurt her, or myself."

He could practically hear his mother's smile over the line. "Have more faith in yourself than that. From what your dad has told me, you've had women coming through your life as if you were a turnstile. I feel certain you would sense the difference in…Jo, is it?"

"Yes."

"Just follow your instincts. And be careful."

Easier said than done.

Hawk began to pace along the length of the counter. "Any chance you could make a trip out here for a couple of days? I'd love your take on the situation, in person, that is."

"Sure, honey, you know I'll be glad to. It'll have to be later in the month, though, because Ryder and I are tied up in meetings for the next three weeks."

"Yes, of course. Whatever you can work out would be great."

"I'll let you know my flight plans as soon as I arrange them."

"Thanks, Mom. Tell Uncle Ryder I said hello, and I'll see you guys in a few days."

"I will. And Hawk?"

"Yeah?"

"Remember that what will be, will be. Sometimes things are decided long before we're even aware they exist. Don't lose your faith."

"Thanks, Mom. Good night."

"Good night."

Hawk placed the phone in the cradle and headed toward the stairs. If he had been asked earlier in the day if Jo would be wrapped in his arms right now, crying his name as he brought her to completion again and again, he would have bet the farm on it. Now it was his mission to make certain his empty arms, and bed, were not an omen of what was to come.

Chapter Six

Glancing over his shoulder, Hawk dropped the currycomb into his bucket of grooming supplies, running his hand over Thunder's flank. He watched as Ray mucked out a dirty stall, pulling a handkerchief from his back pocket to blot his brow.

His father looked old. And tired. Living on and working a cotton farm for nearly half a century would do that. Being stubborn would too. Hawk knew when he moved to Arizona, things would have to change. He would be leaving capital to run the farm and Ray would take the money if Hawk had to shove it down his throat. Which he very well might.

"Hey, Pops," he said, leading Thunder into his stall and latching the door closed. "You sure you're going to be okay running the boarding alongside the cotton farming after I leave?"

Ray leaned the pitchfork against the wall, settling his patient gaze on Hawk. "Son, we've talked about this. Your mama wants and needs you, not to mention all those children who will be affected, and you've spent enough of your life helping to keep things running around here." He walked to the far end of the barn and plucked a hay bale from the corner. He returned to Hawk, dropping it at his feet. "Raven can't do this without you. Or Thunder."

Hawk knelt, pulling a switchblade from his boot to cut the twine from the bale. He shook the hay loose. Grabbing an

100

armful, Hawk stepped into the empty stall adjacent to Thunder's, scattering hay across the floor. He stepped out to retrieve more and Thunder snorted and kicked the living daylights out of the wooden door, its hinges creaking from the impact. Hawk shot him a silent warning with his eyes, holding his firm stare until the animal stepped away from his stall entrance.

"How long you figure you got before you can't breed him no more?" Ray asked, walking around Hawk to peer at Thunder.

"Jo asked the same thing last night." He shrugged and rubbed his chin. "He hasn't shown too much aggression with the mares, but you know as well as I do that he's not hesitant to show the other horses who he perceives is in charge around here."

"How he can complain about the parade of beautiful mares he gets to have his way with is beyond me." Ray laughed, leaning his arm on the stall gate. Thunder turned his head. "Yeah, I'm talking about you. Don't know how good you got it."

Hawk laughed and shook his head before appraising his horse. The corners of his lips dipped down. "It's probably just a matter of time before breeding conditions are unfavorable to prospective clients. Not to mention the fear of hellions being sired."

Thunder turned an innocent look on his owner, rolling his lips back as if he were smiling.

"Uh-huh," Hawk said, eyeing the stallion. "Laugh all you want, buddy. It's not your future on the line." Hawk groaned, sending a look heavenward. "I just wish the timing weren't so stringent. I don't feel right leaving so soon."

Ray stooped to pick up more hay and ducked into the stall on the other side of Thunder's. "Well, time is one thing you ain't got, I'm afraid," he called to Hawk.

"Yeah, I know."

Hawk thought of Jo. As it turned out, the timing with her was just as perilous as that with Thunder. With both, Hawk had to have faith they could hang on long enough to see everything to fruition. The difference with his horse was that Hawk *did* have a backup plan, no matter how unfavorable that option may be. With Jo, he had a very short window to prove to her they belonged together. If he couldn't, there was no Plan B. There was only failure. All Hawk could do was take his mother's thoughts to heart. And believe.

"Hey, Hawk?" Ray asked as he emerged from the stall.

"Yeah?"

Ray wiped his brow once more. "I've been meaning to talk to you about all those hirings you did. You've brought on so many workers I'm going to have to fight just to be able to work on my own farm."

Hawk sighed in exasperation. "And that's just the reason I hired them all. I don't want you to have to work yourself to death. Especially when you don't need to. I have enough—"

"Who said anything about needing?"

"What?" Hawk massaged his right temple where a headache steadily throbbed.

"It's not a need, Silent Hawk. It's a want." Ray walked to him and placed his hand on Hawk's shoulder. "There are only three things in my life I recall ever wanting. For you to do better than your old man, to work this family farm, and your mother."

Hawk focused on Ray's pained expression, the one he had seen countless times since Hawk had become a man and his mother was finally able to escape out west, leaving behind the husband who had drowned both himself and his marriage in the bottle. The lines in Ray's forehead spoke of years of regret.

"The way I see it," Ray continued, "I've only got one thing that I want, and that is for you to do better than me. I lost your mother. I can't lose this farm too. It's what I know. It's what I want."

Hawk nodded, bending to pick up the last of the hay and tossing it into a stall. "You make it hard for me, Pops. I don't feel right leaving you here alone. Even if it isn't permanently."

Ray laughed and slapped Hawk on the back. "I'm not alone. You've seen to that with all those men you hired. And then there's Jo. It doesn't look like she's going anywhere soon with that house of hers. It's like she's trying to prove something by making it whole again."

Hawk cocked his eyebrow, shaking his head.

Ray crossed his arms over his chest and studied him. "What, you don't agree with me? Has something changed I don't know about?"

"No, I agree she's stubborn enough to grab on to that renovation project like a dog with a bone, I just don't know if she'll have the time to finish what she's starting. Not if things go my way." Hawk gave his father a knowing look.

"I take it you're certain about her."

Hawk leveled his gaze on his father. "Yes, I am."

"Does Jo know? About how you feel?"

"She knows I don't want things to end between us, but that's about it."

"And Arizona? Did you tell her?"

Hawk frowned. "Yes. She didn't seem thrilled with the idea."

"I'm sure that doesn't surprise you, son."

"No. I'm giving her some space, at her request, to try to give her some time to wrap her head around all this." He placed his hand on his hip. "Not seeing her until I get back next week is going to kill me."

Ray chuckled. "So, you planning on telling her what you

know when you get back? Let her in on how fate is going to try to pull a number on her?"

"Pops, you know how others are about our beliefs. Hell, you were one of them once upon a time."

Ray nodded. "Before your mama."

"Yeah, before Mom. If I tell Jo what I know to be the truth, she'll fight it. Just like she fights everything else. Faith like ours is difficult to quantify, she wouldn't understand."

"But—"

Hawk began to pace. "And I don't want her to think it's only fate and signs that make me want her. You know as well as I do it has to go way beyond all that for it to be real. It's *her* I want. Everything else just makes me more certain of it."

Ray watched Hawk with an amused smile on his face. "Yes, but she—"

"And is it really that bad if I don't tell her? Knowing Jo, it will only freak her out more. I swear, I've never known a woman so…so…" Hawk looked up at his father's snicker. "What?"

Ray held his hands up. "Nothing. So, what are you going to do about it?"

"I have two months before I leave. Eight weeks to convince her we belong together." Hawk pointed at Ray, shaking his finger. "Yes. I'll make her understand. Or die trying."

Ray shook his head, a smile on his lips. "God help her."

* * * * *

A week had passed since Hawk's confession by the creek, and Jo had done her best to get her thoughts straight and not go crazy all at the same time. Hawk's trip to Arizona had been timely, giving her the opportunity to make decisions without the influence of his presence. As each day passed, Jo realized the importance of putting down roots in her new life. Now she was fragile, far too vulnerable of being plucked away, uprooted and planted somewhere else.

So it was during this time away from Hawk when she strengthened the tender roots she'd planted. She hired one of the contractors Hawk had recommended, satisfied with the timeframe and cost he cited. Refusing alimony from Thomas left her with only her settlement, and she was determined to build her new life on those funds. Jo ventured into Macon to pick out flooring and wallpaper samples. She even boldly walked into a real estate office while in town, just to feel out possible employment opportunities in her area and get recommendations for locations of courses to secure her Georgia Real Estate License.

These tasks and her evening shifts at the diner kept her busy, and anything she could do to keep her mind occupied and off the man who sent her pulse racing with the mere thought of him was a welcome distraction.

Ray dropped by, predictably, after lunch each day to help out. Jo had grown to anticipate his visits in a short period of time. Not only was he one of the most unintentionally funny people she had ever met, but he was willing and anxious to speak of his son. Listening to Ray talk about Hawk was an indulgence Jo allowed herself, a time when she could justify letting him infiltrate her thoughts. Letting go of those thoughts after Ray's departure was always the tricky part, however.

Glancing at her watch, Jo smiled as Ray came bounding into the room, breathless.

"You okay?" she asked in anticipation of whatever pickle he had gotten himself into this time.

Ray bent over, resting his palms on his knees, taking deep breaths. He held up his index finger. Biting back a smile, she waited.

"Whew," he said, rising to his full height. "Mrs. Peterson's damn chicken again."

"What?" She choked on a laugh she couldn't contain.

Ray placed his hands akimbo. "Chicken. Damn bird hates me, she does. Chases my ass all over the place if she sees me."

"The Mrs. Peterson who owns the property that backs up to ours?"

"Yep."

She raised eyebrow. "Lemonade?"

He nodded, following her into the kitchen.

She grabbed the pitcher from the fridge and walked to the cupboard to retrieve two glasses. "So," she said. "Man versus fowl. How long has this been going on?"

"Ever since I stole, uh, I mean, borrowed those eggs of hers. Going on a year now."

Handing him the glass, she gestured toward the table and they both sat. "Borrowed, huh?" she asked, the inside of her cheek raw from their daily visits.

Ray leaned back in his chair, pointing at her. "See, here's the truth. Mary Jane, she was a pistol, she was. Real passionate about everything, especially food."

"Okay…"

"Anyway, she liked her big breakfasts. And me, I'm a gentleman. If by the grace of God I wake up with a woman in my bed, she sure as hell is gonna have her big breakfast if she wants it."

"Let me guess," she said and took a sip of lemonade. "You were out of eggs."

Ray sighed. "As luck would have it. Bacon, biscuits, cheese, but no eggs."

Jo placed her elbow on the table and rested her chin in her hand, concealing her smile with her palm. Ray began to shake his head.

"I thought, what's the harm in borrowing a few eggs? None of the other chickens seemed to care. But this one." Ray slid a long whistle through his teeth. "She's got the devil in her, she does."

"And she's never forgotten you and your stealing ways, right?"

"Nope. I tell ya, she sees me coming across the yard and she takes off running after me. She's fast too. Pecking at my jeans and squawking. Disgraceful is what it is."

Jo laughed, placing her hand over his on the table. "I'm glad I met you, Ray. Every day around you is an adventure."

He covered her hand with his other one. "I'm glad I met you too, darlin'. And so is my son."

She averted her gaze, discomfort enveloping her like an itchy wool sweater.

Ray squeezed her hand before letting it go. "He said he told you about Arizona."

"Yes, he told me."

Rubbing his chin, Ray looked over her head, staring blankly. "I always knew Hawk, his mama and uncle would pull this ranch together and he'd head out west at some point." He took a deep breath, slowly letting it out. "I'd hoped they'd want to open it here, but she wanted to be close to her people."

"So this farm is all yours, then."

"Yeah, been in my family for generations. I would have given it to her though." The corners of his lips turned down. "Wouldn't take it. Catalina is her dream. And with Hawk's help, it will come true."

Jo studied his face, the wistful sadness. "You still love her, don't you?"

His gaze settled on hers and he looked tired. "She was young when we married, had Silent Hawk young. She didn't know what she was signing up for with me. Gentle Raven is a gift, and the best mother you'll ever see."

"How did you meet her?"

Ray's face lit up with a smile. "I was visiting my brother out in Texas and he took me to a rodeo. Gentle Raven was there with her family. Performing." He shook his head, sighing. "I was sitting in the third row, drinking a beer, when the most beautiful woman I ever saw came out riding an appaloosa. Hair was down to her waist, blowing in the wind. I was lost."

"Then what happened?"

"I went up to her afterward and somehow talked her into grabbing a bite with me. I never let go after that." His smile faded. "Well, until Hawk was older and she could leave my drunk ass without beating herself up about it."

She reached across the table to take his hand again. "How long have you two been divorced?"

"Ten years. When Hawk graduated from high school," he replied.

Jo did the math in her head and inwardly winced. That would make Hawk twenty-seven, twenty-eight at the most. *Way to go, Mrs. Robinson.*

"I, ah, didn't know Hawk was so young." Her laugh bordered on hysteria and Ray raised an eyebrow. "Wow. I never asked." She took a sip of her lemonade and choked on it.

Ray rose from his seat and pulled her arm over her head, slapping her on the back.

She laughed as she coughed. When she finally cleared her airway, she looked up at him. "You know that doesn't do anything to help, right?"

"Can't hurt, darlin'," he said, returning to his seat.

"Um, so I guess Hawk is close to his mom, right?"

"Yeah, they're really similar. You'll see what I mean." He took a long swallow of his lemonade.

"I'll see?"

"Raven will be here for a visit in a couple of weeks." Ray rubbed his stomach. "I'm going to try to lay off the pig products between now and then. I'm as bad as that guy on TV…you know the one who's always putting his face close to the food and sniffing?"

"What?" Jo was still thrown by the fact Hawk's mother would be visiting.

Ray snapped his fingers. "You know. He's always putting his face over the pot and yelling when he throws stuff in it."

"You mean Emeril?"

He nodded enthusiastically. "Yep, he's the one. Always says you can never use too many pork products." He pointed to his tiny paunch. "'Course, then you get one of these."

Jo smiled and searched her mind for safe conversation that wouldn't involve Hawk or his mother's impending visit. Or pork.

"I'm interested in learning more about horse breeding."

Ray draped his arm over the back of his chair. "What do you want to know, darlin'?"

"Well, I know Hawk has to be at the farm to work with the horses in the program." *So much for not talking about Hawk.* "But as far as breeding goes, why couldn't they extract Thunder's semen here and send it to Arizona? I've seen documentaries about artificial insemination, it seems like it would be easier."

Ray watched her for a long moment, a smile consuming his features. She flushed clear down to her toes. "Not a thoroughbred racehorse, darlin'."

"Why not?"

Ray crossed his arms over his chest. "Natural conception or no dice." He cleared his throat. "So, my son's needed for more than the training. He's responsible for coaxing as many breeds out of Thunder as possible."

"Yes. Of course." Her gaze hit her lap and she prayed her telling blush had vamoosed.

"And they force the estrus, you know," Ray said matter-of-factly.

"P-pardon me?"

"You know, the estrus. They make it so the mare goes into heat toward the end of the year, instead of the natural spring and summer."

"Why in the world would they do that?" she asked, furrowing her brow.

He raised his glass in a mock toast. "Because of the timing of the races. It makes them the perfect age to run."

Jo nodded, thinking about what Ray said. Hawk was due back that afternoon. If she had enough courage, she would do exactly what those horses did.

Run.

* * * * *

"It's not going to happen."

Jo paced impatiently across her living room floor, cursing under her breath when her big toe encountered a sharp sliver of wood. Leaning over, she plucked it from her flesh, holding the splinter between her fingers as she walked to the kitchen to throw it away.

"You know, Dad, you shouldn't care what he says. I'd think your loyalty would be to me." Jo glanced at the clock. Six forty-five. Fifteen minutes until Hawk was supposed to arrive and she was on the phone arguing with her father. About Thomas.

"Well, maybe that life isn't so perfect for me, did you ever think about that?"

Jo closed her eyes and took a deep breath, trying to remember this was her father, who *thought* he was doing what was best for her. And likely best for him. She wouldn't lose sight of that.

"And what's that supposed to mean?" Her eyes grew wide. "Did you ever run around on Mom?" She stormed back into the living room. "Yeah, I didn't think so."

Tires displacing gravel garnered her attention and her heart burst into overdrive. "Look, Daddy. My neighbor is dropping by to, ah, help me with some things around the house so I really have to go."

Jo finger-combed her hair, switching the phone to her other ear. "Yes, I know you're trying to do what's best for me. But you have to trust that *I* know what's best for me." Okay, that was a lie. She wouldn't have agreed to see Hawk no sooner than his luggage had been dropped in the foyer if she always did the sensible thing. But she knew for sure Thomas wasn't right for her. She'd already tested that theory.

"Fine, I'll think about it," she lied, not wanting to deal with her father any longer. "I love you, Daddy. I'll talk to you later."

Jo tossed the phone into a club chair and walked to the door as a knock sounded. She heard tires on the gravel again and frowned in confusion, pulling the front door open. Her field of vision was obstructed by a giant arrangement of sunflowers, her favorite.

"Delivery for Mrs. Daniels," came from behind the flowers, as well as the telltale thud of boots on the porch.

"Um, yes."

"I'll take those," Hawk said, smiling at Jo over the head of the delivery boy. He relieved him of the vase and leaned down to place a brief kiss on her lips.

"Thank you," she said and glanced over her shoulder to see Hawk placing the arrangement on the coffee table. "Hang on one sec," she said, motioning to the delivery boy. She walked to the kitchen and pulled five dollars from her purse. She returned to the door and pressed it into the boy's hand. "Thank you."

"No problem, Mrs. Daniels. You have a good evening."

Jo cringed at how he addressed her and pushed the door closed. Hawk was by her side in three long strides, pulling her into his arms. She could hear his heart hammering against her ear as he held her, rubbing her back in long strokes.

"I missed you," he said. "Thank you for having me over." His mouth captured hers in a heated possession and she clung to his shoulders, meeting each hungry kiss with one of her own. "Mmm," he murmured. "I missed this."

"Me too." She'd been every form of fool to entertain the thought, even for a moment, that she might be able to keep her distance. Despite everything she knew, one touch from him and she could forget it all. She wrapped her arms around his neck, her toes lifting from the ground when he pulled her against him.

"I brought a bottle of Shiraz for us to share, but clearly," he looked over his shoulder at the embarrassing display of flora on the table, "I undershot the mark. Whose ass do I need to go kick down at the diner?"

Jo smiled without humor. "No one, I'm sure."

"Hmmm," he mused. "Probably not. Since I doubt no one there refers to you as Mrs. Daniels."

Jo shook her head and took a step toward the table after Hawk lowered her to the floor. Dread consumed her. She could only pray the flowers were from her father. Or mother. Or Meg. She knew they weren't, though.

She closed the distance to the table, removing the card with a trembling hand. She pressed her finger under the flap of the envelope to slide it open. The paper sliced into her flesh. "Crap," she muttered, placing the tip of her finger in her mouth. Paper cut. Perfect.

Jo extracted the card and her heart sank.

An allied attack; she shouldn't have expected any less. Thomas probably asked her father to call her *this* particular afternoon. Jo's eyes skimmed across the handwritten card. Funny, when they'd been married, it was either typed by the florist or written in the loopy cursive of her husband's executive assistant. Never once had Thomas taken the time to write it himself.

Give me the chance to be the husband I always wanted to be but didn't know how. All my love, Thomas

Jo crumpled the card in her palm, taking a deep breath. She jumped when Hawk placed his hands on her shoulders.

"Sorry," he said, kneading her muscles. "You okay, baby?"

She nodded. Silence ensued and Jo was at a complete loss as to what to do. The card in her hand made her feel guilty, as if she had betrayed Hawk somehow. Which was, of course, ridiculous.

His lips brushed her ear. "Jo, you don't have to tell me who they're from." She could feel his smile against her earlobe. "I'll just have to go out and get you an arrangement twice as big, that's all."

She smiled, turning to face him. She had no desire to lie. "They're from my ex-husband. It's nothing." She waved her hand. "Actually, let me go toss this." She held up the card. "Do you want to bring that wine in here and open it while I get the glasses?"

He pressed a kiss to her nose. "Absolutely."

Hawk trailed Jo into the kitchen, holding his expression in check. Her ex-husband? He didn't know who this Mr. Daniels was, but he sure as hell would find out. Thank God for the internet. There shouldn't be too many Josephine Montgomery

Daniels in existence.

A muscle ticked in his jaw. Hawk knew his behavior bordered on juvenile, but Jo was his, and he'd be damned if some ass who had lost his chance was going to try to swoop back in with expensive flowers. This man had no idea who he was up against. Hawk had paid witness to the scarred woman Jo was when she'd arrived in Georgia, and he'd bet just about anything this loser was responsible. He didn't plan on allowing him to get within an inch of her. And it was time for Jo to come clean with him about her past.

Hawk watched as Jo tore the card to pieces, letting them flutter into the trashcan. She opened a drawer and handed him the corkscrew with a smile.

He set to the task of uncorking the wine, pushing his thoughts of homicide away. He had work to do. The walls of one Josephine *Montgomery* needed to be breached. He was running out of time, and with another player on the field…

He pulled the cork with a pop, pouring the wine into the awaiting goblets Jo had placed on the counter to his side. He picked them up and motioned to the living room with his head, giving her the warmest smile he could. "Shall we?"

She preceded him and sat on the sofa, adjusting a cushion behind her. Hawk joined her, handing Jo a goblet. "To plastic-free furniture," he teased, raising his glass in a toast.

She smiled, tapping her glass to his. She sipped the wine, the fingers of one hand clenched in her lap. Jo looked around the room, glancing at Hawk and then staring at the coffee table in front of them. She placed her wine by the flowers and abruptly stood.

"You know," she motioned to the elephant in the room, "I should just throw these out." She grasped the vase but Hawk stopped her with a hand on her wrist.

"No, don't do that. They're a beautiful gift from nature, regardless who they're from. There's no reason we can't enjoy them." He stroked his hand up her arm. "Sit."

She eyed him hesitantly but did as asked. Hawk would just have to distract her the best way he knew how. Leaning close, he brushed his lips against hers, a soft, feathering caress along her jaw. He nuzzled her neck and heard her gentle sigh. He returned his mouth to hers. *Mine.* All he could think, could feel with Jo pressed so intimately against him, was *mine.*

She withdrew slowly from the kiss, settling her toffee-colored gaze on his. She opened her mouth to speak but closed it again. The words came out on her second attempt. "Hey, Hawk, how old are you?"

He pulled back from her with a smile on his lips. He'd been prepared for an onslaught of difficult questions, and this one, by comparison, seemed fairly…benign. But this was Jo, so he knew to tread carefully. "Old enough, I'd say."

"Hawk," she sighed. "Be serious."

He retrieved his glass and sampled the wine before settling his attention on her, only hoping his amusement wasn't apparent in his eyes. "And give you more ammunition to fire all the reasons we shouldn't be together? No way."

A tiny crease appeared between her brows. Hawk caressed it with the tip of his finger before taking her hand in his. "Look, Jo. I'm guessing from the length of your marriage you're probably a couple years older than me. Who cares?"

"How old, Hawk?"

He pushed his hair off his forehead. "Twenty-eight."

She groaned, leaning back against the pillows, draping her forearm over her eyes.

"Come on, Jo. You can't be more than what…thirty?"

She raised her free hand, splaying her fingers.

A laugh he tried to restrain as best he could rumbled in his chest. "Thirty-five. Well, you don't look it."

She removed her arm and peered at him. "That doesn't make it not so."

Hawk leaned over her, brushing the hair from her face. His gaze held hers as he let out a deep breath. "Our age difference doesn't matter, Jo."

"I know," she said on a sigh, a sheepish look on her face. "It's just—"

"Let me ask you something. Do you look for reasons why we shouldn't be together?"

"I don't have to look, Hawk. They're there."

He pulled back, his lips set in a firm line. "And you really believe that?"

Standing from the sofa, she ran her hands up and down her arms and started to pace. "Is reality any different than what I see?"

Hawk kept his voice even, controlled. "What do you see, Josephine?"

She turned to face him and stared for a long moment, her eyes drifting over his face, dropping to his chest before she looked away and rubbed her temple. "I see an impossible situation. You and me," she gestured between the two of them, "we don't make sense. And the timing, well…"

Hawk shot to his feet, grasping her upper arms. "What do you mean we don't make sense?"

She balled her fingers into fists and released them, closing her eyes. "Hawk," she said, barely above a whisper. "You're a wonderful man, with a life you need to live. You don't need to be burdened with me. With all the issues that could arise. There's more to the situation than I've let on." She shook her head and pulled back from his grasp, walking to the bay window.

Hawk followed, tentatively placing his hands at her waist. "Jo, what did he do to you?"

Her laugh was sarcastic and cutting. "Nothing. He didn't do anything to me."

"I don't believe that." Her shoulders rose and fell with her breaths. Hawk wrapped his arms around her, pulling her against his chest. "You can trust me. You told me once your past would always follow you to some extent. Care to elaborate?"

She leaned her head back and Hawk studied her reflection in the glass. The corners of her lips turned down and she stared off vacantly into the front yard.

"Well…have you heard of someone named Thomas Daniels?" Her voice shook slightly as she spoke.

Hawk searched his memory for the familiar name. Her chest expanded on a deep breath as she waited for his reply. Then it hit him. "You mean *Senator* Thomas Daniels? The Republican from Arizona, right?"

She turned to face him, crossing her arms over her chest. She held his gaze but didn't speak.

"Your ex-husband?"

She nodded and a look of relief flooded her features, but it was short-lived. "So, now surely you see why this is a bad idea. I came here to disappear, not to embroil someone else in what looks to be an ongoing problem." She gestured to the flowers, a disgusted sigh escaping her lips. "Our marriage didn't exactly end well, and I'm housing an ugly secret."

The mere thought of what that could be caused Hawk's blood to boil. He pried her hands from her arms, taking a step closer to her. "I'll ask you again, Jo. What did he do to you?"

She averted her gaze, shifting her weight to her other foot. "Hawk, no one knows but my sister." She shook her head. "Well, and my parents now, unfortunately."

He guided her chin so she would have to look at him. "Tell me, Jo."

"If any of this gets out…" She ran her fingers into her hair, fisting it in her palms.

Hawk put her wariness of him aside. He would have to earn her trust. He'd always known that. "Baby, I would sooner give up my prize stallion than hurt you. Talk to me."

"Okay." She let her hands drop from her hair, its honey mass falling in disarray. "I discovered Thomas in bed with another woman. Not exactly a transgression to be overlooked by the conservative voters who put him in office."

Hawk's back molars ground together and he placed his hand on his hip, shaking his head. "And he…" Hawk put his fist to his mouth and took a deep breath. "He what, paid you to keep it a secret?"

She snorted. "Hardly. I didn't agree to keep it quiet for *his* benefit."

Hawk narrowed his eyes. "I'm afraid I don't follow."

"We lived a very public life, obviously. My husband was known for taking chances in his career, so he was always in the spotlight. And as his wife, I was too." Jo rubbed her temples. "He always came out on top, though, casting himself into the role of some kind of savior. You can imagine the hysteria the media would create if the great senator fell."

"So you lied?"

"Only by omission. I was so anxious to get away from him, I wanted as few ties as possible. Admitting his infidelity wouldn't have been conducive to that. I'd be in the news until it all blew over, and as long as he holds office, that wouldn't happen."

"And what did you say about your parents?"

"They, ah, didn't know about the affair. Until Thomas told them. He confessed it as the biggest mistake of his life. One he plans to remedy." Jo looked defeated.

Hawk drew a deep breath through his nose, trying to relax

his jaw. "And they support him, I take it?"

"Unfortunately." She grimaced.

"Why would they do that? If I had a daughter—"

"My father is the DA. He helped put Thomas in office. If Thomas falls, well…" She shook her head. "It's just a clusterfuck all around. I couldn't possibly ask you to get involved in something that's so screwed up. I need to get my own life in order and I'm not even ready…" She tried to turn from him.

No. She was not going to use this as an excuse to walk away. As long as she wanted him, and every instinct he had said she did, he'd stop at nothing to have her.

Hawk pulled her roughly into his arms and she gasped, placing her hands against his chest. "Josephine, listen to me." He pinned her beneath his stare. "I don't care who you were married to. Or where you came from. I don't even care that you tried to disappear right next door to me. I only care that you're here." He cradled her jaw in his palm. "With me."

He crushed his lips to hers, sliding his hands to cup her ass and pull her flush against him. Her arms wrapped around his waist, her hands spanning his lower back. "I only care about you," he said against her lips between kisses. "Only you, Jo."

Hawk sensed the moment she relaxed into his embrace, and it felt like coming home. As if he'd just passed over the threshold of his dream house, knowing it belonged to only him. He swept Jo into his arms and approached the stairs. He placed one booted foot on the first step and looked down at her with a smile. "Are these going to hold?"

She pulled his lips down to hers. "God, I hope so because the bed is upstairs." She kissed him with such hunger he nearly lost his footing, and had to put her down. He backed her into the wall, bracing her hands above her head in one of his. As Hawk looked down at her, her eyes laced with passion and trust, he knew he would be forever lost.

119

Jo stared into Hawk's eyes, his irises a midnight blue. He made her feel safe, and cherished, and desirable. Three things she never recalled feeling outside of him. As he lowered his mouth to hers, she knew. She had fallen in love with this man. And as his lips moved over hers, she realized he would wait for her. Everything about the way he touched her, looked at her, assured her of that fact.

His lips left a wake of heat as they passed across her skin, skimming along her neck to the hollow at the base of her throat. His hand disappeared beneath the skirt of her dress, its calloused texture caressing the skin of her thigh. Jo moaned as his finger edged along her lacy thong, dipping beneath the flimsy fabric.

Her head snapped back as he slid a finger inside her, his thumb seeking her pebbled arousal. She groaned, rocking her pelvis against his touch. She struggled to release her hands but Hawk only gripped tighter. "Not yet," he whispered against her lips.

He captured her mouth, sliding his tongue inside. She began to pant, her release building to its breaking point. "Let it go," he murmured, wedging her body more tightly between him and the wall, his erection against her abdomen as he slid a second finger in her slick heat and sent her tumbling over. She cried out his name as she came, shuddering with the intensity of her climax. Hawk released her hands, picking her up so she straddled his waist. His arousal nudged her aching center and she dug her fingers into his shoulders, pressing against him.

"Damn, Jo," he said. "I've got to get you upstairs before I have to take you right here."

Although that idea appealed to her, she was pleased when her back touched the mattress and Hawk had the entire length of his body stretched over her. He pushed her skirt up, removing her panties with one quick tug. He kissed her as he started to unbutton his shirt. "I can't even wait to get our clothes off," he said as his mouth moved over hers. "See what you've reduced me to?"

He may be in a hurry, but she certainly wasn't. Not with the landscape of his magnificent body so close to being revealed. She pushed his chest until she could gain purchase and get him on his back. Just where she wanted him. His look of surprise was quickly replaced with molten heat when she freed him of his shirt and undid his belt and the zipper on his jeans. He eased his hips up enough for her to tug the denim down his thighs and then her mouth was on him.

Hawk hissed as she grasped his erection and worked it in tandem with her lips and tongue. An expert in this act she was not, as she'd only suffered through Thomas' lukewarm reaction to her attempt to bring him off in this manner a few times, but that was clearly not the case now. Hawk plowed his hands into her hair, holding her against him as she applied suction to his cock head.

"Fuck, Jo." His hips arched and she reveled in her power. His taste was intoxicating, the salty flavor of his pre-come and his rumbling groans urging her on. Relaxing her throat, she took as much of his steely length as she could handle and made it her life's mission to give this man the kind of pleasure he'd given her—devastating and complete.

His grip tightened in her hair, almost painfully so, but she found the bite of pain turned her on even more.

"Jo," he panted, loosening his grip on her hair. "Baby, you've got to stop. I can't—" He sucked in a sharp breath. "God. I'm not going to make it."

Just what she wanted to hear. And when he tried to ease up the bed away from her eager mouth, she clamped down on him, sliding her tongue along his hard length. She also used her slight weight in what would have been a useless attempt at holding him down if he hadn't been so far gone.

But he was. And *she'd* done that.

She squeezed his sac and swallowed down as much of his length as she could handle and he was there. He continued to pulse for a few seconds and then he went lax beneath her. She released him and crawled up his chest, a satisfied smile on her face.

She met his lips in a lingering kiss, so turned on she was certain she'd come within seconds if he touched her. And quite possibly even if he didn't. She felt his smile beneath her mouth before he whispered, "Damn, baby. That was quite the homecoming."

Jo gasped as his fingers found her wet slit and entered her in one rough thrust. He curled them and, oh God…there. She threw her head back, moaning as pinpoints of unfamiliar pleasure shot through her. She leaned back, bracing her hands on the mattress on either side of Hawk. Grinding against his fingers, she began to chant his name, thrusting her hips, seeking whatever destination he was taking her to. When he abruptly withdrew his hand, her eyes flew open.

"Not this way," he said as he gently lifted her from him and kicked off his jeans and boxers. She made fast work of removing her dress as he fumbled in his pocket for a condom and rolled it on. He settled her on his lap, and with his hands firmly on her hips, drove into her in one powerful thrust. They moaned in unison as they rushed toward release. The fire he'd kindled with his fingers moments before reignited and she came apart in his arms, trembling as her orgasm took her.

"Oh God," she sighed as she ran her fingers through his hair. "I've never come twice with anyone but you."

Hawk did his best not to behave like a caveman and point out that her ex had to have been a stupid, selfish bastard for that to be the case, and decided to make light of it instead. "Well, lucky for you I'm such a *young* man and will be able to come again without having to make love all night." Her eyes grew wide and he laughed. "On second thought, perhaps age has its merits."

She kissed him long and deep then, and he dug his fingertips into the flesh of her ass. Damn, she felt like heaven. And he was close. He drove home one last time and toppled over, drawing her against his chest as his release pounded through him.

Jo tucked her head under his chin and he knew she could hear his heart thundering in his chest. But could she interpret what that meant? That it beat only for her? Now more than ever, Hawk knew she would be his at any cost. There was no other option. He leaned back and tilted her chin up so their eyes would meet. "So beautiful," he whispered, running his finger along the curve of her breast, down her side and across her abdomen.

She blushed beneath his regard, and her attention dropped to his chest. She traced the edges of his muscles with her hand, following the perimeter to where his abdomen cut into sharp angles. He drew a deep breath.

"Josephine," he said, taking both her hands in his. She looked at him and he decided to take the chance now. He swallowed, his heart hammering behind his ribs. "Come with me to Catalina."

CHAPTER SEVEN

Jo didn't say yes, but she didn't exactly say no, either. The constant state of indecisiveness in which she found herself foundering had become the background music of her life for the past two weeks. She had neither the will nor the desire to walk away from Hawk, even when the darkest hours of the night slipped by and she lay awake, wondering if her love could overcome the obstacles that surely lay ahead.

When she was near him, when he touched her, she easily shut out all her worries. Thoughts of her future, and her past, didn't exist when his mouth moved over hers, his hands caressed her body. When he held her motionless with his stormy gaze as he slid inside her, all her torment melted away. In those moments, her only reality was the man who had erased years of pain and self-doubt with one utterance.

I only care that you're here. With me.

So Jo took things day by day. She worked her shifts at The Whistling Dixie Café, watched as the contractor slowly transformed her crumbling farmhouse, and fielded annoyances from Arizona that jangled her cell phone and filled her living room with every flower available to hack down and wrap in cellophane.

And the letter. God, that infuriating letter from her father. She'd read his argument, all two pages of it, and shoved it into her kitchen drawer. She'd always idolized her dad. And to see

124

him so desperate, so willing to look for any solution to conceal what was truly going on, broke her heart more than any other man could have. But she couldn't worry over that now.

Another thing she tried not to think about was the forty-two days left before Hawk packed up Thunder and drove across the country. At least if she could help it. Most of the time that was an exercise in futility, and with Hawk's mother coming to town, it was an impossibility.

As Jo placed the baked brie she had just prepped into the fridge and bumped the door closed with her hip, she allowed the gravity of what she had offered to do today really wrap around her. Having Hawk and his parents over for dinner meant more than just a meal, she was aware of that. But she had offered without hesitation.

The more time Jo spent with Hawk, with his family, the more she tied herself to an uncertain future. She was really backing herself into a corner with very little opportunity for escape. Perhaps that was the point.

"Hey, Jo?"

She was so lost in thought she didn't hear Ray enter the kitchen or realize tears were clinging to her cheeks. She swiped at the betraying moisture and turned to face Ray.

"You okay, darlin'?"

"Yeah. I was chopping some onions a few minutes ago. Fumes were terrible."

He eyed her suspiciously but let it go. He held up two shirts, a sheepish look transforming his features. "Which of these do you think would look the best?"

"Hmm, let's see." Jo studied her two choices. Both plaid. Both bad. Rubbing her chin, she met his expectant expression. "Tell you what, Ray. I've got to get some things for the table setting tonight after my shift at work." She walked to him, placing her hands on his shoulders. "I saw a cobalt-blue dress shirt in a store window the other day. It would be perfect with your eyes."

Ray's blush nearly matched the crimson hue of the tartan number he held in his right hand. "Oh, you don't have to do that, Jo."

"It's not every day Raven comes to town." His flush grew deeper, if that were possible. "Besides, if I'm cooking dinner for all of us with my fancy new appliances and getting the dining room all gussied up, I can't have you any less sparkly."

Ray shrugged, sighed and laid the shirts across the kitchen table. "If you say so." He reached into his back pocket, extracting his wallet.

"No," she said, placing her hand over his. "This is my treat. It's the least I can do with all the work you've done around here."

His look placed him on the fence, his fingers thumbing through the bills in his wallet.

She squeezed his hand. "Really, Ray. It would make me happy if you let me do this for you."

"It ain't right, but I know not to tangle horns with you. Once you set your mind to something…"

"Yes. And don't you forget it." She winked at him and turned to walk to the stove to stir the marinara sauce for the lasagna she was making for Hawk and his parents. "Hey, Ray?" she called over her shoulder.

"Yeah?"

Jo tapped the spoon on the side of the stockpot, placing it in a holder on the counter. She turned to face him and put on her best impish grin. "Who do you think is more nervous about seeing Raven? Me or you?" She could see the red tips of his ears even from across the room.

"Well," he said, shoving his hands in his pockets. "It *should* be you."

"But?" She bit the inside of her cheek.

Ray laughed. "Are you trying to kill an old man from embarrassment?"

She walked to him and kissed his cheek. "You're not old. And yes, I'm trying to kill you with embarrassment. Takes the heat off me."

"I see how you are." Ray narrowed his eyes playfully.

"So. When does the love of your life arrive?" Jo wiped her hands on her apron.

Ray glanced at his watch. "Hawk should be on the way back with her from the airport now."

Jo took his wrist in her hand to check the time. "And I have to get to work." She smiled at Ray. "Do you mind dropping by here to pick up the shirt later? I'm going to be cutting it close, time-wise."

"It's the least I can do. Thanks, darlin'."

She gave him a quick hug. "Anything for you."

After he'd left, she transferred the sauce into a container and put it in the fridge. As she was washing the pot, a wave of nausea hit her. Perhaps she was the one more nervous about meeting Raven, after all.

* * * * *

"So, whose idea was it, having dinner at her place?"

"Jo's," Hawk said, smiling at his mother.

"Well, well, well," Raven replied. "Brave woman, having the mother over right out of the gate." She turned in her seat to face Hawk.

He glanced over his shoulder before pulling his truck onto the highway. "She's very brave, although she'd never say so." He tightened his grip on the steering wheel. "She's got a lot being thrown at her right now."

"And not just from her ex-husband, I presume."

Hawk slid a glance to his mother. A gentle smile curled the corners of her lips. "It's taking every ounce of control I have not to throw her over my shoulder and drag her back to my cave. I don't want to make things more difficult for her, but it's hard to keep it all to myself."

"You love her." It wasn't a question.

"Of course." He turned to look at her. "But you already knew that."

"I know," she said in a singsong voice. "I just wanted to hear you say it." She placed her hand on his arm. "But you haven't told her."

Hawk shook his head. "I have to ease her in, Mom. I don't want to lose her." He pressed his ear to his left shoulder, trying to stretch the tight muscles in his neck. "I'm sure she knows she has me completely turned inside out. Anyone could see that."

Raven laughed. "Well, *I'm* certainly looking forward to seeing it. I can't wait to meet her."

"I just hope you see what I've seen, and I'm not just losing my mind."

"You're not, Hawk. I can already sense that." She squeezed his arm affectionately and returned her hand to her lap.

"But still…" Hawk signaled when his exit came into view, veering his truck toward Vidalia. He turned to his mother with a grin. "Dad's excited you're here."

Raven nodded and Hawk swore he saw a blush rush across her russet skin. "Yes. I'll be glad to see him. It's been too long."

"Dad said you've been talking a lot on the phone." He bit back a smile.

"Yes. We've had things to, ah, discuss." She looked out

the window.

"Like?" he prodded.

Again, she turned in her seat to face him. "We do have a child together. And you're coming to live with me. We have details to work out."

His eyes widened and he laughed. "Mom, I'm twenty-eight years old. What details could you possibly have to work out? A schedule of my bedtime and snack preferences, perhaps?"

A flush clearly slashed across her high cheekbones and she crossed her arms over her chest. "What *is* your bedtime, anyway?"

Hawk snickered. "Whenever Jo falls asleep." He raised an eyebrow at his mother. "And I'm on a hummus kick right now. Does that help you out?"

"Tremendously," she said, narrowing her eyes at him. "But seriously, Ray's doing okay? He's ready for your move?"

"Yeah. I've hired a lot of help. He's not happy about it."

"That sounds like him." She tugged on her braid. "I feel bad, pulling you away from the farm. And now with Jo…"

"Oh, not you too. Dad already laid the 'I feel bad for keeping you here' speech on me. You two forget I do have freedom of thought."

"Well, make sure you use it. Do what's right for you. I'll be okay—"

"Mom. Stop." He waved his hand in the air. "You wouldn't be okay and you know it. You need Thunder and my training to get this off the ground. End of discussion."

"But Hawk…"

"I loved Rayne, too. It's just as important to me as it is to you." Hawk turned onto the dirt road that led to his farm. "And as for Jo, weren't you the one who said what will be, will be?"

She nodded. "I did."

"So it will all work out, right?"

"Absolutely." Raven smiled.

Hawk wished he could be as certain as his mother. She had unfailing faith, but she hadn't seen just what Hawk was up against. He could only pray her take on the situation wouldn't change after this evening.

He made the turn at his driveway and drove up the long, dusty stretch. When he pulled up to the house and cut the engine, Ray appeared on the porch, bounding down the steps, his face lit up like a carnival.

Subtle.

Hawk tried in vain to suppress a laugh as he undid his seat belt and got out of the car. Before he could even round the truck to open his mother's door, Ray was already there, helping her down.

"Hi, Raven," his dad said, pulling her in for a hug.

"Hello, Ray. You look well." Raven wrapped her arms around his shoulders, pressing a kiss to his cheek.

Hawk walked to the bed of the truck to retrieve his mother's suitcase. Ray had somehow managed to beat him there as well. He leaned close to Hawk, a huge smile on his face. "Scram, kid," he muttered under his breath. Hawk held up his hands and stepped back from the truck.

"Hey, Mom? I've got to go check on the horses. Just make yourself comfortable."

She waved to him. "Sure thing, hon. See you in a bit."

Hawk watched the two of them walk up the steps, Ray gripping the suitcase with one arm and Raven with the other. He smiled as they disappeared into the house.

He turned and looked over the tree line to Jo's place. The day would stretch on endlessly until that evening. Anticipation curled around his heart and stomach at the thought of seeing her. Of introducing her to his mother. Of loving her…forever.

* * * * *

"Damn, Jo. This place looks like a funeral home."

Jo sighed as she tossed her purse in a chair and looked around the room. "I know. But beautiful gifts of nature or not, these things have got to go." She turned to Kristy. "Thanks for taking them for me."

"No problem. It gave me an excuse to swipe the car for the day, anyway. I'm going to go shopping after I leave here." She gestured around the room. "Hey, maybe I could sell some of these in town. I bet some of the boys would love to take them home to their wives. Split the cash?" She rubbed her hands together, smiling at Jo.

"You keep it."

Kristy looked around the room, a frown pulling the corners of her lips down. "So, these are all from your ex-husband? What'd he do, knock over a flower shop?"

Jo nodded and rolled her eyes. "It would appear that way, wouldn't it? But I tell ya. I'll take flowers over a phone call from my ex any day." She pointed to a simple arrangement of daisies tied in a ribbon on the coffee table and smiled. "That one's from Hawk."

Kristy walked to the table and ran the organza bow through her fingers. "Where'd he get these?"

"He snuck into Mrs. Peterson's garden late one night and took them." She shook her head. "Apparently the Stephens men have a penchant for pilfering things from her. All in the name of love, of course."

"Love?" Kristy crossed her arms over her chest and smiled bigger than the Grand Canyon.

"Well." Jo's cheeks felt as if she could cook an egg on them. "What I mean is, both he and Ray have, um, borrowed

131

things from her to give to women." Her backpedaling was keeping her in the same place. Kristy only raised an eyebrow.

"Do you love him, Jo?"

Jo scratched her neck. "Oh, I don't know if…what I mean is…"

Kristy walked to Jo and drew her into a hug. "You love him," she said, heaving a wistful sigh.

"I shouldn't," Jo said with regret.

Kristy pulled back abruptly, her eyes wide. "The hell you shouldn't."

"It's too soon. I don't know if I'm whole enough to give myself to someone yet. And look at all this crap." She swept her arm toward the table full of flowers. "What man in his right mind would want to deal with this kind of baggage?"

"But Jo, you can't help who you fall in love with. Or when."

"I know. Things are just…complicated." She'd endured yet another phone call on the way home from her father, defending his actions and trying to lay a guilt trip. "It's not fair to Hawk."

"If the look on his face whenever he comes into the diner is any indication, I don't think he's suffering."

"But the things he wants. I don't know if I have them to give. At least not now."

Jo's confession left her more than a little lightheaded, her stomach beginning the unsteady rolling indicative of the truly distraught. She leaned her palm on the back of the sofa.

"You okay, Jo? You're kind of pale." Kristy's brow creased in concern.

"Yeah, I'm fine. I've just got a lot going on today. Dinner with Hawk's mother." She gestured around the room. "This."

"He's still calling?"

Jo rubbed her temples. "He hasn't left a voice mail in

about three days…or sent flowers. His silence worries me more than anything."

Kristy took her hand and pulled her to sit on the sofa. "And does Hawk know everything?"

"Well, the flowers, obviously. I've told him Thomas has called, but I haven't told him how frequently. Nor have I gone into detail about my dad's ridiculous behavior. It's embarrassing. The situation upsets him. He tries to hide it, but I can tell."

"Of course it upsets him. No wonder he wants you to come to Catalina with him. I would too, if I were him."

"I know." Jo put her head in her hands.

Kristy rubbed her back. "Have you made any decisions on that yet?"

"No," Jo mumbled.

"The last thing you need is to pressure yourself. You've got time. Just enjoy tonight, and don't give another thought to your florist. Or your father."

They rose from the sofa and Jo gave Kristy a hug. "Thank you for taking care of all the flowers. And thank you for being my friend."

"You're welcome." She stood back and held Jo in a loose embrace. "Now go upstairs and get gorgeous for that man of yours." She winked. "You lucky bitch."

Jo gave her a small smile. "See you at work tomorrow."

Kristy grabbed a large bouquet of roses from the sofa table and shooed Jo. "Go. I'll get these." She took a step toward the door before she turned back to Jo. "Oh, and I'll be expecting a full report tomorrow, of course."

* * * * *

"Damn it."

Jo groaned in frustration as she repositioned an uncooperative pin in the chignon she was trying to construct out of her badly behaved hair. Her second attempt pulled it too tightly, the sharp tug a warning of an imminent headache if she left it in place. She yanked it out again and dropped it on the vanity top, resting her head in her hands. Tears pricked the backs of her eyes. Now was not a good time for her emotional dam to decide to break, letting out all she'd been struggling to contain in a rushing gush of hysteria.

"Jo?"

His velvet-like voice stroked her from across the room. She glanced over her shoulder, willing her negative energy away. He walked to her and she swiveled in her seat to face him and it was then she got the full visual assault. His hair was pulled back into a braid that dropped over his shoulder. He wore black dress slacks that clung to the bands of muscles in his legs, a white silk shirt opened at the neck revealing a leather-and-stone necklace flush against his throat. Polished black dress boots with gleaming silver tips finished off the devastating picture.

She traced her finger over the necklace. "This is nice," she said, still staring at his throat.

"Thank you. My mother brought it to me. It was my grandfather's."

She dropped her hand and began to absently pick at a cuticle. Hawk placed a finger under her chin, tilting her head up.

"What's wrong, baby?"

She shrugged. "I'm just a little nervous about tonight, I guess."

"You needn't be." He kissed her gently and tucked her hair behind her ear. "I saw all the flowers are gone. All but mine. You didn't have to do that for my benefit, you know."

She nodded. "They remind me of what I don't want to

think about. And with your mother coming…" She let out a shaky breath. "I gave them to Kristy."

Hawk knelt on the carpet in front of her, placing his hands on the back of her chair, and leaned close. "Let me help you relax." His lips met hers, one hand sliding up her thigh. He kneaded the muscles of her leg gently before running the tip of his finger over the silk of her panties. She could feel the wet fabric clinging to her skin. He pulled back to look at her, his pupils wide and his lips parted. He hooked his finger beneath her panties and pulled them aside. His finger grazed her slick flesh.

"My God, Jo. You're so wet. When?" His fingers commenced a slow, circular caress, his mouth taking hers in a heated capture. He drove his hand into the hair at her nape, dragging her even closer to him. "I only just touched you. When did you get so hot?"

Jo went up in flames at his words. His voice was so raw, so insistent as he continued to kiss her, murmuring "when" every time he released her lips for a breath. She moaned, letting her thighs fall farther apart.

"Tell me," he said as he slid two fingers in her channel.

Her head fell back as she felt the tight coil inside her begin to break loose. His palm closed over her breast and she shattered, gasping as her orgasm took control of her body. When the tremors subsided, she raised heavy eyelids to look at him. His face was clouded with desire, his gaze intent and probing.

"When you walked in the room," she whispered. "That's when."

He groaned and kissed her again, sliding his tongue inside her mouth. She pulled him to her, hands at his buckle. He drew back gently, halting her endeavor. "Are you relaxed now?"

Her body was coiled like a panther about to pounce, so she couldn't say she was relaxed, exactly. But he certainly knew how to obliterate any negative thoughts. "Ah, I'm not as stressed, if that's what you mean."

He smiled like the devil and rose to his full height. She stared up at him in dumb confusion. "Wh-what are you doing?"

"I'm going downstairs." He glanced at his watch. "It's time for my parents to arrive. Can't have them walking in on us like guilty teenagers while your lovely dinner burns." The corner of his lip trembled.

"But Hawk, I'm…you're…" She gestured to his erection straining against the fine fabric of his trousers.

He leaned down and kissed her deeply, placing her hand against his arousal. "Yes, I am. And I'll probably stay like this all night, just thinking what I'm going to do about it later." He brought her palm to his mouth, kissing her and nipping her flesh gently with his teeth. "I'll see you downstairs?"

"Yes," she said, tugging gently on his braid to bring his mouth back to hers.

"Thank you for tonight," he whispered against her lips.

"It's my pleasure."

Hawk ran the backs of his fingers across her cheek. He smiled and she watched as he walked out into the hall, pulling the door closed behind him. Jo turned in her seat to face the mirror.

She hardly recognized the woman staring back at her. Her cheeks were flushed, her hair tousled. She was beautiful, desirable. And in love.

* * * * *

"Now, Jo here has done a lot of the work. The contractor, Hawk and I just step in on the things she can't handle on her own." Ray raised his arm in a toast, grasping the stem of his water glass between two fingers. His crisp blue shirt intensified the aqua of his eyes—eyes that sparkled every time he looked at Raven.

Nerves elicited a strangled laugh in her throat. "Well, all of you have to step in a lot, but thank you." She skirted around the end of the table to take her seat. Smiling, she picked up her wineglass and raised it to Ray before she took a sip. She could feel Raven's regard on her, as it had been for most of the hour she had been in Jo's home.

When Raven had first entered the house, her beauty had taken Jo aback. She had expected her to be beautiful, but she wasn't prepared for how stunning she truly was. As Ray had said, she was a vision. Long, thick black hair cascaded down her back to her trim waist. Sharp, angular features comprised her face, with warm brown eyes softening the bone structure. Her lips were full, and when she smiled, straight white teeth stood in contrast to the deep tan of her skin, just like her son.

Raven's dress skimmed along gentle curves, its hem just shy of her knees. Her skin was a deeper hue than Hawk's, and nearly free of wrinkles. Jo discovered this wasn't so much a result of good genes, which they clearly had in spades, as it was the fact she was barely ten years older than Jo. That little tidbit of information had sent her tender stomach surging into full-blown nausea.

But there was nothing about Raven as a person that didn't invite Jo in. She was gracious and warm. Open and accepting. And she watched Jo with interest, a smile always curling the corners of her lips. Jo suspected Raven was privy to all her baggage, the messy state her life was currently in. The thought Hawk's mother could see through to her thoughts and emotions unnerved and intrigued her all at the same time.

Raven placed her wineglass on the table. "So, Jo. Hawk tells me you were a real estate agent back in Tucson."

Jo nodded, placing her fork on her plate. "Once upon a time. I haven't done it in years."

"Have you ever thought of going back to it?" She tossed

her hair over her shoulder.

"Yes, I've toyed with the idea." Jo took a sip of wine and cleared her throat. "I'm licensed in Arizona, but I would have to obtain one here. I looked into a position at an office in Macon. It won't be too difficult an ordeal." She felt Hawk's regard on her. She could guess he didn't like that last part, since it would require her to move. Her stomach pitched. "If it comes to that."

The table fell silent, and Jo fought the urge to slither underneath it.

"So," Ray said, breaking the awkward silence. "This dinner is delicious."

Jo smiled warmly at him, pushing her food around on her plate. She felt her stomach contract, the natural precursor to what inevitably became the main gastrointestinal floor show. She hadn't willed nausea away so fiercely since she'd thrown up on her pre-pubescent date on the Mad Hatter teacup ride in seventh grade. She clenched her napkin in her lap as heat pricked her skin and clamminess enveloped her.

The wave mercifully abated and Jo wiped her damp palms on her skirt. "Um, where did Hawk's name come from, Raven? He's never told me."

She glanced at Hawk, pride in her eyes. "Well," she said, resting her forearm on the table. "When Hawk entered this world, he didn't cry. Not a peep." She looked at Ray and smiled. "Remember how I panicked? I thought something was wrong."

Ray took her hand, squeezing it. "I remember."

"Anyway," Raven said, facing Jo again. "When my mother handed him to me, he locked those intense eyes of his on mine. He was alert. I knew then he would be Silent Hawk—coming into this world in silent alertness, just like the predatory bird he's named for."

A shiver ran down Jo's spine and she looked at Hawk. The

eyes Raven spoke of were on her, their heat piercing her skin, sending her heartbeat skittering. Silent and predatory. And sexy as hell. She tore her gaze from his, her stomach beginning to roll again.

"Jo." Raven's voice was soft. "Are you all right? You're awfully pale."

"You okay, darlin'?" Hawk asked, ushering her hair behind her shoulder.

"Yes, of course." She slid the wineglass away from her. "Raven, you said your mother was with you when you gave birth?"

"She delivered Silent Hawk. She's a curandera, an energy healer." She took a sip from her water glass. "So am I."

Hawk took Jo's hand, twining their fingers together in his lap. "A curandera is a natural healer, a woman trained in medicinal herbs and energy healing," he said, running his thumb in circles over the back of her hand.

"Fascinating." She looked at his mother. "And you grew up learning this?"

She smiled. "It's been passed down from generation to generation for as far back as my Apache heritage has been recorded."

Ray laughed, his eyes adoring as he glanced at Raven. "Poor thing had her work cut out for her with me. Try as she might, I never could seem to get things right."

"Sometimes change doesn't reveal itself immediately. That doesn't mean the path hasn't been cleared." Raven placed her hand over his on the table.

Jo turned her attention to Hawk and the look on his face as he watched his parents caused her heart to flip over in her chest. The apparent love he had for them and the pleasure he was receiving from their pleasant camaraderie was a private family matter. If she were a tap dancer crossing the stage

139

during the middle of *Swan Lake*, she couldn't feel any more out of place.

Pushing her chair back, she stood from the table. "If you all will excuse me for a minute, I need to go check on the mulberry pie. I'm still getting to know my new appliances. I don't trust the heat settings yet."

Hawk and Ray rose from their seats, Southern gentlemen through and through. She smiled at them. "Please sit. I'll be right back."

She strode toward the swinging door and pushed it open, receiving comfort from an empty kitchen on the other side. The pie was fine. She was not. She walked to the oven anyway, slipping on an oven mitt. She made a point of creating a lot of busy noise to conceal her true purpose—momentary escape. Leaning over, she grasped the oven handle.

The room started to spin and beads of sweat popped out on her forehead. Placing her hand against the counter, she steadied herself, taking deep breaths. Her heartbeat echoed loudly in her ears, her stomach pitching. Blackness crept into her periphery and then…nothing.

* * * * *

"She was fine earlier."

Jo heard the voice through what sounded like wads of cotton stuffed in her ears.

"Well, she ain't now."

Ray. It was Ray…talking to Hawk?

A cool cloth was placed on her forehead, a soft hand enveloping hers. "Can you hear me, Jo?"

She blinked her eyes open, trying to focus on the faces hovering above her. The room was dim—odd for a kitchen so full of windows. And what was she lying on? She tried to sit up, her head spinning.

Hawk's hands pressed on her shoulders gently. "Oh no you don't. You stay right there on the bed where I put you."

She looked around in confusion. Her bedroom. Hawk sat on one side of her, his mom on the other. Ray stood at the foot of the bed, a panicked look on his face.

"Wh-what happened?" she stammered.

Hawk brushed her hair from her cheek. "You went into the kitchen to check on the pie and then we heard a crash. You fainted, and must have pulled down all the mixing bowls with you as you fell because they were scattered all over the floor."

"I did?"

"Yes." He smiled at her tenderly.

"Scared the crap out of us, is what you did," Ray said, grasping the bedpost and leaning against it.

Raven squeezed her hand. "Silent Hawk, go join your father down there and give me and Jo some breathing room."

Jo's eyes followed his movement as he obeyed, standing next to Ray. Her attention darted to Raven when she stood, her left palm flat, hovering near Jo's head.

"What are you doing?" Jo asked in a tiny voice, wary of the expression on Raven's face.

"Shhh," she said, soothingly. "I'm just opening the chakra of my non-dominant hand so I can read your energy field. See what's going on."

Jo glanced at Hawk and Ray. They watched as if this were nothing out of the ordinary. She relaxed against the pillows, willing to let Raven do whatever it was she thought would help. What harm could there be?

Raven started at Jo's head, her hand slowly skimming across her body very close to her skin, but not touching it, her eyes closed in concentration. Jo's steady breaths echoed in the silence of the room. Raven passed over her chest, pausing for a brief moment before moving to her left arm, then her right. Her hand hovered over Jo's stomach, perfectly still. Nausea continued to churn, so if this was supposed to alleviate it, it wasn't working.

Raven took a deep breath and moved a few inches down over Jo's pelvis. Heat radiated from her hand and infused Jo's flesh with warmth, as if hot water had been poured on her. She placed her hand against Jo's abdomen, its high temperature discernible even through the fabric of the dress. Raven opened her eyes, locking her gaze on Jo. Leaving her left hand on Jo's stomach, she placed her right hand on her arm. Her skin was cool as she touched her there.

"Do me a favor, will you, boys?" She removed her hands, turning to face Ray and Hawk. "Go back to the house and get my satchel of herbs. I'll also need the mortar and pestle."

"Both of us?" Hawk asked, stepping toward Jo.

"Yes." Her voice was firm and Hawk stopped. "Jo needs to rest for a little while. You can come back later on."

Hawk hesitated but eventually nodded, and he and his father left the bedroom, shutting the door behind them.

Raven sat on the bed next to Jo, taking her hand in hers again. She took a deep breath, her brow furrowed. Brown liquid pools stared down at Jo, concern clouding their warm beauty.

"Does my son know yet?"

CHAPTER EIGHT

"But we used condoms. Lots of them." Jo stared in disbelief at the two glaring blue lines that verified what Raven already knew. She was pregnant.

"Well, that one time by the stream, we were a little...careless." Hawk ran his hands up and down her arms and Jo shook her head.

"No. We used one then. I remember."

Hawk took the stick from her trembling fingers and placed it on the sink. He drew her into the bedroom, helping her to sit on the bed. "We finished with one, sweetheart, but we weren't very careful starting out. And they're not a hundred percent effective."

She stared at him blankly, swallowing down a surge of nausea. He took her hands in his. "Jo, I hate to even bring this up because I know how it upsets you to talk about him." He edged closer to her on the bed. "In all the time you were married...you never tried to get pregnant?"

"Um." She rolled her head back, staring at the ceiling. He was right. It did upset her to talk about her marriage. Especially with Hawk. She took a deep breath and looked at him. "I went off birth control after we'd been married a couple of years, but I never conceived. I always thought there was something wrong with me, my cycles are very irregular."

"Or wrong with *him*."

Jo shrugged. "My doctor couldn't find anything, and as time went on I just wrote it off to not having sex." She laughed without humor.

Hawk didn't join her. He had an expression of forced control on his face instead. "And he never got tested? Not once in all that time?"

Jo looked down at her lap, shaking her head.

"So, he wouldn't take the time to see if he was at fault. He just let you think it was something wrong with you."

She looked up at him. "I guess." She waved her hand. "It doesn't matter now. Clearly it wasn't me."

Hawk gathered her into his lap. "Tell me, Jo. Is this good news for you? Or bad?"

She looked into his eyes—the eyes she wanted their child to have—and knew she could never regret this move, this man, this child. Whatever became of them, this baby was a gift. And she'd never regret it. "It's scary news. But I wouldn't change it."

His lips touched hers, tender and searching. She felt secure in his embrace, despite the curveball fate had just thrown at her. They would be forever bound to one another by this child. The thought both comforted and terrified her. All choice had been taken out of her hands—stalling for time was no longer an option.

He continued to kiss her, his possession slow, restrained.

Deliberate.

Hawk broke the kiss, staring into her eyes. Cradling her face in his hand, he stroked her cheek with the pad of his thumb. "I guess it's safe to assume you'll stop fighting what we both know to be the truth—we're meant to be together, Jo." He searched her face. "You'll come to Arizona?"

Jo drew in a shaky breath, turning her cheek into his palm. "Yes," she whispered.

Hawk gently guided her mouth to his. "You will never regret this decision. I promise you that." He placed his hand over her abdomen as he kissed her.

And she believed him.

* * * * *

"Is Jo okay?"

Hawk dropped his keys into the pewter bowl on the table and walked to the seating area to join Raven. He sighed as he dropped into the leather club chair. "I hope so." He leveled his gaze on his mother. "She's sick as hell. Thinks she's going to work later." He shook his head, leaning forward to rest his forearms against his knees.

Raven's brow creased in concern. "I'll have your father take me by on our way to the airport. I'll make a tea for her to help with the nausea." She leaned toward Hawk and tapped him on the arm. "I'll leave written instructions for you so you can make her some more."

"Thanks, Mom." Hawk reclined into the seat, running his hands down his face. He looked at his mother. "She's coming with me."

"I thought she might." Raven smiled.

Hawk nodded, the corners of his lips tugging down. "I can't help thinking that she might not be if it weren't for the pregnancy."

"Do you really believe that?"

He groaned, leaning his head against the back of the chair. "I don't know what to think." He rolled his head to the side to look at her. "Talk about divine intervention."

"That's right," she said. "You can't fight destiny. No matter how hard you try."

"I guess not."

Raven took his hand in hers. "And how are you doing, son?"

He sat upright in the chair. "The woman I love is carrying my child. I can't even describe what that feels like."

Hawk and Raven turned at the sound of boots thudding against the hardwoods. Ray walked into the living room, stopping to stand behind Hawk's chair. He placed his hand on Hawk's shoulder. "It feels like your heart has expanded so much that you can hardly breathe, like you'll suffocate from pure joy alone."

Hawk turned to look at Ray. "Well put, Pops."

"Well, I've been in your shoes." He cleared his throat. "Ah, Raven darlin', we need to get going soon if you're going to make your flight."

She squeezed Hawk's hand and rose. "Yes, and I've got to swing by Jo's on our way out. Make her a tea."

"Still sick?" Ray directed his attention to Hawk.

He stood from his seat. "Very. She'll never make it through her shift."

Ray put his hands on his hips. "You're going to let her go to work, Silent Hawk? A pregnant woman—"

"Whoa, watch it boys." Raven laughed. "She's not an invalid. She's pregnant."

"But it ain't right. She's in a delicate condition." Ray shook his finger at Raven. She snatched it in her grasp, smiling at him.

"It's not terminal, Ray." She rolled her eyes and looked at Hawk. "Even if it feels that way for a while."

Hawk's brow creased. "So it's okay for her to be on her feet for hours, running around?"

"Hawk, you're already pacing around outside the delivery room and she isn't even past her first trimester. She'll be fine." She pushed her hair off her face. "Speaking of which, do you

146

have any idea how far along she is?"

"It was a little over a month ago."

Raven retrieved a hair band from her pocket and began to twist her hair into a loose braid. "So, that would put her about six or seven weeks along, gestation-wise. Make sure you get her to a doctor soon, okay?"

"I'd have her there today if she wasn't insisting on going to the diner." Hawk clenched his jaw.

Raven let out an exasperated sigh. "God help her. You're going to drive her crazy." She stood on her toes and kissed Hawk on the cheek. "You'll be a good dad, though."

Raven turned to Ray. "I guess I'm all set. Would you mind grabbing my bag from the guest room?"

"Of course not, darlin'."

Hawk gave his mother a hug. "Okay, so call me and let me know when I need to fly out in the next few weeks."

She patted his back. "I'll try to handle as much of it as I can. I know you don't want to be away from Jo."

"Thanks, Mom. And she and I will be out there in six weeks or so."

"I can't wait. Take care of her." She stepped from his embrace and poked him in the chest with her finger. "But don't smother the poor girl."

Hawk's face lit up with his smile. "I'll try my best."

* * * * *

"Are you sure you're up to this, baby?"

Jo groaned, leaning her head against the back of the seat in Hawk's truck. She was quickly beginning to regret her decision to allow him to bring her to work. "For the hundredth time, yes." She glanced to her left and smiled at his frantic expression. "The tea Raven gave me worked wonders. I feel much better."

"But you'll call if you get sick again?"

"Yes." She looked out the window to the diner before turning back to him. She bit back a smile. "Can I go now?"

He undid his seat belt. "Here, let me help you."

She grabbed his face in her hands and pressed a fast, hard kiss to his lips before abruptly releasing him and clicking her seat belt open. She had the door ajar and was sliding down before he had a chance to carry her into the diner. "Bye, Hawk," she called over her shoulder, daring a glance at him before she went inside. He didn't look pleased. Jo bit back a smile.

She walked to the counter and stowed her purse beneath it. Kristy appeared from the kitchen. "I clocked you in when I saw Hawk pull up." She strode over to Jo. "Where's your car?"

Jo scowled. "In my driveway."

"O-*kay*." Kristy leaned a palm on the counter. "How did last night go?"

Jo held back a laugh. "It was…interesting."

"And?"

"Well," she said. Jo walked to the bussing station with Kristy on her heels. She grabbed a tray of table set-ups and headed to the first booth, placing condiments at the rear of the table against the wall. A sugar caddy toppled off the edge of her tray, bounced off the seat and clamored against the floor. "Great," Jo muttered, kneeling on the seat to reach below the table. Her head began to spin when she reached down and her stomach rolled on a violent wave of nausea. Jo slithered into the seat, leaning her head against the back of the bench. "Oh no, not again."

Kristy dropped next to Jo, the movement jostling her.

Jo put her hand on Kristy's arm. "Sit still."

"Jo?" Kristy asked, peering at her face. "What's wrong?

148

Are you sick?"

"Not exactly," Jo mumbled, clutching her stomach. At least not in the way Kristy probably intended. "Excuse me," she said, pushing at Kristy frantically. She darted to the bathroom and barely made it to the stall before she threw up.

Jo heard the door push open. Kristy's pink high-top sneakers appeared to the side of the stall. "Hon, are you okay?"

Define okay.

Jo weaved toward the sink, washing her hands and rinsing her mouth with cool water. Kristy rubbed her back. "You *are* sick, Jo."

Jo turned to face her, leaning her hip on the vanity. "No, I'm pregnant."

"What?" she gasped.

Jo didn't think a human's eyes could open so wide. She nodded, rubbing her temple.

"When did you find out?"

Jo choked out a sarcastic laugh. "You'll love this. You ready?"

Kristy nodded.

"Well, I passed out while Hawk's mom was there and woke up in my bedroom with all of them surrounding me." Jo wrapped her arms around herself. "And as my luck would have it, Raven is an energy healer."

"What in the heck is that?"

"Oh, it's someone who can read your energy field and pinpoint exactly what ails you."

"No-oo-o." Kristy made the word into three syllables.

"Oh, but yes," Jo said, recalling the look on Raven's face just before she laid the news on her. Jo shook her head. "The only saving grace was that she asked Hawk and Ray to leave the room before she told me."

"So Hawk's mother knew before either one of you?"

"Yeah, isn't that great?" Jo turned to the sink to wet a paper towel. She placed it against her throat.

"My God. That must have been awkward. Did his mother seem…upset?"

"Quite the contrary," Jo said. "She seemed concerned about my reaction, but she didn't seem the least bit out of sorts. She looked almost, well, pleased, I guess."

"And what did Hawk say?" Kristy pulled a section of hair that had fallen from Jo's ponytail and tucked it behind her ear.

"He said I needed to stop fighting what we both know is the truth—that we belong together."

Kristy placed her hand over her heart. "Oh, I can't stand it! And what did you say?"

Jo swallowed down a rush of queasiness. "I, ah, told him I would come to Arizona."

"I'm so happy for you." Kristy threw her arms around Jo and squeezed tightly.

"Uhhh," Jo groaned, pushing at Kristy. "Move, move, quickly." She rushed past her back into the stall.

"Kristy?" she called weakly.

"Yes, hon?"

Jo grimaced. "Can you call Hawk for me? I think I need to go home."

"Um, he's still here, actually."

"What?" she asked, pushing her ponytail over her shoulder.

Kristy walked to the stall, peering around the open door. "He was just coming in the diner when I came in here after you. I told him to wait out there." She snickered. "I'd probably clock him if I tried to push the door open right now."

"Geez," Jo moaned. "Okay, will you go tell him I'll be out

in a minute? Oh, and what about Bobby?"

"I'll take care of it. You take your time."

"Thanks."

Jo waited until the nausea abated enough to leave the ladies' room. She opened the door slowly, walking into the narrow hallway that led to the dining room. Hawk stood a few feet down, holding her purse. He closed the distance between them quickly, drawing her to his side. "Let's get you home, okay?"

She nodded and stepped out of his reach when he tried to pick her up. "Forget it, Silent Hawk. I'm walking." She looked at him—all six-foot-three inches of solid male, holding a small red leather Gucci handbag. "Give that to me." She snatched it from him and smiled. "I'm not letting you walk through there carrying this."

He grinned down at her. "Really? I always thought red was my color."

She took his hand and tugged him down the hall. "Come on, let's go."

Jo stopped to hug Kristy on the way out and waved to Bobby as Hawk led her outside. Once they were in the truck, he turned to face her.

"I spoke to Bobby while you and Kristy were in the ladies' room. He said you didn't have to come back if you didn't want to. There's a girl who would like to take the position."

"Oh, Hawk, I don't know. This nausea may not last too long." She rubbed her tummy.

Hawk leaned across the cab, placing a kiss against her lips. "Please, Jo. Will you do this for me?"

She leaned her forehead against his and let out a long breath. "Okay."

Relief flooded his features and he kissed her nose before drawing away and starting the truck. Jo stared at his profile.

Anyone paying attention would realize she would do just about anything for him at this point.

Hawk pulled from the parking lot and turned onto the side street that led into the main square. She sent him a questioning look.

"I need to pick up a few things my mom listed so I can make the tea for your nausea. It'll only take a sec."

"Oh, okay." She settled back into the seat and closed her eyes. "I'll just stay here and try not to throw up again."

"Do you need me to take you back first? I can come—"

"Noooo." She shooed him away. "I was kidding. I think."

"Jo…"

She laughed. "Get out of here. I'm fine. If I throw up, I won't do it in your pretty truck."

He didn't look convinced, but he left.

Jo dug around in her purse in search of peppermints. Nothing like the taste of vomit. Disgusting. She'd just popped the candy in her mouth when she noticed a black Town Car parked at the other end of the square. With tinted windows.

Her heart sped up. *Certainly not…*

Jo slid down in her seat as she dug around in the Gucci for her sunglasses. After placing them on her nose she faced straight ahead but cut her eyes to the left. With the bright sun, she could just make out the outline of the driver. The telltale shape of a chauffer's hat came into view. The candy disintegrated as she ground her back molars. She doubted very seriously anyone in this small slice of Georgia drove a car like that. Which could only mean—

The driver door opened and Hawk slid in, dangling a bag from his finger. "One hurling kit in the making, my love."

Jo schooled her features and forced her panic away. She pasted what she hoped was a convincing smile to her face. "Perfect. Let's get out of here so you can put your potion-making skills to work."

Hawk leaned over to place a quick kiss to her cheek before backing out and driving toward home. Right past the Town Car. He was oblivious to the out-of-place vehicle. But she sure as hell wasn't.

* * * * *

The next month was a flurry of details. And as shaken up as Jo had been from the sighting that day in the square, she hadn't seen the car again. And she'd looked, pretending to be soaking in every detail of the little town as she went with Hawk on errands or to the occasional restaurant when she wasn't feeling too queasy. But there were no black Town Cars with tinted windows in sight. Only a plethora of pickups and small sedans.

She had mapped out her plans, and did her best to focus on that and leave the past where it belonged—even if it did try to thrust itself into her new life.

Hawk had assured Jo they would eventually return to Georgia, and considering the simple fact she wouldn't be able to sell her house if she tried, renovations went on as usual, with one exception—Billy Crutchett. He had been thrilled to take her place in the project. Staring at his butt crack when she was on the verge of vomiting on a regular basis already wasn't a thrill, but like Ray said, he did fine work.

Jo leaned back into the sofa cushions, clutching her cell phone to her chest. She had tried to make this phone call countless times, too many to remember, but she always ended the call before depressing the final digits. She had spoken to her sister, of course, but never with the intention of divulging her news.

Her sister was dealing with enough of Jo's drama, what with running reconnaissance to discover what was going on between Thomas and their father while digesting the fact Jo was more than friends with her sexy neighbor—information she'd received well after the fact. It had been two weeks since Jo had received yet another message from Thomas, begging her to let him plead his case in person, and she just couldn't bring herself to ask her sister to find out why. There was more important news to discuss. With her move only two weeks away, she couldn't put off telling Meg any longer—her sister would be hurt enough by her omission already.

Jo closed her eyes as her sister's phone rang, drawing a deep breath. "Hi, Meg."

"Hey! How goes it?"

"I'm fine." Jo leaned her head against the back of the sofa. "Listen, Meg. I have some news."

Brief silence followed. "Has something happened with Thomas that I don't know about?"

"No, all quiet on the western front." She grimaced from a swell of nausea, something she thought she'd shaken a few days ago. "It's about Hawk and me, actually."

A relieved laugh echoed in Jo's ear. "Thank God. I was afraid I'd missed something on my end. I've been spending a lot of time at the house, but nothing seems out of the ordinary. Just lots of talk about the election. So what's going on with Hawk?"

"Well, you remember that I said we were kind of seeing each other?" Jo switched the phone to her other ear, dread consuming her.

"Yeah..." Meg drew the word out.

"It's, ah, a little more involved than that."

"Jo, hon, do you think you're ready for anything serious? I mean, in light of all that's going on."

Jo slammed her eyes shut. "I don't have a choice in the matter. Not anymore."

"What's that supposed to mean?"

"What it means, Meg…" Jo steeled herself for her sister's reaction. "Is that I'm pregnant."

A gasp, then silence traveled over the line.

"Meg?"

"How far along are you?"

Disappointment laced her sister's voice, but for what reason in particular she couldn't know—because Jo had rushed into a physical relationship, or because she had kept it all from the one person who was supposed to be her best friend. "I'm right at eleven weeks."

"Eleven—Jo! How could you keep this from me? How long have you known?"

"About a month."

Jo could hear the rush of her sister's breath over the line, and knew Meg was trying to calm down. "Why didn't you tell me?"

"I know I should have." She rose from the sofa and began to pace. "But, Meg, I just couldn't handle any more stress at the time. What with Thomas and the crap Dad pulled and learning of the pregnancy, I just…" She pressed the heel of her hand to her forehead. "I just couldn't handle your reaction. You weren't exactly on board with me coming here in the first place."

"Jo—"

"And I've burdened you so much lately. I hate to think how much time I'm taking away from your studies while you keep tabs on Thomas and Daddy." She bit her bottom lip.

"Jo, you know I would do anything for you. I just wish you had told me, but I can't fault you for worrying about my reaction. I wasn't exactly supportive of your move. I'm sorry about that."

Tears threatened. Damn hormones. "You certainly don't need to apologize. But Meg, there's more."

"Do I need to sit down?"

"Probably," Jo mumbled. "Hawk is moving to Arizona for an extended period of time. And I'm going with him."

"Where?"

"Catalina." Jo waited for it.

"But that's practically under Thomas' nose! You can throw a rock from there and hit us. If the press catches wind of it…"

There it was.

"I'm aware. It was one of the reasons I was reticent about moving there in the first place. And then I found out about the baby." Jo leaned her hip against the sofa. "Well, that should get Thomas off my back, at least."

"What? Your involvement with another man? I wouldn't count on it, Jo. It might just make him try that much harder."

"But I'm carrying Hawk's baby. Certainly…"

"I don't know. I've never seen such raw determination in my life." A strained laugh carried over the miles. "You'd probably have to marry Hawk."

Jo's stomach pitched.

"Has he asked you?" Meg asked.

"No," Jo replied.

"Do you think he will?"

Jo rubbed her arm, beginning to pace again. "Knowing Hawk, yes."

"And what will you say?"

Jo turned to face the window when she heard tires on the gravel and saw Ray's truck approaching. Her heart fluttered frantically in her chest as her answer passed her lips. "Yes. I would say yes, Meg."

"Because of the baby?"

"No." Jo gripped the phone tightly in her hand. "Because I love him."

An unexpected chuckle vibrated through the phone. "Well, you'd better marry him then."

Jo laughed and walked to the door to open it for Ray. "Hawk's dad just got here with my lunch. Can I call you later?"

"Sure. And Jo?"

"Uh-huh?"

"I'm really happy for you."

Jo smiled. "I'm happy for me too. I love you."

"Love you too."

Jo ended the call and held the door open for Ray to pass.

"Here it is, darlin'. Just what you wanted." Ray gestured toward the sofa and closed the door after Jo stepped away. He plopped down on the cushions next to her and handed her a bag from the deli. "Tuna salad on sourdough with extra pickles."

Her mouth began to water as she extracted the sandwich from the bag. Unwrapping the paper, she sat back into the sofa, taking a bite. She sighed in culinary ecstasy.

"Um-hmm. I've heard that before," Ray said, tossing his hat on the coffee table. "Next thing you know, you'll be puking, telling me to cross tuna fish off the list of things you can eat."

She popped a chip into her mouth, shaking her head. "Not this time. I haven't thrown up in four days."

"Well, thank the Almighty for that." He ran his hand over his abdomen. "My stomach ain't the strongest. If I see anyone vomit, I can't help but join in."

"You're taking your chances with me, then. I'm like a time bomb. Despite my days of good fortune, I could go off at any moment."

Ray patted her tummy. "You're worth the risk, darlin'. You're carrying my grandbaby in there."

She placed her hand over his on her belly, smiling. "You know, Ray, I think—"

"Pops, you're not moving in on my woman, are you? I *believe* you have one of your own."

Jo's pulse accelerated at the sound of his voice.

Ray flushed scarlet at the mention of Raven. "Just checking on our girl, son." Ray rose from the seat. "She said she wasn't planning on hurling her lunch today."

"Progress," Hawk said, his grin nearly reaching his ears. He drew Jo from her seat and placed a kiss on her lips. "How are you feeling?"

"Tired. Oh, and bored. Definitely bored." She glanced over her shoulder at Billy laying a piece of hardwood flooring in the dining room, his ever-present crack grinning at her. She gestured in his direction with her head. "That's only entertaining for so long."

Hawk threw his head back in laughter and pulled her against him. "Hey, Dad, do you mind meeting with the Grants for me? They're interested in boarding their daughter's gelding here over the winter."

"Sure son. What time?"

Hawk's attention dropped to Jo's lips. "How's now?"

Ray cleared his throat, a poor cover-up for his snicker. "Now's fantastic. As a matter of fact, I think I'll grab my two buddies here and get some lunch. I reckon I shouldn't expect the Grants for about..."

"Two hours." Hawk's eyes danced with mischief as he looked down at Jo.

"Well then. Two hours it is." He snatched his hat from the table. "Hey, Billy. Grab Dan and let's get us some lunch."

Billy sat back on his heels. "But I ate already."

"Like that's stopped you before," Ray said sarcastically, crossing his arms over his chest, a smile pulling up the corners of his lips.

"Well, that's the damn truth," Billy replied, standing and wiping wood dust from his jeans. "Hey, Dan," he yelled into the kitchen. "We're eating again."

The other contractor appeared and shrugged. "All right." He unhooked his tool belt, draping it over a ladder.

Jo watched the trio leave and turned her attention to Hawk. "You sure know how to clear a room."

He scooped her up, walking toward the stairs. "Well, you said you were tired, and you can't rest with all of that banging going on."

"You're taking me to nap?" she asked, narrowing her eyes at him.

He entered her bedroom, placing her on the bed and stretching out along her side. He yanked off one boot and then the other, dropping them noisily on the floor. "You'll nap." His lips found the sensitive skin at the base of her throat. "Eventually."

She encircled his neck with her arms, wrapping her leg around him. The pregnancy had made everything more sensitive, including her body's reaction to Hawk. A mere look, let alone a touch, flooded her with want, her skin on fire for his touch. He never disappointed, bringing her to peak over and over. She knew this time would be no different and her blood surged through her veins at the thought.

He removed their clothing—his quickly, and hers at a pace meant to drive her insane. Each article of clothing came off maddeningly slow, with his hands and tongue caressing skin he exposed. She was desperate with need by the time he finally settled himself between her thighs, the tip of his erection pressing against her inflamed flesh. He teased her, sliding back and forth, grazing her clit. He knew from experience in the last month that, with the pregnancy, that alone could make her come very quickly. But he didn't give it to her today. She got an evil grin instead.

"You're going to make me suffer?" she asked, tilting her hips in search of his cock.

He eased down her body, placing kisses against the upper curve of a breast. "In only the best way possible, darlin'."

She groaned as his lips closed over a pebbled nipple. Her breasts had not only gotten larger, but just as sensitive as the rest of her. Each pull on her nipple shot pleasure straight to her womb, and she writhed beneath Hawk, desperate for any sort of release. He left her breast and pressed kisses down her abdomen, his destination obvious. His eyes locked on hers just before he made one long swipe with his tongue along the length of her sex.

"Oh sweet Jesus," Jo moaned. He continued to lap at her and she squeezed his head between her thighs, uncaring that it hindered his movements. She didn't want to risk his tongue going anywhere but exactly where it was. But he wasn't having it. He pried her thighs apart and pressed kisses to both of them. She whimpered at the loss of his mouth, but the displeasure was short-lived when he quickly changed position and drove his cock home.

She came instantaneously but held on for more. She knew it was only a matter of moments before he would have her on edge again.

Hawk placed hot, open-mouthed kisses against her throat as her breathing accelerated and she hovered on the brink of orgasm once more. One final thrust and she tumbled over, her arms wrapping around his back as he joined her, his lips at her ear. The rush of his breath fanned across her skin as he quivered in her arms.

"God, I love you," he whispered and brought his mouth to hers, kissing her deeply.

Jo's heart flipped over in her chest. She knew he loved her, could feel it every moment he was near her. But to hear him say it unleashed myriad emotions—joy, overwhelming relief, fear.

Hawk continued to kiss her, comforted by what he felt in her response. Her lips were eager, possessive, and she melted beneath his touch, molding her body to his. She was everything he'd ever wanted, and she was his. He would do everything in his power to keep it that way.

He trailed kisses down her neck, across her chest, before he settled his lips against her abdomen, letting them linger. He placed his ear against her skin, resting his head over his child. "I hope she's petite, like you."

"What makes you think it's a she?" Jo ran her fingers through his hair.

"It's a she." He twisted his neck to look up at her, the expression on her face nearly halting his breath. She gazed down at him with such peace, her eyes following the movement of her hand as it glided through the length of his hair, the corners of her lips slightly upturned. She was radiant. He took her hand and brought it to his mouth, pressing a kiss to her palm. "You'll see, Josephine. Come spring we'll have a daughter."

"Come here," she whispered.

Hawk eased up the bed, hovering above her. She stared at him, her eyes caressing his features. "No," she said, gripping his hair gently in her hand and pulling him toward her. "Come here." He complied, bringing his mouth to hers.

Her kiss was unlike any he'd ever experienced. Her lips were insistent but tender, her hands cradling his face. She sighed as their mouths parted for breath and then she drew him in again, her hands moving into his hair, winding it around her fingers to pull him even more tightly against her. Her voice was so soft as she spoke he could barely make out what she said, but as he drew back and saw tears glistening in her eyes, he knew he'd heard her correctly.

Always feel this way about me.

He searched her face, wiping a tear away from her cheek with his thumb. "Yes." He kissed her, easing his body over hers. "Always, Josephine."

CHAPTER NINE

"And you're doing it tonight?"

"Yes." Hawk tested the security of his saddle atop Thunder and wasn't the least bit surprised when it slid easily under his grip. He looked over to Ray, shaking his head. "Bloated his stomach again while I was tightening the cinch. Next thing you know, he'll start cribbing and I'll be up all night walking him around."

Ray waved his hand in the air, impatience stamped across his features. "You're going to ask her. Tonight."

"Didn't I just say that?" Hawk pulled the leather strap tautly, meeting resistance. "Thunder..." he warned. His horse relaxed his abdomen and Hawk secured the saddle to his satisfaction.

"But I thought you were afraid of rushing Jo, of scaring her." Ray rubbed his chin.

"Well," Hawk said, placing his boot in the stirrup and raising himself into the saddle. "That was before my baby was growing inside her."

"And you think she'll be open to the idea? I mean, I wouldn't hurl too much at her at once, Silent Hawk." Ray stroked Thunder's neck.

Hawk withdrew his hat, placing it on the horn of his saddle. He took a rubber band from his shirt pocket and secured his hair at his neck. "Well, honestly, I don't like the

163

idea of putting Jo in such close proximity to her ex-husband without giving her some outward sign of my commitment."

And he *really* didn't like that letter he'd found in her kitchen drawer when he was looking for a strainer to make his mother's nausea remedy.

Ray chuckled. "So basically, you're metaphorically peeing on her, marking your territory."

"Call it what you like." A muscle ticked in his jaw. "I found a letter from her dad in the back of her kitchen drawer last week. A whole bunch of garbage about family loyalty and reaping rewards for playing her part in sealing the upcoming election."

Ray's humor quickly faded. "Rewards?"

Hawk stroked Thunder's mane. "From what Jo has said, and from what I read, her dad seems pretty desperate to protect his name. He's in deep, career-wise, with her ex. I think that senator has him brainwashed. Jo's too good a person to have come from a man evil enough to use his own daughter. And I don't want that ex of hers anywhere near Jo."

"Are you genuinely concerned with that politician, Silent Hawk? I thought you said he's been leaving her alone."

"Yes. Recently. And why is that, do you think?" A bitter taste coated Hawk's throat.

"Maybe he…" Ray scratched his head. "Well, he might have figured out…"

Hawk narrowed his eyes. "Uh-huh. You see? No man in his right mind would give up on a chance with Jo. Especially one with ulterior motives. The fact he's gotten quiet doesn't comfort me in the least."

Ray placed his hand on his hip, shaking his head. "You think he's just regrouping before he comes at her twice as strong?"

"That's what a smart man would do. Of course, he cheated

on Jo, so intelligence might not be a factor after all." Hawk ground his molars together. "What I wouldn't give for Mom's ranch to be in New Mexico, Utah, anywhere but the one place Jo swore she'd never go back to."

"But she's going. Because of you."

Hawk gave Ray a curt nod. "And I want my promise on her finger before we get there." He shook his head. "Hell, I'd drag her off to the justice of the peace if I didn't think that would terrify her beyond all reason."

"And you think she'll say yes, when you give her that ring?"

Hawk plucked his hat from the saddle and placed it on his head. "With the way I plan to do it, she won't have to give me an answer. Not tonight."

Ray sent him a questioning look but Hawk chose to ignore it. "Wish me luck, in case I don't see you after my ride."

"Good luck, son." He took a step back. "Not that you need it."

Hawk dug his heels into Thunder's flanks and leaned low over the saddle as the horse took off in a gallop. He hoped his father was correct.

* * * * *

Jo checked the clock and noted Hawk should be arriving in five minutes. She rushed to the closet, pulling her jeans from a shelf. She stepped into them and began to close the fly. Two buttons up she stopped, sucking in a deep breath. The denim cut into her on the third button and she looked down. Her jeans were too tight. She yanked them off and placed her hand over her abdomen, a smile on her face. Her tummy protruded ever so slightly beneath her fingers.

She rifled through her clothes, searching for a skirt that sat lower on her hips. She plucked one from a hanger and drew it

165

on, satisfied when it fit just below her tiny belly. She grabbed a pink blouse that matched the floral design of her skirt and stepped into silver sandals. Two minutes later she had dusted on a little blush and was in her living room, awaiting Hawk.

He was right on time and she rushed to the door, anxious to have him verify that he, too, saw a change in her body. She threw her arms around him when he entered, standing on her toes to get as close as possible.

"Well, hi," he said, laughing against her hair. "Miss me?"

"Yes." She tilted her face up for his kiss.

Hawk lifted her from the floor, wrapping his arms tightly around her as their lips met in a long, needy capture. She pulled at the elastic in his hair, freeing the mass and running her fingers through it. He smiled against her lips. "You don't like it pulled back, do you?"

She shook her head. "I do. I just like the feel of it in my hands. Very sexy."

"Mmm." He pressed a kiss beneath her jaw. "I'll keep that in mind." He lowered her to the floor and she took his hand, placing his palm against her tummy.

"I couldn't get my jeans on," she said, smiling up at him.

Hawk rubbed his hand over her pelvis, a smile spreading across his face. "You're starting to show a little."

Jo looked down at his hand against her. "It's kind of early, though."

"Well, you're so tiny, baby. There's probably not much room for anything in there."

"Ugh," she groaned. "I'm going to be huge."

"And beautiful." He leaned down and pressed a kiss to her forehead. "Let's sit." He drew her toward the sofa.

"Do you want a glass of wine or anything? I'd be glad to fix it for you," she said as he towed her behind him.

"No, I'm fine. Maybe in a little bit."

"Okay." She took a seat next to him.

"I brought you something," he said, cupping her cheek. "And I hope you'll like it."

"Of course I will." She took his fingers from her cheek and kissed his hand before enveloping it in hers.

"Jo, you and the baby mean everything to me. I don't know what I did to deserve this great fortune, but here you sit. And I know that I want to feel this way forever."

Jo's eyes tracked the movement of his hand as he pulled it from hers and reached into his shirt pocket. Her heart fluttered erratically as light from the fixture on the sofa table met the object in his hand, setting off sparks of color. He extended his palm.

A large, square diamond flanked by two emeralds sat atop a slender white-gold band.

Jo placed the backs of her fingers over her mouth, her other hand resting above her heart. Her attention darted to his face, the aquamarine pools of his eyes deepening to a midnight blue. They spoke of love and security. Of trust and forever.

Pure joy surged in her chest. She had finally found the one person who could make her whole. "Hawk…"

"I don't want you to answer me right now. I know things are moving too fast for you." He placed the ring in her palm and closed her fingers around it, bringing her closed fist to his lips for a kiss. "If you'll just wear my ring, you'll make me the happiest man in the world. We don't have to make any concrete plans now."

Jo uncurled her hand and looked down at the exquisite ring in her palm, and then up at the man who loved her so much he'd given it to her, without assurance it would lead where he intended. She grasped the ring between her fingers and extended it toward Hawk. His brow furrowed and his hand dropped into his lap.

"Of course I will," she whispered, extending the ring farther. "Will you put it on for me?"

Jo heard his breath as he exhaled and reached for the ring, taking it from her. She held out a shaky hand and he placed it on her ring finger, leaning toward her. He stopped mere inches from her lips, holding her hand in his, his thumb toying with the ring. "I want you forever, Josephine." His lips brushed against hers before he drew away and looked down at her hand. "It looks beautiful on you. I knew it would."

"Why emeralds?" she asked, smiling at him when he looked up at her.

"Because they're the birthstone for May, and that's the month my life changed forever. That's the month I met you."

* * * * *

Before Jo knew what hit her, they were three days away from their departure date. With the contractors working nearly around the clock, her little rambling shack of a farmhouse had been transformed into a charming, downright livable abode. No more broken floorboards or rotting trim. The aged wallpaper had been replaced with fresh coats of paint. And the kitchen? Martha Stewart would be envious.

So quaint was this house that she hated to leave it. But it would be in good hands. Dan Jenners' daughter and son-in-law promised to keep it cozy for her while she was gone, and the rent money would help to fund the bed-and-breakfast Jo hoped to open once she and Hawk were back in Georgia, living on his farm.

Jo and Kristy already had their tearful goodbye two days prior, just before Kristy left for her trip to the beach with her boyfriend. Next to Ray, Jo would miss her the most. But it wouldn't be forever. That was the one thing Hawk had assured her of over and over. She could endure stepping within a stone's throw of who she used to be if she could be with Hawk.

168

No sacrifice would be too great for him and their baby.

She walked to the screened-in back porch, on a hunt for Ray. He was just finishing replacing the door that had annoyed Jo to within an inch of her life with its loud banging. She stepped outside.

"There you go, darlin'. Quiet as a church mouse now."

She gave him a kiss on the cheek and handed him a glass of lemonade she had just squeezed. "Thanks, Ray."

He took long swallows of the beverage and wiped his forehead with the hem of his shirt. "I can't believe you two are leaving so soon. Man, time rushes by."

"I know. Hawk flies back from Arizona tomorrow, and then we'll start packing up the truck. He already has three clients coming the week we arrive to breed with Thunder. That will put enough money in the bank to get them through the first year."

"And let's hope our resident hothead behaves his sorry ass after the trip out there. Damn horse…" Ray narrowed his eyes, shaking his finger. "And as for you, you're not packing up anything. You're gonna have your little behind parked on that sofa while me and Hawk load things up." He let out a disgusted sigh. "Damn pregnant women thinking they can run about all normal-like."

"Yes, sir." She held her hands up in surrender. "I'll just sit on the sofa and let my rear spread some more."

Ray smiled, placing his hand on his hip. "You're probably, what? A hundred pounds soaking wet?"

"A hundred and ten, actually."

"Whatever," he said and pointed at her tummy. "You've got to eat for that baby, now."

"The doctor said my weight is fine." She bit back a smile as she saw his lecture winding up.

"Now, Gentle Raven, she's a tiny woman, as you know."

169

She nodded, walking to the porch swing to sit. Ray followed, plopping down to her left.

"Well, she put on a good fifty pounds with Hawk. Was even more beautiful." He pushed his toe against the porch floor, setting the swing into gentle motion. "Nothing like the feeling of watching the woman you love grow big with your child." He turned to her, a wistful look on his face. "Hawk'll know what that's like soon enough."

Jo placed her hand over the tiny mound on her tummy. "I'll only get bigger from here, that's for sure," she replied, taking a sip of lemonade, the cool rush of liquid a relief to her hot, dry throat.

"If you eat enough, you will," Ray scolded.

She rolled her eyes playfully. "I tell you what. Let's go inside and I'll fix us a huge lunch and you can supervise as I eat every last bite."

He grinned. "I reckon that'll shut me up for a little bit, but I'm gonna ride you about it." He shook his finger. "And don't you think you'll be safe from me out there in that heat. There are phones in Arizona, you know. Raven will keep me posted."

Jo saluted him. They rose from the swing and headed into the house. "So, Ray." She drew out the words. "You and Raven have been talking a lot lately, haven't you?"

His cheeks flushed tomato red. "Well, we do share a child, Jo, and he's headed out her way. There's details to see to."

"Um-hmm." She pointed to a kitchen chair. "Sit." Walking to the refrigerator, she paused, twirling on her heel. "And these details are…?"

"Geez, Jo. Just things to coordinate."

She raised her eyebrow.

"Well, there are some details about farming, and, uh, Hawk's flight schedule. And…" His face lit up and he pointed at Jo. "And your pregnancy. I need to let her know how you've

170

been faring. Stuff like that."

Jo turned back to the refrigerator. "Ray, go sell that someplace else," she said, grabbing turkey and cheese from the refrigerator before bumping it closed with her hip. "You know as well as I do Raven doesn't need to know anything about this pregnancy. She'll probably sweep her hand over me as soon as I arrive and determine what college this kid will go to."

Ray tried to pout, but his lips curled up. "Fine."

"You love her," she taunted in a singsong voice.

"You don't get any detective points on that one, missy. Anyone with eyes in their head can see that. Including Raven."

She smeared a generous amount of mayonnaise on the bread, stacking turkey and cheese on top. "Well, I for one am thrilled." She placed sandwiches on plates and brought them to the table. "Looks like Hawk and I will be seeing you more than we planned."

"If Raven wants me to visit." He sighed. "We all know I love her. How *she* feels? That's anybody's guess."

"Oh, I don't know about that..."

He took a big bite of his sandwich and pointed at hers.

She complied, nibbling on the turkey and cheese dangling from the corner of her sandwich. She and Ray ate in companionable silence. She was going to miss him, but it wouldn't be forever. And if Raven felt even half of what Ray did, there was a strong possibility he would be a frequent visitor to the ranch in Catalina.

She chased down her lunch with the last of her lemonade and rose from the table, gathering their empty plates. As she was walking to the sink she felt the familiar but uncomfortable leak of fluid. Those pregnancy books weren't lying when they said to keep a lot of panty liners on hand. Jo should own stock in the company by now.

"I'll be right back, Ray. I've got to go to the little girls' room."

She walked down the hall and entered the restroom, closing the door behind her. She reached into the cabinet and pulled out another liner before easing her panties down.

Jo froze, her heartbeat suspended in her chest. She grabbed the vanity as dizziness overtook her.

"Ray!"

* * * * *

"Okay, Josephine, just try to relax if you can. Your blood pressure is elevated quite a bit." The nurse removed the cuff from her arm, patting her hand. "I know this is scary, but the best thing you can do is stay calm. Dr. Brooks has been paged and she should be arriving any moment."

The curtain slid back and a lab technician entered, stepping around the departing nurse. He glanced down at the form in his hand. "Ms. Montgomery, I need to draw some blood."

"Darlin'." Ray squeezed her hand. "I'm going to have to turn my head. I can't do needles."

"Can you go and try to call Hawk again? See if he's gotten the message and gotten on a flight?" Tears pricked the backs of her eyes, but she held them at bay. "Why hasn't he called yet?"

Ray kissed her on the forehead. "Cell reception is patchy out there." He took her hand in his. "Nothing would keep him away from you if he knew what was going on. As soon as he gets the message, he'll be on the first plane back. Promise."

She nodded, a tear squeezing past her defenses. "I'm scared, Ray."

"Now, don't you go thinking the worst. We don't know anything yet." He gave her a good attempt at a smile, but she could see the fear behind his eyes.

"I know. I'm trying." She fidgeted with the edge of the bed

sheet.

"That's my girl. I'll be right back."

She watched him leave, turning her head to the side as the lab technician prepared her vein. She shut her eyes at the prick of the needle, taking deep breaths as the blood was drawn.

"Josephine."

Jo's eyes focused on her doctor when she pulled the curtain behind her and took the chart from the end of the bed. Dr. Brooks nodded at the tech as he took his vials and she read over the nurse's notes, her eyes narrowed in concentration.

"How heavy was the bleeding when you first noticed it?" she asked.

"It was just a trickle at first, but then it became heavy."

Dr. Brooks made notations in the file. "And now?"

"I-I can't tell. I can't feel anything."

She patted Jo's knee. "Let me do a quick examination, see what's going on."

Jo scooted down the table and felt a hot rush of fluid between her legs. Abruptly she sat up, peering apprehensively at the examination table. Fresh tears spilled down her cheeks at the sight of blood—blood that had soaked the pad they had given her and leaked through onto the bed sheet.

"Am I losing the baby?" Jo asked, her voice rough. Nausea gripped her stomach as she looked at her doctor and knew the answer before she could tell her.

"Josephine, it appears you're miscarrying."

She sucked in a breath, her heart slamming against her ribs.

"But," Dr. Brooks continued, "I can't know anything for sure until I get your blood work back and we do an ultrasound."

Jo nodded numbly. "Okay."

"Let me do the manual exam and then we'll get you in for the ultrasound." She walked to the side of the bed, placing her hand on Jo's arm. "We'll take good care of you. Are you alone?"

Shaking her head, she gripped the metal rungs of the bed railing. "My...fiancé's father is here. He's gone to call Hawk—the baby's father—to let him know. He's in Arizona." And she was rambling. Her doctor already knew all these things, Jo had only seen her three days ago.

She squeezed Jo's hand. "I'm sure he'll reach Hawk soon." She took her seat at the foot of the table and started the exam. "Take deep breaths, Josephine. Try to relax as much as you can."

Jo nodded, trying to do as she asked. But how was she supposed to relax when she was losing Hawk's baby was beyond her.

* * * * *

Jo watched through the hospital window as nightfall slowly enveloped what was left of the day. She had been moved to a private room, required to stay overnight for observation. It had nearly taken dynamite to blast Ray out of the chair beside her bed, but she had finally been successful in persuading him to go home and rest. He'd been with a woman in fits of hysteria for the better part of a day. He needed rest almost as much as she did.

The door creaked as it opened and she rolled to her other side, relief and dread flooding her. Hawk rushed to her bed.

"Baby, are you okay?" He sat and drew her into his embrace.

His arms around her eased some of the pain from the day. Something about being within the circle of his embrace screamed home to her—a home she knew would no longer be hers. Could no longer be hers. At least for now.

The impending miscarriage would keep him here, potentially ending the success of Raven's ranch. Jo would not be responsible for that. Her fingertips dug into his shoulders, fresh tears brimming her eyes.

"I've been worried sick. The hospital would only say you were resting, and my dad's damn cell phone kept going to voice mail." He stroked her hair and pulled back to look at her. "Are you okay? The baby?"

Jo took a long, shaky breath. "Don't be upset with your dad. I told him I wanted to tell you. I'm sure he turned his phone off."

His Adam's apple bobbed as he swallowed. "You wanted to tell me what, Jo?"

She averted her gaze, willing her tears not to fall. She needed to be strong now. She'd never be able to do what she needed to do if she fell apart. Pulling up all her reserves, she looked him in the eye. "I'm losing the baby."

He pulled her to him, his arms like steel around her back. He held her in complete silence, his deep breaths as loud as a marching band to her ears in the stillness of the room.

"How?" His word feathered the hair at her temple.

She eased back from his embrace. "There's no way of knowing. The doctor said these things sometimes happen. Even as far along as I am. Nature's way and all that…"

Silence dragged out and she watched the emotions cross over his features. He closed his eyes and nodded, gripping her upper arms lightly. Leaning forward, he placed his forehead against hers. "And you're going to be okay?"

"Yes," she whispered. "They're just keeping me here for observation tonight. I have to wait for things to run their course. And then I may need a D&C." If only things were that simple.

He placed a kiss on her lips, his hand cradling her face.

"Thank God you're okay." His thumb traced her cheekbone. "I'll stay here with you tonight and then take you home tomorrow if they'll release you."

She cast her gaze to her lap.

Hawk heaved a weighted sigh. "Damn. This isn't fair." His fingers brushed against her cheek. "Look at me, Josephine."

She looked at him, her stomach rolling with nausea. Some things in life were difficult, but the means could sometimes justify the end. Dread nearly choked the breath right out of her as she raised her eyes to his, calling upon every ounce of courage she could muster. This was something she had to do. She couldn't live with herself if she didn't. And hopefully God would be merciful and she could come clean sooner rather than later. If Hawk was the man she knew him to be, he'd understand and they could move on.

Hawk tucked a stray wisp of hair behind her ear. "I'll call my mom tomorrow. Tell her we'll be delayed for as long as you need to rest. I'll, ah…cancel the breeds we set up. We'll figure it out."

"I'm not going," she whispered.

"What?" His eyes widened and he leaned closer, turning his ear toward her as if he hadn't heard her correctly.

She cleared her parched throat, swallowing down the enormous lump of regret lodged soundly within it. "I said I'm not going."

He stared at her, his eyes changing from their cool, icy blue to a stormy gray. "What are you saying, Jo?"

She scooted back on the bed, trying to gain as much strength as she could by distancing herself from him. "I'm saying since I'm losing the baby, making this move to Arizona might not be the best decision."

Hawk shot off the bed, running his hands through his hair. He whirled on his heel and stared down at her in disbelief. "You're serious."

176

"Hawk—"

He gripped the bedrail, leaning down over her. "After all this time, you're serious."

She inched back against the pillows, mentally bracing herself for the lie she had to tell. "Hawk, a lot has been happening while you've been away. My father has brought some things to light that I can't turn my back on."

"What things, Jo?" His knuckles were white against the metal his fingers were wrapped around.

"My, ah, father helped to put my ex-husband into office last term. He went to bat for him, and as a result, is tied very closely. If Thomas falls, my father could too, in the eyes of the community at least."

Hawk pushed off the rail, his eyes hard as he stared down at her. "And what does that have to do with you?"

"I've been selfish." She ran the bed sheet through her fingers, grasping it in her palm. "Running away. Not considering how this would affect my family. We're moving into an election year. I don't have the right."

"What in the hell are you talking about? I don't see how this has anything to do with you. With *us*."

She pressed her fingers to her eyes. "I have to think of my father, his reputation. If I don't stand by Thomas during this election year, he hasn't a prayer of maintaining the Senate seat." She forced herself to look at Hawk, the expression on his face nearly breaking her resolve. "The affair never hit the press, but people will go digging—especially his opponent. We have to put up an allied front. It's the only way to safeguard all my father's worked for his entire career."

Hawk stared at her in silence, a muscle ticking in his jaw. She suffered his reaction, watching it play out over his features, until he finally spoke. "And what's in it for you, Jo? What could they possibly offer you to make all this worthwhile?"

She looked away from him, unsure of how to answer. She thought of that letter from her father. Had Hawk seen it somehow? Did he read the same ridiculous crap she had? If so, she could use that to her advantage—as much as it pained her to have him think of her in that way. The future, his and his mother's future, made it worthwhile, however painful it may be.

His cutting laugh drew her attention back to his face. "So how much does that kind of sacrifice go for these days?" His eyes were like steel as they pinned her beneath his accusation.

She slid his ring from her finger, grasping its delicate band. Extending her hand, she did the most difficult thing she'd ever had to do. She gave back her second chance at happiness. She could only pray it wouldn't be lost forever once the truth came to light. "This belongs to you. Thank you for giving it to me, but I can't keep it now."

He stared at the symbol of his promise at the tips of her fingers. He stood completely still, until she thought she would perish in the moment. Mercifully, he reached out and took the ring, curling his fingers around it.

"I'll never understand this, Jo. If I live to be a hundred and two, I'll never understand."

His tone chilled her, its delivery as cold as the look in his eyes. "I gave you this ring because I love you, not because I got you pregnant." He held up the fist holding the ring. "I didn't realize there was a chance I could be outbid. I guess that's my mistake."

Before she could speak he turned on his heel, yanking the door open and disappearing into the hall. As the heavy wood clicked back into place, she released the emotions she had been stoically keeping at bay. Sobs racked her body and she curled into the fetal position.

Hawk had asked what the price of sacrifice was. Jo knew it could cost her everything.

CHAPTER TEN

As Jo was gathering what few belongings she had with her and shoving them into the standard-issue plastic hospital bag, the door opened. She turned to look at Ray, preparing for the expression she knew she'd find on his face. He stood in the doorway, silently frowning.

"How are you feeling?" he finally asked.

She shrugged, fighting back tears. "I'm okay, Ray. Thanks for coming to get me."

"Like you gave us any choice. I can't recall when I've seen Hawk so upset. And you couldn't even find it in your heart to let him come and get you, considering it's *his* baby. It's..." He shook his head, dropping his gaze to his scruffy boots.

"Horrible," Jo finished for him. "I just didn't know any other way. Seeing Hawk would only make things more difficult for both of us. What else could I do?"

"Stop all this nonsense and go to Arizona with him!" He held her motionless with the pure ire in his voice. Never before had Ray spoken to her in this manner. Never before had she deserved it.

"I can't, Ray. For a lot of reasons. Trust me, this is for the best. You'll see." She tried to instill confidence in her voice, if not for him then to convince herself.

179

"Jo, what I see is a woman who is so afraid to take a chance that she's throwing away her future. My son…" Ray pushed his shoulders back, his chin tilting up. "Hawk is a good man. He'd be a good husband—much better than the one you fancy yourself helping. And he loves you."

"I know," she whispered.

Ray narrowed his eyes at her. "And I'm not buying this hoopla you sold Hawk about your family. The world just isn't worth living in if someone like you could be that cruel."

Jo looked away from him, resting her hip against the foot of the bed.

"You're afraid, Jo. You can't move beyond your own fear and give your heart to Hawk. Damn stupid mistake if you ask me."

Of course Ray was right. This could prove to be the worst mistake of her life. She knew it. He knew it. But there were other things she knew. Things she couldn't tell him, couldn't tell anyone. She dared a glance at him, clasping her fingers together across her lap.

Ray walked toward her, taking a seat next to her on the bed. "Look, Jo. You feel like a daughter to me. I had hoped you *would* be my daughter." He placed his hand over hers. "I can't make you change your mind. I don't agree with your decision, and my loyalty is to my son."

She nodded. "I understand."

"Jo," he said softly. "I'm not saying we can't be friends anymore. I'm just going to need some time to get used to the way things are now. You've hurt all of us."

Jo swiped at a tear. "I'm sorry. I'll take any kind of friendship you're willing to give me. It's more than I deserve."

The door pressed open. "You all set?" A nurse entered with a wheelchair and walked toward the bed.

"Yes," Jo said, easing into the seat.

"And you understand the instructions from the doctor. You're to call if anything changes." The nurse handed Jo the discharge folder.

"Change like how?" Ray asked, his gaze darting between the two of them.

"Oh, if my bleeding becomes heavier than it is." So that was a partial truth. She snuck a glance at Ray and he seemed satisfied with the answer. Thank God."Okay, all set."

The nurse pushed her through the open door and entered the sterile hallway.

Ray walked alongside, resting his hand briefly on her shoulder. "Let's get you home."

Home. Such as it was.

* * * * *

"Hawk."

At the sound of his father's voice, Hawk turned, the flask of aged Kentucky bourbon he kept hidden between the ledgers in the file cabinet suspended halfway to his lips. He raised it in a mock toast. "Sorry, Pops. Seemed as though the occasion called for it this morning."

Ray dismissed his apology with a wave of his hand. "You've got more sense than I do. A drink or two ain't going to send you down the road to perdition."

Hawk brought the flask to his lips for a long swallow, wincing. "She get home okay?" The thought of Jo burned nearly as much as the amber liquid that left a scorching trail down the back of his throat.

"Just now." Ray withdrew his hat from his head and dropped it on the desk, leaning a hip against the edge. "Wouldn't even let me walk her inside."

Twisting the top back on the tarnished flask, Hawk

dropped it into his shirt pocket. "Now why doesn't that surprise me?"

"I guess it shouldn't. Headstrong one, she is."

"There's a word for it," Hawk muttered under his breath.

"I'm so sorry, son."

Hawk rose from the chair and plucked a box off the floor, dropping it on the desk. He began to place the breeding ledgers into it.

"We gonna talk about this, Silent Hawk, or are you just going to disappear to that part of yourself that drove you to the Black Hills last summer?"

Hawk leaned his palms against the desk, his head bowed. He drew in a deep breath. Thoughts of that journey had plagued him as he lay awake all night after leaving the hospital, remembering the spiritual awakening he had experienced, which had all but convinced him Jo was the one from the first moment he had touched her.

Four days he had fasted and cleansed last summer, all in preparation to visit the sacred place. To find the answers he sought, to seek the salve to heal the abraded soul his mother convinced him he had. He'd traveled to find the comfort of the premonition of Jo. Now everything he had believed to be the truth fell into question.

Running his hands through his hair, he leveled his eyes on Ray's. "Perhaps I misinterpreted my meditations. The female energy, and the peace that came with it, could have been about Mom, or Rayne, or this move I'm about to make."

"I don't think you believe that. What about your beliefs? The prophecies? You can't just turn your back on them."

Clenching his jaw, Hawk suffered through the same thoughts that had tortured him from the moment Jo had returned his ring. He had a lifetime of beliefs his mother had taught him, her unfailing faith a catalyst to what he accepted as the truth. But along the way he had learned other things also.

He had acquired the ability to see beyond what he knew, to the ugly realities that existed, and he had the nagging suspicion that he had fallen back on tradition as a means to escape it all.

Hawk's laugh was bitter as he looked at his father. "Prophecies? Dad, we live in the woods. We're surrounded by wildlife. Deer are bound to wander into the yard."

Ray crossed his arms over his chest, the corners of his lips dipping down. "Seven days in a row? And what of the buck at Jo's?"

"What of it? He probably prefers to eat weeds. Unlike the doe, whose delicate sensibilities drove her to destroy my flowerbeds."

Ray shook his head. "And the Black Hills? You know as well as I do that the peace you received there has nothing to do with you moving to Arizona to be with your mother."

Hawk turned from his father and rested his elbow on the file cabinet, dropping his forehead into his palm. "Fasting for four days and going into the sweat lodge must have messed with my head. It doesn't mean anything."

Ray's boots thudded as he approached Hawk, his grip rough on Hawk's arm as he forced him to turn. "Your mother would be devastated if she heard what you just said. Don't you ever speak of it in front of her, do you hear me? I don't want her thinking I had anything to do with your nonsense. I won't break her heart twice."

"Dad…"

Ray placed his finger mere inches from Hawk's face, his hand shaking. "Tell me one thing you know for certain, Silent Hawk. Just one thing that is unfailing and true."

He stood to his full height, his look daring his father to press him. "One thing? Fine. Jo Montgomery doesn't love me."

Ray stared at him, his eyes full of anger. "For the first time in my life, Silent Hawk, I'm ashamed of you." With that, he left him alone in the office.

Hawk ran his hands down his face. If a white man whose only tie to native tradition was through love could believe, then why couldn't the Apache blood running through his veins convince him what he once believed was true? Turning to look out the window across the pasture to the tree line in the distance, he found his answer.

"Because she turned her back on me," he whispered to no one. Certainly not to the doe outside the window with the last of the marigolds dangling from her mouth.

* * * * *

The first few days home from the hospital had stretched on endlessly. The day Hawk left was the worst, to be sure. Jo had attempted to distract herself with an all-day movie marathon, but she only curled into a ball on her bed, crying through every comedy she owned. Ray had dropped by the first couple of days to check on her, concerned she was still in bed, but she had asked him not to return for a while. It was just too much to see him, his blue eyes a mirror of his son's. Somehow she made it through the first two weeks, which was nothing short of a miracle as far as she was concerned.

On the morning of her follow-up appointment with Dr. Brooks, sunlight streaked through the slit in her curtains, nearly blinding her when she opened her eyes. Glancing at the clock, she cursed. She would be late for her appointment if she didn't get her day started. Crawling out of bed, she padded to the bathroom like a ninety-year-old. She peered into her panties, hopeful, as she did every morning. She groaned when she saw streaks of red. Her heart raced with fear, but all she could do was change the sanitary pad and get dressed. It was out of her hands.

Thirty minutes later she was hobbling out to her Cadillac to make the drive to the doctor's. This was the first time she had left the house, and as she backed out of her driveway, sadness consumed her. The tops of Hawk's magnolia trees were visible across the property line and she remembered the long walk she had taken up his drive the day she met him. Images of him in the training ring, as he'd been that first day, assaulted her. Tears began to roll down her cheeks but she brushed them away. This was helping nothing. She had made her decision. And hopefully because of it, the breeding would go on as planned over the next few weeks and the ranch would have a hefty sum in its account.

Shaking the memories away, she pulled onto the gravel road that led to the main street out of this miniscule piece of Georgia. The sky was dark and menacing, streaks of lightning like arrows in the sky disappearing into the hills in the distance. The weather suited her mood just fine.

Flipping on the radio, she searched for any station not playing country music. The last thing she needed was to hear a pained artist singing about lost love. *We all lose things. No sense yammering on about it.* Classic rock blasted through the speakers and she relaxed against the leather seat. Mick Jagger begged for satisfaction as she merged into the highway traffic. She would be at the office soon.

Forty minutes later she was in her drafty paper gown, reclining on the examination table.

"Okay, Jo, this will be a little cold."

She winced as Dr. Brooks squirted a glob of clear gel across her abdomen, distributing it across her skin with the ultrasound transducer. The doctor moved the instrument in slow circles, searching. Jo held her breath, prickly fear skittering along her skin. Just because the bleeding hadn't gotten heavier didn't mean she'd dodged a bullet.

Dr. Brooks smiled. "Ah-ha. Here it is." She pointed at the monitor where a mass moved fluidly, a fluttering motion within it. "Strong heartbeat. This one's a fighter, Jo."

Jo stared at the screen, mesmerized. This tiny part of her and Hawk was nestled deep inside her womb, fighting with everything it had to hang on, to beat the odds and survive. Tears welled in her eyes as she watched her baby. Their baby. The doctor had told her there was an ongoing risk of miscarriage, and with all the blood, Jo had resigned herself to this fact while in the hospital. But with each day that passed, a glimmer of hope had begun to unfurl.

"I'm going to take a couple of pictures for you." Dr. Brooks smiled as she clicked away at the keyboard with one hand, her other holding the transducer that allowed Jo to view her reason for everything she'd done. Everything she'd continue to do.

Dr. Brooks removed the wand, wiping Jo's belly with a warm, damp cloth. When she finished, she draped a sheet over Jo's abdomen. "The baby looks good, but all this bleeding concerns me. You *are* staying in bed all the time except to go to the bathroom, right?"

Jo ran the sheet between her fingers, bracing for what was surely to come. "Um, for the most part."

Dr. Brooks leveled her gaze on Jo. "What do you mean, for the most part?"

"The, ah, kitchen is downstairs, but I limit how often I go as much as possible."

Her pen paused against the chart and her brow furrowed. "Josephine. Complete bed rest with bathroom privileges means just that. Complete bed rest. You may get up to use the toilet and take a quick shower, but that's it."

Jo nodded, guilt strangling her.

"The baby's heartbeat is strong, but you are by no means out of the woods." She placed her hand over Jo's. "Like I told you before you left the hospital, we can't be sure what's causing the bleeding. Oftentimes the placenta moves, causing this kind of thing. But rest is imperative."

"I know. I'm being as careful as possible," she replied.

"If you're going up and down those stairs, you're not. I'll be glad to speak to your fiancé if I need to. I can explain—"

"We broke our engagement. He's in Arizona."

She frowned again. "I'm sorry to hear that, Josephine. This must be very difficult for you." She made a notation in the file. "What about your parents?"

Jo nearly laughed. The last people on earth, besides Thomas of course, she wanted to know about her current situation were her parents. They'd be at her home, with her ex in tow, before Jo could even turn around. "They're unable to travel," she lied.

"Friends, relatives, anyone close by?"

Meg and Kristy, that was about it. Jo would not interfere with her sister's schooling, and Kristy couldn't take a leave of absence from work, even if she could get the car. Jo shook her head.

Dr. Brooks placed the chart on the edge of the examining table. "We've got to get someone in that house with you. Will your insurance cover private care?"

"I don't think so."

Dr. Brooks' eyes were edged with concern. "I'd hate to have to admit you."

Jo drew in a deep, calming breath. "There is one person I can call. I'd hoped to keep him out of it, but desperate times…"

She nodded, picking up the file. "Josephine, if you promise me you will get help immediately, I'll let you go home. If not—"

"I will. I promise. Consider it done." Jo gave her what she hoped was a convincing smile.

"How'd you get here today?"

She felt like a child caught with her hand stuck in the

187

cookie jar. "I drove."

"Uh-huh. Don't want to hear that again." She scribbled in the file.

"You won't. I promise." Jo placed her hand on Dr. Brooks' arm. "I can't lose this baby. My entire future depends on it. I'll do just as you say."

She patted her hand. "That's a girl." Rising from the stool, she smiled down at Jo. "I'll see you again in two weeks. If the bleeding becomes heavier, call immediately. Understood?"

"Yes."

Dr. Brooks walked toward the door and turned. "You can get dressed and my nurse will be in with some printed instructions for you...just in case you forget." She winked and turned to leave.

"Dr. Brooks?" Jo called to her.

"Yes?"

"Thank you. For everything."

She tucked her pen in her pocket and smiled warmly. "You're welcome."

She left and Jo dressed before perching on the edge of the table, waiting on the nurse. She was dreading the phone call she would have to make. Dreading it like nobody's business. Deciding it was never going to be any easier, she withdrew her cell phone from her purse. She punched in the numbers and waited. One ring. Two. Three. Jo sighed and then a voice came on the line.

"Hi, it's Jo. I have a huge favor to ask you."

* * * * *

"It ain't right, Jo. It just ain't right."

She lay propped against the pillows, her eyes tracking Ray's movement as he paced back and forth at the foot of her bed. "Ray, please listen to me. There isn't any other way."

He halted in his tracks, his hands on his hips. "So, you're asking me to just keep my trap shut. Not tell my son that *his* baby is still growing inside you. That you lied about the whole thing. That the gist of it?"

"Basically," she mumbled, wiping her sweaty palms against the duvet.

His eyes grew wide. "How? How does a father do something like that to his son?" He threw his arms up in the air, wearing a path in the hardwoods.

"If you'll just hear me out, maybe you'll understand," she pleaded. He kept walking, shaking his head. "Please, Ray. Just come over here and sit down and let me explain. Okay?"

He stared her down, indecision written all over his face. He conceded, edging around the side of the bed to take a seat next to her. "You better explain real good, Jo, because what you're asking of me is just plain crazy."

"I will. Just calm down and listen, okay?"

He ran a hand through his thinning hair. "Let's hear it."

She let out a relieved breath. At least he was open to hearing her out and hadn't run to the phone to call Hawk as soon as she had revealed her pregnancy, as she had expected him to.

"That day in the hospital when I thought I had miscarried was one of the worst of my life. Thinking I had lost Hawk's baby, it was just...tragic."

Ray nodded, rubbing his thumb against his pointer finger.

"When the doctor detected a heartbeat during the ultrasound, I was elated. I can't tell you how relieved I was." She placed her hand over his fidgeting ones, stilling them. "But that relief was short-lived. Everything pointed toward an impending miscarriage. She told me about the danger I was in and what was necessary to keep the unthinkable from happening, if by some miracle I didn't lose the baby."

"Bed rest?" he asked.

She nodded, grasping her hair at her nape. "Complete bed rest until I stop bleeding or miscarry, whichever comes first."

"You're still bleeding, I take it?"

"Yes, but the baby's heartbeat is strong." She smiled at him. "That's a good sign, but until I stop bleeding, this is where I have to stay."

"How long do they think?"

She nestled farther into the pillows, placing Ray's palm over his grandchild. "That's the problem. There's no way of knowing." She looked him in the eye. "Now do you see why I couldn't go to Arizona?"

"That's clear, Jo, but what you did to Hawk. It's—"

"Because I love him."

"If you love him, you can't keep something like this from him."

She shook her head, placing her hand over Ray's. "It's *because* I love him, and Raven, that I'm keeping this from Hawk. For now. I never intended to keep the secret any longer than necessary."

His eyes pleaded with her. "You're planning on telling him, Jo. I'm begging you to do it now."

"Ray, what do you think would happen if you or I get on the phone and call Hawk, telling him what's going on?"

He sat up straight, a look of pride on his face. "My son would come and take care of you and that baby of his, is what he'd do. What any man worth his salt would do."

She raised her right eyebrow. "There's my reasoning in a nutshell. He would come running back, because that's the kind of man he is."

"Damn straight," Ray said, accentuating his point with a curt nod of his head.

"And what would happen to their ranch if he came back here right now, while they're in the midst of breeding Thunder?"

"They'd, ah…"

"How safe of a gamble do you think it is to give Thunder the luxury of time, to just go ahead and wait until *next* season to breed him to fund the ranch? Think he's only going to become more docile as time goes on?"

Ray took a deep breath and rubbed his hand over Jo's tummy. "Not likely."

"Exactly. I can't be responsible for that. Timing is everything, remember? You told me that."

He dipped his head. "That I did, Jo. That I did. If I'd known it was going to come back and bite me in the ass, I'd have kept my damn mouth shut."

"Don't take that burden, Ray. Hawk and I talked a lot about the ranch. I would have known anyway."

"So what are you planning on doing?" Ray asked.

"As soon as the doctor clears me from bed rest or, God forbid, I lose this baby, I'll be on the first available flight to Tucson."

Ray twined his fingers with hers. "You hurt him, Jo. Maybe fatally so."

"I know I did." She blinked back threatening tears. "But because of the man your son is, I knew the only way to make him go was to hurt him. And…" She drew a shaky breath. "He hurt me too. It's my fault, obviously, but it still hurt."

Ray brushed a tear from her cheek. "He did?"

"Yes. He believed my lie a little too easily." She looked down at their joined hands against her belly. "Of course, if I had told him I loved him instead of letting fear clog my throat, there wouldn't have been as much opportunity for doubt."

"For a man who was raised to believe in the intangible, my son has a tendency as of late to view things in absolutes." He shook his head.

"Nothing I told him is the truth. You do believe all I did was because I love him, right?"

"Of course I do, darlin'. He's luckier than he'll ever know."

She smiled through her tears. "So you'll help me? Keep my secret?"

"Don't see that I have a choice. You're right, Jo. This ranch means everything to Raven. And to Hawk. I wish it didn't have to be this way, though…" He drew in a deep breath, letting it out slowly. "God help us when he finds out. He's going to skin us both."

She trembled at the thought. "But you're his father. He'll forgive you in time. And me…"

"And you're the mother of his child." Ray drew her into his arms, rubbing her back. "We'll make him see, Jo. We'll make him see."

CHAPTER ELEVEN

"He looks good." Raven shielded her eyes from the sun as she watched Thunder.

Hawk joined his mother in her perusal, their eyes following the stallion as he ran the length of the pasture. He was a black blur as he closed in on the final yards of land before the fence line. Abruptly he stopped, his tail swishing back and forth as he shook his head.

"He seems happy enough," Hawk said, draping his arm around Raven's shoulders. "The last three breeds have gone much better than I ever could have anticipated."

Raven chuckled. "You should have seen Mr. Kendrick's face when he saw Thunder run. I thought he was going to fall out. He has high hopes for the potential offspring."

"Hmm." Hawk's attention was drawn to a horse ring where Ryder was working with a group of children. "The director from the hospital seemed pleased with our first session last week."

"Yes," she agreed, sliding her arm around his waist. "Rayne's memory will live on as long as we see the smiles on those children's faces."

Hawk looked at Thunder as he took off running in the opposite direction. "And his cooperation will make things so much easier. Hopefully he'll be in it for the long haul. I guess only time will tell."

"That's true," Raven murmured. "Speaking of time, Silent Hawk, how long are you going to keep trying to hide what happened in Georgia?"

He leaned his forearms against the fence, letting his mother's arm fall away from his waist. "I'm hardly hiding, Mom. There's not a lot to it. Jo lost the baby, and I lost her."

Raven turned, leaning on the fence behind her. She studied his face in silence, her eyes raking over his features. "Hawk," she said finally, crossing her arms over her chest. "There's more to it than that. I saw you with Jo. What aren't you telling me?"

He kicked at a loose rock, silently cursing this turn in the conversation. He focused on Ryder in the distance, walking with a group of children to the eastern edge of the fence to watch Thunder.

"Hawk?"

He turned to her, looking down at her patient features. He wouldn't tell her the path his thoughts had been taking. He couldn't let her know he had considered turning his back on all he once believed in, all she had taught him to believe. It would devastate her. And worse? He'd be a fool in her eyes. He laughed without humor. "It's about political scandal and family loyalty. It's about bribes." He nearly spat the last part. "The stuff of movies, right?"

"Hmm," she said, studying his features. "I don't know if I believe that. Not from what I've seen of you two."

"And you see all, right?"

"No, Silent Hawk, not all. But I see enough." She placed her hand on his forearm. "Do you want to know what I see now?"

"Could I stop you from telling me?"

"Probably not." She smiled.

"Fine." He placed his palm on the fence.

"Something in you changed over the last few months. I could hear it in your voice on the phone and could sense it the moment I laid eyes on you. I sense it still."

"Well, I thought I was in love. That would bring about a change in most everyone, I would think." He shifted his weight from one foot to the other.

"*Was* in love?"

Tapping his fingers against the smooth aged wood of the fence, he focused his eyes on the Catalina Mountains in the distance. "Yes. Things weren't as they seemed. That's obvious now."

The sound of laughter closed in on them as the group Ryder was working with drew closer. Raven glanced at them before she turned back to Hawk. "You know to look beyond what's in front of you. There's always something more, if you just search hard enough for it." She stood on her toes and kissed his cheek. "And when you allow yourself to become blind, fate has a way of reminding you to open your eyes."

Raven adjusted his hat, pushing the brim up. "Okay, I've got to prepare the ring for the next group of children. Dinner's at seven, okay?"

"See you then," he called and pulled his hat from his head, placing it on the fence post. He leaned over to stretch his back and two white tennis shoes with heart laces appeared in his line of vision.

He rose, looking down at a little girl with porcelain skin, green eyes and sparse blonde wisps of hair just beginning to grow from her bald scalp.

"Well, howdy there, ma'am," Hawk said, placing his hat back on his head and tipping it down at her.

A smile lit up her face and she lowered herself into an exaggerated curtsy. "Kind sir," she said as she rose.

"So, tell me, little lady. What brings you around these parts?"

She blushed. "Ryder told me the black horse belongs to you."

He nodded. "That's right, he does. His name is Thunder. And I'm Hawk." He extended his hand and she wrapped her small one around his.

"I'm JoAnna," she said, shuffling her toe in the dirt. "But I like to be called Jo." She wrinkled her nose. "JoAnna is so fussy, don't you think?"

Hawk's chest ached as he listened to the tiny voice. He knelt down, resting his arm on his knee. "Well, I don't know. I think it's beautiful, just like you." He reached into his shirt pocket and withdrew three sugar cubes. He gestured to the pasture with his head. "Thunder over there has a wicked sweet tooth. He'll love you forever if you give these to him."

"Really?" Her eyes grew wide and she smiled as big as the endless sky that stretched on around them.

Hawk stood and whistled, raising his hand in the air. "Absolutely." Thunder strolled to the fence and stopped in front of his master. Hawk placed the sugar cubes in Jo's hand. "Now, hold your palm flat, just like this." He demonstrated and she did as he asked, laughing as Thunder's lips tickled her hand.

"Thank you, Hawk," she said and waved as she skipped off to join the group again.

He watched her as she blended in with the other children, waving his hand at Ryder when he looked his way. Hawk thought of the child he had lost, the woman he had lost. It had been two months and the pain could still bring him to his knees if he gave in to it. Which he did. Every single day.

* * * * *

Two months had stretched on for what felt like forever, with doctor visits every two weeks. Ray had waited on Jo hand and foot, insisting she only leave the bed to answer the call of nature. Negotiating showers was a daily struggle, but she managed to finagle one at least every other day. He refused to stay at his own home, setting up camp in her guest room where he could keep an eye and ear on her at all times. He only ducked out a couple of times a day to check on the farm, content to let all the help Hawk had hired take care of things.

Her bleeding had become lighter and lighter, much to their relief. And because of her small frame, her belly protruded noticeably, a visual reassurance the baby was growing and viable. When she went a solid week without any bleeding her doctor allowed her a little more time out of bed, but still issued stern warnings about overdoing it.

Countless times Jo had picked up the phone to call Hawk. Him not knowing was killing her, but she and Ray both agreed the news she had to deliver had to be in person. If she were to have any chance of soothing his hurt and starting their lives off on the right foot, she needed to do it face-to-face.

The news she had been waiting for finally arrived, giving her the freedom to go about her life like any normal pregnant woman. Including air travel. She and Ray chose to celebrate with a bottle of sparkling cider. They sat in her cozy kitchen, her plane ticket resting on the table between them.

"So, you know what you're going to say?" he asked, taking a sip from the delicate champagne flute that looked out of place in his large, calloused hand.

"I've run it through my head a million times, but I think when I see him, I'll know how to go about it." She took a long swallow of the cider, the bubbles tickling her nose. "At least that's what I hope."

"And you don't want me to come with you?"

She shook her head. "No, I think I need to do this on my

own. When he finds out you were involved, he's going to be even more upset."

"He's a good man, Jo. Even if he's ornery as a bull at first, he'll calm down. You two love each other. In the end, it's gotta work out."

"True love wins in the end?"

"If there's a God above, it will." Ray rotated his left arm, squeezing his shoulder.

"You okay?" she asked, pointing to his arm.

He opened and closed his fist, wincing. "Yeah, damn horse I worked with earlier kept yanking on its reins. Nothing but a barn sour pain in the ass, if you ask me. Should have just stayed here with you."

She smiled at him and placed her glass on the table. "How about some dinner? I think we have some leftovers in the fridge." She started to rise from her chair but quickly plopped back down when he stood and pointed to her seat.

"You're still on my watch. Sit your pretty little behind down and I'll heat up some pasta."

She laughed. "Okay. I know who I'm calling to come take care of this baby when it arrives, Nurse Stephens."

"Damn straight," he called over his shoulder as he leaned on the open fridge door.

She took another sip of cider, contemplating again how she would convince Hawk what she'd done had been for the best. Surely he would—

She whirled in her seat at the loud thud behind her. Ray lay sprawled on the kitchen floor, motionless.

"Ray!" she yelled, rushing to his side. Kneeling down, she felt for his pulse. It was weak. She sprang to her feet. "Oh God, no," she cried as she grabbed the phone.

* * * * *

The steady beep, beep, beep of the monitor echoed in the quiet of Ray's private room. He and Jo had been at the hospital going on eight hours. Ray was conscious upon arrival and quickly informed the triage nurse of *Jo's* condition, which landed her in the waiting room under the careful watch of one Miss Derringer. Scary woman, she was, eyeing Jo every time she dared to move.

Jo was relieved when her keeper came and got her, escorting her to Ray's bedside. When Jo arrived, the nurse informed her that Ray would be okay, he had just suffered a mild heart attack, and that a message was left hours ago for the next of kin. Hopefully the hospital staff's voice mail had been more coherent than hers had been when she'd dialed Hawk's cell in a panic.

Jo slithered into the chair by Ray's bed, overcome by relief and fatigue. She took Ray's hand in hers, studying his peaceful face. His breathing was steady, rhythmic, and the sound of it made her drowsy. She leaned her head against the back of the chair, closing her eyes. Sleep encroached upon her, a welcome visitor after the stress of the last few hours.

Jo.

In her dream, Hawk's silken voice enveloped her. She fell into his outstretched arms and his lips met hers in a tender caress. A kiss of understanding, of forgiveness.

Jo.

She placed her hand over their baby and he smiled, the promise of forever in his eyes.

"Jo, wake up."

Groggily, she opened her eyes. Her dream loomed above her, but he wasn't smiling, or kissing her, or promising forever. He was frowning, lines of worry creasing his brow.

"Hawk," she whispered and jumped from the seat.

She watched in panic as his gaze dropped to her abdomen,

where her cashmere sweater clung to the bulge of her stomach. Her pulse galloped as he raised his eyes to hers.

"What the hell?" he asked, gesturing to her.

She placed her hands over her belly instinctively. "Hawk, I—"

"You're still pregnant." His tone was glacial, just like his eyes.

"Y-yes. I can explain."

He turned, leaning against the footboard of the bed. She stood there, fear smothering her, before taking a step toward him and placing her hand on his arm.

Hawk spun around and her hand fell away. "And just when did you plan on telling me you were still carrying my child?" Ray stirred in his sleep and Hawk glanced to him before turning his attention back to Jo. "Ever?" he hissed.

When she'd envisioned their reunion, never once did she paint Hawk to be so volatile, so unreachable. But he was. And deservedly so. Her heart fluttered out of control. "Of course I was going to tell you. There's a—"

He grabbed her shoulders, his fingers digging into her flesh. Anger contorted his features. "How could you do something like this, Jo? You tossed me out of *your* life, but out of our *child's*? How could you?"

Icy dread consumed her. "Oh Hawk. I wouldn't do something like that!"

"You *did* do something like that." His lips settled into a firm line, his eyes on fire.

Before she could reply the door swung open and the doctor entered, followed by Raven. Hawk's mother took one look at Jo and her gaze shot to her son. The doctor glanced around the room, focusing on each of them before he cleared his throat and walked to Ray's bedside, opening his chart.

"I'll, ah, give all of you some privacy," Jo stammered,

stepping out of Hawk's grip. She walked to the door, meeting Raven's gaze hesitantly as she passed, and grabbed the handle.

Hawk's hand closed over hers and he pulled the door open, ushering her outside.

"I appreciate what you've done for my father, Jo, but I think it best if you go." His tone was as harsh as the florescent lights in the hallway. "I'll deal with this later." He motioned between the two of them.

"But Hawk…"

He slammed his eyes shut, clenching and unclenching his fists. "Please, Jo." He looked at her. "You've done enough. Let me take care of my family without having to look at you, look at the evidence of our child and how you betrayed me."

She nodded, holding her tears at bay. She turned from him and walked down the hall, each step taking her farther and farther from where she knew she belonged.

* * * * *

Jo had awoken close to noon, after finally drifting to sleep from sheer exhaustion just as the sun had begun to rise. She'd kept her cell phone by her bed, but it had remained as silent as the room around her. She hadn't a clue what to do from here. Nothing was going as she'd hoped and prayed. She had known Hawk would be upset, but the look he'd had on his face terrified her. Having him discover, in such a crass manner, that she'd lied to him had been a strike against her case she wasn't prepared to deal with. She'd never intended for her pregnancy to be revealed so painfully.

Kristy had begged her to come to the diner when Jo had called, telling her of Ray's health issue and the resulting fallout. The diversion had been tempting, but the thought of missing Hawk, should he come by, was unthinkable. Jo's sanity was hanging by a very slender thread, and until she was able to speak to Hawk, to try to make him understand, she feared her tenuous grip just might snap.

Jo was in the kitchen trying to force herself to eat something when a knock sounded at the front door. Her heart raced as she approached the living room, her mind a jumble of all the things she wanted to say to Hawk. She drew the door open in anticipation—

And froze.

"Hello, Josie."

She took a step back, her hand resting over her heart. "Thomas. What are you doing here?"

"Aren't you going to invite me in?" he asked and glanced over his shoulder.

Jo peered around him to the familiar Town Car parked next to her Cadillac, the hat of the driver the only thing she could discern through the tinted window. She looked back at him and stepped aside, gesturing inside the house. Thomas smiled and entered, the bite of his aftershave wafting past her, churning unpleasant memories.

When she had closed the door and turned to face him, she was grateful she had chosen the full blouse she was wearing. His eyes swept the length of her, skimming past her torso and settling on her face. He smiled. "Wow," he said, gesturing to her. "You look amazing."

She ran a hand through her hair, shaking the mass of blonde waves. "Georgia must agree with me, I guess."

"I guess so," he said. "Can we sit?"

She looked to the sofa and back to him. "Care to tell me what you want first?"

He raised an eyebrow. "I would think that would be obvious by this point, Josie."

She crossed her arms over her chest. "Yes, quite. Perhaps a better question is *why* do you want me back?"

The corners of his lips quirked and she narrowed her eyes at him. "Can't we please sit?" he asked again.

"Fine." She walked to a side chair and pointed to the sofa. "Sit."

She watched as he walked toward her, the image something she had seen every day of her life for years. He appeared exactly the same now. His blond hair was cropped short, his eyes she had once thought were a pretty topaz color, but were actually just plain brown, had tiny creases in the corners from too many years in the Arizona sun. His suit was immaculate, his shoes an expensive Italian leather.

He unbuttoned his suit jacket and sat, edging as close to her chair as the sofa would allow. "Why do I want you back? I would think that would be obvious as well." He reached for her hand but she drew it farther into her lap. He shook his head slightly before settling his attention on her face. "I made a terrible mistake. First by my unfortunate transgression, and then by letting you go."

She tilted her head, resting her chin in her hand. "And which was the worst of the two? For you, I mean."

He looked at her for a long moment. "The latter, obviously. Losing you was the most difficult part for me. I just live with guilt on the first count."

"Mmm-hmm." She kneaded a muscle in her shoulder. "And tell me, Thomas. Just how important did your campaign manager tell you it was to get me back?"

He twined his fingers together and rested them on his knee. "Honestly, Josephine. I have no idea what you're talking about. This is about me and you."

Her sarcastic laugh cut through the room. "Man, I must have been more of a doormat during our marriage than even I realized. Just how gullible do you think I am?"

"I'm afraid I still don't follow."

"Fine then," she said, rising from the chair and looking down at him. "I'll spell it out for you." She began to pace. "Let's begin with your reasons for marrying me in the first place, why don't we?"

"Josie, really…"

She silenced him with a glare. "Humor me."

He sat back in the cushions and waved her on.

"Thank you," she said. "I was quite the catch, no? Or at least my father was. The perfect match for a man with aspirations to be a senator."

He opened his mouth to speak but she stopped him with a raise of her hand.

"Now, let's flash forward a few years. Said man becomes a senator, with the help of his wife's well-respected district attorney father, of course, but finds his personal life lacking. This wife of his, he doesn't really want *her*, only what she can afford him."

Thomas set his lips in a firm line, his arms crossing over his chest.

Jo stopped in front of him. "You following so far?"

"Jo—"

"Let's move on, shall we? So, this senator decides to, um, participate in some social activities that go completely against all the conservative values of the people who put him into office." Jo put her hands on her hips. "Now, his wife finds out, but is so desperate to rid herself of him she disappears, taking the secret of his infidelity with her rather than be tied to him for one moment longer."

Jo returned to her chair and sat. "Here's a question for you, Thomas. What do you suppose happens to this senator when he has to run again for his seat? Only this time, he doesn't have his naïve wife there to project everything his past supporters demand in their candidate."

Thomas rubbed his temple and glared at her.

Jo sat on the edge of her chair, leaning toward him. "Just how desperate do you think he would be to get his wife back?"

"You've got it all figured out, don't you?" His voice was laced with sarcasm.

A smile spread across her lips. "I believe I do." She sat back in the chair. "But I really can't fault you for thinking your strategy would work. The woman who used to be your wife would have fallen for it." She shook her head. "No, not fallen for it. Tolerated it, because she didn't think she deserved any better."

She thought of Hawk, and all the things he'd taught her about herself, about strengths she hadn't known she possessed. As she looked at her ex-husband, she realized the woman who had been kicked to the curb no longer existed. Coming to Georgia had changed her life, and because of the love Hawk had given her, *she* was changed. She'd never go back to who she'd been. No matter what happened.

"All right, Josephine." He drew out her name. "Let me pose a question for *you*." He steepled his fingers. "How much do you suppose it would cost this senator to purchase a lie? To create a falsehood to help win him his seat, and protect the reputations of many who helped him earn said seat in the first place?"

Jo rose from her chair. "I'm afraid you've made a wasted trip. I'm not for sale, Thomas."

"Don't be so hasty." He stood slowly, leveling his gaze on hers. "You need only name a price, Jo. How much do you think an illusion is worth?"

She pulled her shirt tightly against her abdomen, molding the fabric around her protruding belly. "Somehow, I don't think this would fit into your plans very well."

Thomas glanced down and then looked back at her, his

brow furrowed. "Are you married to the father?"

"No," she said. She'd seen him work out a quandary too many times to count to miss the fact he was rolling solutions around in his brain.

He pushed his shoulders back, hands resting on his hips. "We could say the baby is mine. That we've been working on reconciling. A child would definitely sway the voters."

Jo's mouth fell open. This was too much, even for him. She walked to the door and yanked it open. "Get out, Thomas. We've finished our conversation."

He stared at her for a long moment before walking past her out the door. He turned slowly. "I hope you don't regret this, Josephine. Time is a small price to pay for the better good."

"I already did twelve years' time for 'the better good'. You used me to get where you are. Now it's your responsibility if you want to stay there." She leaned against the doorjamb. "I won't be hearing from you again, I trust."

"No," he replied curtly and walked to his car. "I'll send your regards to your father, since you won't be returning as expected," he called out to her before disappearing behind the tinted glass in the back of the limousine. Jo watched as his driver turned the car around and drove out of sight.

She would deal with her father in time. She knew he truly loved her, and despite his desperate attempts to sway her, he would eventually understand that nothing is worth the cost of happiness. Not a political reputation, and certainly not her. And that was the truth. There was another male who needed to be told the truth, and that took precedence over all else.

Jo glanced over the tree line to Hawk's. She'd give him until tomorrow to contact her and then she would go and find him. And he would listen to her. She wouldn't accept anything less.

* * * * *

"All I'm saying is that you shouldn't be too hasty to judge."

Hawk drew a deep breath, reminding himself he shouldn't raise his voice to his father while Ray was in this condition. But damn, it took every ounce of strength he had. Even the calming presence of his mother wasn't helping.

"Let me get this straight, Pops. My fiancée thinks she's losing my baby, lies to me, convinces *you* to lie to me, and I should be fine and dandy with it all because it was for my own good."

"Not just your own good, son. But for me and Ryder and the countless children we'll be able to help." Raven took Hawk's hand and pulled him to sit in the chair next to hers.

He stared at her, saucer-eyed. "You too? You think this is acceptable? To keep something like this from me?"

"I know this has hurt you," Raven said, squaring her shoulders as she faced him in her seat. "And you have every right to be hurt. But this was not something Jo did without reason. Without a very good reason."

"But she—"

"Let me finish, Silent Hawk."

Ray's attention shot to Hawk's face, as he, like Hawk, knew that tone. Feeling like a petulant child, he kept the rest of his sentence to himself. "Sorry, Mom. Go ahead."

"Jo is the one. You know it. I know it. Hell, nature knows it. And because of that, you don't have the liberty to be careless, or to get so wrapped up in your own pain to not consider there is a possibility you aren't seeing the entire picture. She's not some girl you picked up in a bar, Hawk. She's destined for you. That's not something you fuck around with."

The color rose on Raven's cheeks and Hawk tried his best not to smile at his mother's use of the word fuck. Not once had it ever crossed her lips before. At least not that he was aware of.

Hawk drew a deep breath. "But it wasn't her decision to make. Why does she get to decide what's right for me? For my life?"

"And you think the decision is yours and yours alone?" Raven shook her head. "Hawk, you lost that right the minute you gave your heart to her. The moment you stopped fighting all I've taught you. Now, you may not like her method, but her intention came from love. And I cannot even imagine the pain it caused her to let someone she loves go, in the hopes that love would come back to her."

Hawk ran a hand down his face. "But if I had known, we could have worked something out. It just seems cruel to let me think I'd lost my child. To suffer that loss."

"Jo left that hospital assuming she'd miscarry," Ray said. "I was with her, remember? That much blood, it was just…" He shook his head. "She thought what any woman would think and prepared for the worst. But since they detected a heartbeat, she went home, expecting to have to come back for a D&C."

"Again," Hawk nearly bit out, "something I should have known."

"And what would you have done, had she told you?" Ray asked.

What kind of dumbass question was that? "I would have stayed with her, obviously. Supported her."

Raven's hand was warm on his arm. "And what of Thunder? And the ranch?"

"Mom, how could you ask that?"

She gave him a gentle smile. "I'm not asking for the reason you think. I would never put our ranch, no matter how important it is to us, above my child and the woman he loves. I'm asking you to think of it as Jo would. What of Thunder and the ranch?"

His mind spun about and a sick feeling seeped through his chest. "A delay in the opening. A strong possibility Thunder wouldn't be a viable stud next season." He pinched the bridge of his nose. "Fundraising that could take years to produce what Thunder could in a month."

"That's right," his mom said. "And if you were Jo, and you had the ability to make a very stubborn man do what needs to be done not only for the good of that man, whom she loves, and his mother, but for sick children, would you do something?"

Love. Jo had never said she loved him. But if what his parents said was true, perhaps her actions spoke louder than any word ever could.

"And furthermore," his mother continued. "Could you live with yourself if you were Jo, knowing that, even if not intentionally, you were responsible for what could potentially be the downfall of someone else's dream?"

Well…shit.

The steady beeping of the heart monitor accelerated slightly and Hawk turned to his father to find tears in his eyes. "Silent Hawk, don't make the same mistake I did. Don't let anything get in the way of a good woman. And despite everything, Jo's a good woman."

* * * * *

The rest of the day stretched on endlessly with no word from Hawk. Jo had been reassured that Ray's condition hadn't declined when she'd phoned the nurse's station, and that he was alert and with his family. She tried to take comfort in that one piece of encouraging news.

When the first streaks of pink and orange ignited the sky, Jo settled into the rocker on her front porch with a glass of raspberry lemonade, tipping the chair into motion with her foot. She stared out at the sunset disappearing behind the line of trees in the distance. A fluttering sensation rippled in her abdomen and she jumped in her seat, placing her hand over her belly. She smiled, tracing the area with the tip of her finger.

"You've finally decided to let me feel you, huh?" Jo was certain her baby understood every word she said.

"She must sense I'm nearby."

Jo nearly dropped the lemonade when she heard his voice. She placed it on the table with trembling hands and stood from her chair. Hawk was leaning against the porch rail, watching her.

"Where'd you come from?" she asked.

He motioned toward his house. "Home. I just got back a little while ago. I wanted to walk; it's such a nice night."

She nodded and glanced around the porch, her stomach turning summersaults. "How's Ray?" she asked.

"As opinionated as ever." Hawk's dimple appeared by the side of his mouth. "He's sitting up in bed and complaining as much as possible. My mother's a saint."

She gave him a small smile and her pulse thundered in her veins when he approached her. "S-so, she's staying with him then?"

Hawk stopped in front of Jo, his eyes intense as he stared down at her. "She won't leave his side. It's sweet, actually." He reached out slowly and traced his finger over her cheekbone. "I've missed you, Josephine." He lowered his head, his lips brushing hers in a soft caress.

"Hawk—"

He shook his head and drew her closer. "Kiss me, Jo," he whispered.

She melted into the embrace, the kiss she'd dreamed of since she'd sent him away with a lie consuming her. Her lips parted under his, her arms wrapping around his neck. His mouth's possession of hers became desperate, his hands weaving into her hair to hold her against him. He kissed her deeply, murmuring her name with each breath he took.

His lips gentled and he drew back. "Can we go inside and talk?"

She nodded and reached for his hand, walking inside. He led her to the sofa and sat, pulling her down beside him. "I hurt you yesterday," he said, his eyes full of remorse. "I'm so sorry." He leaned his forehead against hers. "I didn't know."

"What didn't you know?" she whispered, running the tips of her fingers down his cheek.

Hawk pulled back, taking her hands in his. "I didn't know you love me. And I certainly didn't know how much."

Jo's heart swelled. "Ray talked to you."

"Ray. My mom." He laughed. "They tag-teamed me with a pretty solid argument."

"That was…"

He stroked the back of her hand with his thumb. "That what we have is too important to walk away from. That what you did, however painful, was done out of love."

"I do love you, Hawk. Enough to risk everything."

He brought their joined hands to his lips and kissed the backs of her fingers. "I know." He drew a deep breath. "I wish I'd had the opportunity to help make the decision, but I know what my parents claim my reaction would've been is, in fact, true."

"That you would have sacrificed everything to stay here with me?" She brushed his hair off his forehead.

He nodded. "So you made the sacrifice instead."

"I never saw it that way. I had faith that the part of you that would have abandoned what was so important to you, to Raven, to stay here with me would be the part that would understand why I did it." She framed his face in her hands. "Will you forgive me, Hawk? For making this decision?"

He pulled her into his arms. "I'll never forget what you did for me, for my family. Never." He trailed kisses across her cheek to the corner of her lips. "Say you'll spend your life with me, Jo. Be my wife."

She looked at him, tears blurring her vision. "Yes."

Hawk withdrew her ring from his pocket and slid it on her finger. "I love you, Josephine."

"I love you," she said, easing into the cushions as Hawk leaned over her, his hand splayed across her abdomen. He lowered his head, brushing his lips against hers. He edged even closer, his mouth moving across her jaw to settle near her ear.

"I've missed this," he whispered as his arm slipped around her back, pulling her flush against his torso. "The taste of you against my lips, your body beneath my hands." He cupped her breast as he trailed kisses down her neck.

She ran her hands into his hair, dragging his mouth back to hers. She sought his tongue with her own, moaning through their kiss as he began to undress her. She tugged at his clothing, sighing with pleasure when he settled the long length of his naked body over hers, skin warm as he nestled his cock between her thighs.

He stared down at her as he thrust gently. "Is this okay with the baby?"

"Yes." She ran her nails down his back and smiled when he groaned. "The doctor has given me the all-clear for any activity a normal pregnant woman can do. So, full steam ahead."

He grinned as he rolled onto his back, positioning her to straddle his lap. With a firm grip on her hips, he lowered her heated passage onto his erection. She rode him, relishing the angle and friction this position created. She placed his hands over her sensitive breasts and held them there as she moved her hips, moaning when his pelvis rose to meet each movement she made.

Before long the first waves of orgasm built and with one hard thrust, she was there. Hawk soon followed, grabbing her hips to hold her stationary as his cock pulsed inside her. She collapsed on his chest, both their breaths coming in pants. She lifted her head and pressed a kiss to his mouth.

"Jo," he murmured against her lips, sliding his hands down her back.

"Yes?"

He looked into her eyes. "Thank you."

"For what?" she whispered.

He sat up, settling her in his lap and cradling her face in his palm. "For knowing what I need and making sure I got it, no matter what the cost."

"I'm just intuitive that way." She sent him a knowing look.

His smile lit up her heart. "I guess you are, baby. I guess you are."

EPILOGUE

The sun was just about to set across the Catalina Mountains, casting a pink glow against the surface of the stone. It was the perfect evening for a wedding. The fall temperatures enabled the men in the wedding party to don their jackets without suffering a heat stroke, and the women would make it through the ceremony without wilting hair and makeup.

As the music started, Jo glanced down the aisle at the groom, standing tall, proud and handsome. His suit fit him like a glove, and even from this distance she could see his sparkling blue eyes. He smiled at her and winked. Her bouquet of lilies shifted slightly as the treasure she carried in her womb gave her abdomen a sound kick, as though her hands resting there were a nuisance. She smiled, glancing down at her bulging belly.

Jo saw trouble out of the corner of her eye, gobs of rose petals being dropped in the grass behind the white aisle runner. She grabbed the tiny hand, guiding the unpracticed flower girl back to her designated place.

"No, no, Spirited Rayne. If you drop all the pretty flowers now, there won't be any for the bride to walk over, will there?"

Her cherubic lips pursed into an adorable pout, her black ringlets swaying with the shake of her head. Suddenly her face lit up like Christmas and she jumped up and down, pointing toward the gazebo. "Daddy!"

Jo glanced down the aisle at her husband as he joined his

father. He stood next to Ray, his hands clasped casually in front of him.

"I love you," Hawk mouthed, locking his eyes with Jo's. He lowered his gaze to their daughter, who was tugging at Jo's hand, trying to get to her daddy. "You too," he mouthed to Rayne, winking at her.

They got the go-ahead from the wedding coordinator and began their walk down the aisle, Rayne throwing petals with wild abandon. Taking their place to the right of the minister they turned...watching Raven walk down the aisle on the arm of her brother toward the man she'd never stopped loving.

Thank you for reading Thunderstruck.

This book had many different elements that required research, and I enjoyed every minute of it. Especially the trip to Paris, Kentucky, where I got an in-depth look at the day-to-day operations of horse breeding. The characters came to me soon after with their complicated relationship. I hope you enjoyed their love story, and that Ray was good for a laugh or two. If so, I would greatly appreciate your help in spreading the word, either to friends or by leaving a review or rating at your favorite online book retailer. I appreciate you taking the time to read my work, and hope I can entertain you again in the future.

On the following pages, please enjoy an excerpt of **Charlie Sierra Tango.**

Charlie Sierra Tango

Merilee Diego is desperate. With only days left to save her late father's charter company, she must seek aid from the one man who can help her. A man her father treated like a son. A man whose raw sex appeal never fails to send her pulse racing. Too bad he seems to hate her.

Lawson Manning isn't pleased to discover his final charter before branching out on his own is none other than his mentor's spoiled daughter. He's nothing if not professional, and decides to grin and bear it until he can rid himself of her in the Bahamas. His plan is thwarted when storms create an unwelcome detour to the hurricane-ravaged island of Walker's Cay.

Isolated, with only their tempers and simmering attraction between them, the two do their best not to kill each other. It isn't long before they discover a more creative, and hotter, outlet for their anger. But this detour creates a complication neither is prepared for.

CHAPTER ONE

"This will be our last time together."

Lawson Manning ran his hand lovingly along her smooth lines as he completed the last of his flight check. The Cessna 210 gleamed in the early-afternoon sun. She was still shiny and new, with less than a thousand hours on her. But she wasn't his.

Not that he was complaining. He'd scrimped and saved for three years to buy his baby, his escape from this hellhole job and its asshole boss.

Diego Charters had once been a blessing for a man whose aspirations of becoming a fighter pilot had been shattered by a damn eye exam—and the discovery that his particular issue couldn't be corrected with surgery. Amazing how much power the letter *S* could have when it was mistakenly identified as a *Z*. And not being able to see targets clearly was a problem for the United States Marine Corps, but not so much for shuttling clients to and from business meetings and to their sunny Florida and Caribbean vacations.

But what had been a hell of a Plan B screeched to a halt when John Diego senior passed away suddenly from a heart attack and his dickwad son took the helm. John junior expected his employees to jump at the word go, probably from lack of any other sort of management skill. And they did. Lawson included, until he'd saved enough to buy his Piper Cherokee 6 and get the fuck out of there. He was nearly thirty. Not too late for his life to really get started.

He'd agreed to this last charter because John was in a bind. And if the truth be told, he wanted one last ride with the lady. He'd flown her maiden trip, after all, and he wasn't one to leave a ladybird without a proper goodbye. Lawson smirked. He'd stuck it to the man too, demanding twice his normal pay to take this charter to Treasure Cay.

Lawson was just putting the stepladder he'd used to check the fuel into the cargo hold when he heard a vehicle pull onto the tarmac. He closed the door, engaged the lock and turned. A limo. He heaved a weighted sigh.

Just one more and then I run my own show.

The driver opened the rear passenger door and one long, tanned leg followed by the other unfolded from the interior. His gaze traveled up in appreciation as his client emerged from the vehicle. Her mahogany hair whipped across her face in the wind and she slid her sunglasses atop her head, pinning the hair back.

Lawson sucked in a breath.

"Oh hell to the no."

Merilee Diego's vision was perfect, and she could see Lawson's scowl from thirty yards away. He could frown all he wanted. She wasn't happy about this trip either. But from the look on his face, clearly her brother had failed to mention she'd be Lawson's last charter. That was *so* a John thing to do. She was convinced he had the devil in him—fucking around with people for his own asinine amusement. Her fingers tightened around the leather handles of her bag. She jumped when the limo's trunk slammed, and turned to face the driver.

"Shall I take this to the plane for you, Miss Diego?"

"Yes, Charles. Thank you."

He gave her a nod and a smile and rolled her Louis Vuitton toward the Cessna. She reluctantly followed, second-guessing herself. Perhaps there was another way to gain the information she needed besides putting herself at the mercy of a man who clearly didn't care for her. What in the hell she'd done to him, she had no idea, but it was what it was. She shook her head.

Lawson Manning was the only person she could turn to.

She watched as he crossed his arms over his chest and planted his feet in a defensive stance. *Fantastic.*

She trailed behind Charles, feeling the heat of Lawson's glare intensify the closer she got. He'd given her looks of distaste before, but not like the one he was laying on her now. If her father hadn't thought so highly of him, she would have likened him to an animal and been done with it. But Daddy seemed to have loved him like a son, and his name had been spoken of reverently in their home. *Lawson did this. Lawson said that.* It irked the hell out of her brother. If she were a betting woman, she'd go all in that her father had secretly wished his own son were more like Lawson.

She rolled her eyes. Her brother was an ass, but at least he didn't look at her like a piece of gum he'd just stepped in. When she got within spitting distance of Lawson and the ice-blue of his gaze pierced her, she began to regret her plan. It was too late now though.

"Merilee," he drawled in that thick South Georgia accent she'd deny to her grave that she loved. Even laced with irritation it sounded appealing, wrapping around her like a warm blanket out of the dryer.

"Lawson."

"Would have been nice if John had mentioned this was your charter." His voice dripped with sarcasm.

4

"Wouldn't it just?" She dug in her purse for her wallet as Charles strolled toward her, either oblivious to the tension or outright ignoring it. She couldn't blame him for the latter. She extracted a twenty and pressed it into Charles' palm. "Thank you for the ride."

"My pleasure." He tipped his hat at her and walked toward the limo. She let her gaze follow him, anything to delay what she was sure would be the longest four hours of her life. When the limo door closed and the vehicle pulled up to the exit gate, she reluctantly turned toward Lawson.

He was within inches of her, and she sucked in a sharp breath.

"What're you about, Merilee? I'm sure this isn't a coincidence. From the way John was going on, I thought he had his balls to the wall over a demanding client. That you, princess?"

She straightened her shoulders and tilted her chin. "I requested you, yes."

"Well..." He drew the syllable out until it was almost two words. "Aren't I the lucky one?" He pulled his aviators out of his pocket and settled them on the bridge of his nose. His dark-blond hair was disheveled from the wind, sticking up in delicious disarray. Why was it the assholes were the ones who were always so good-looking? He stalked to her suitcase and withdrew a set of keys from his pocket. He unlocked the cargo door and tossed her bag none too gently inside. "This it, or is another limo coming along with the rest? Perhaps we should phone John and see if one of the larger planes is available."

The corner of her lip twitched at his juvenile behavior. If this was how he wanted to play it, fine. When he was trapped in the air with her, he'd have no choice but to listen. She made a show of studying her nails. "I may not be a pilot, Lawson, but my father *did* own this company. I know a thing or two about airplanes. I think you'll find the weight of my suitcase is within

5

the safety guidelines for this Cessna." She pulled her sunglasses from her hair and put them on. "Of course, you would have had to have bothered weighing it to know that." She clicked her tongue. "How careless of you."

She turned her back with that remark and walked around the front of the plane to the passenger door. She bit back a smile. She really shouldn't goad him. She needed him, after all. But he had that smug, superior thing going on and she couldn't help herself. There had been a time when she'd thought Lawson had hung the moon, had literally pined over him, but those days were gone.

Merilee opened the door and carefully planted her stiletto on the narrow step above the landing gear wheel and hauled herself into the plane as gracefully as she could. Not that it mattered, as Lawson was now avoiding looking at her altogether. She pulled the door closed and pressed the lever to lock it.

The pilot's door opened and Lawson climbed into the plane, closing the door a little more firmly than necessary and jamming the lever into place. He pulled out his clipboard from the side of the seat. "So, to what do I owe this esteemed honor?"

No way in hell she was telling him now. He'd have her back on the tarmac with her suitcase in a skinny minute if she revealed her true purpose. "Just a vacation in Treasure Cay, Lawson. Not unlike your many other charters."

He snorted. "Visiting the flavor of the month I take it?"

She turned in her seat to look at him. A muscle ticked in his jaw as he adjusted the wing flaps for takeoff. He didn't seem to care that she hadn't answered him as he opened the window and yelled, "Clear." He started the propeller and the plane began to shake, the noise near-deafening in the small space.

Lawson already had on his earphones and pointed to hers.

Once she had them in place, she heard his mocking voice. "Seems if you knew a thing or two about planes you would have put those on already."

She adjusted the mic and ignored him until he drawled in her ear once more. "So, am I right?"

She let out a long sigh. "About what, Lawson?"

"You headed down to see whatever man you've roped into providing you a distraction? From what, I'm not sure."

And there it was. She always suspected Lawson thought of her as a daddy's girl with no purpose in life. Dumping her business degree at the University of Georgia and heading to Julliard after her father's death might make her appear selfish. Leaving John in charge was probably looked upon poorly by the employees, but she'd only been nineteen, damn it. She rubbed her temple. "If you must know, I'm visiting my friend Elizabeth. Her parents own a home on the island."

"Of course." Lawson continued his preflight checks while she stewed over his reaction to her. It really shouldn't matter what he thought, but it did. That need for approval wouldn't be an ally for her when she talked to him about her concerns. She must remember that technically she was the one in charge. He was her employee, for now, and if her plan was successful it would stay that way, and she needed information he could provide. All this other nonsense didn't matter. "Law—"

"Peachtree clearance November 2-4 Charlie Sierra Tango has romeo information. We're IFR ready to copy."

She knew enough to keep her mouth closed from here on out. She could only imagine what Lawson's reaction would be if he had to radio back in if he missed something because she was jabbering. She listened as their clearance was read back and watched as Lawson wrote down every detail in surprisingly neat handwriting.

He tapped the pencil's eraser against the clipboard and continued ignoring her. "Ground, November 2-4 Charlie Sierra

Tango is at Epp's Aviation, ready for taxi."

"Charlie Sierra Tango taxi to runway 2-0 right."

Lawson eased the plane onto the runway and pulled to the side to do his run-up. She'd watched her father do this countless times. Everything was so methodical, a synchronized system that was followed to the letter every time. Lawson pushed in the throttle and the plane shook with the effort. She eyed the gauge as the RPMs rose. He turned the yoke, looking out each window at the rudder. He continued on in his process and she could almost hear him ticking off items in his head.

He finally turned to her. So he hadn't forgotten she existed. "You ready?"

"As I'll ever be." She checked her seat belt and fisted her hands, tucking them under her thighs. She didn't like takeoff. Her knowledge of planes made her aware this was the most dangerous part of the flight. If he noticed her discomfort, he didn't say anything. Not that she expected him to.

For someone who acted so ballsy, Merilee seemed nervous. Whether it was from his uncalled-for behavior or the flight, he wasn't sure. John senior never mentioned his daughter being afraid to fly, so it must be the former. He'd try not to feel like an ass about it. He had his reasons for judging her as he did.

All her father had wanted was for his children to follow in his footsteps, to continue the business he'd built from his own sweat and tears. He'd given them everything and asked for very little in return. John Diego senior was the finest man he'd ever met. Hell, he was more of a father to him than his own waste-of-space alcoholic old man. That's why Lawson had gone military. It was a fast way out of the hell he was living in. And when his aspirations were shot down, John had been there to give him a chance.

The thought of John's own flesh and blood not respecting

his one wish tore at Lawson's gut. His mentor had worked so hard to build this company for his children's future. But John was gone, his pain-in-the-ass son was in charge and Lawson was carting the princess around. He rubbed his jaw. "Tower, November 2-4 Charlie Sierra Tango finished run-up and we're ready for takeoff."

"Charlie Sierra Tango, stand by for clearance."

He looked at Merilee. Her fists were still under her thighs, her eyes were closed and she was breathing so heavily he could hear it through the headset. He prayed she wasn't a vomiter.

Since she couldn't see him, he took the opportunity to study her profile. She wasn't a spitting image of her father like John junior, so he could only assume her delicate features were a result of the mother who passed on when Merilee was just a young girl. She had high cheekbones and a small, upturned nose. Her father's heritage gave her olive skin and dark hair, but her eyes were sea-glass green, a definite gift from her mother.

He could remember the first time he'd seen them—he'd been in John's office when Merilee had excitedly entered the room, holding a thick envelope from Julliard. Her incredible eyes had sparkled with excitement, but Lawson had sensed distress in John senior. It became clear to him then just how much John longed for his daughter to work by his side.

She'd always been the one her father had faith in, and John had expressed his concerns to Lawson about his son's reckless behavior and apparent lack of direction. Getting John to complete college had been a feat in itself and Lawson knew John senior was counting on his daughter one day taking over. But she'd had other plans. That was clear when she took off like a shot after her father's death.

Did no one appreciate family and understand what loyalty meant? It was Lawson's own loyalty that kept him on with John junior, despite the miserable working conditions. He'd taught John all he knew, made certain the business was stable, and with only a small amount of regret had decided to move on. As much as he admired and loved John Diego senior, he couldn't sacrifice his own future forever. And honestly, it was John's children's responsibility to run Diego Charters. As much as he loathed John junior, he had to give the guy credit for at least realizing that.

Unlike some people…

Lawson jumped when static hissed through his earphones. "Charlie Sierra Tango, you're clear for takeoff runway 2-0 right, heading 1-8-0."

He eased the Cessna onto the active runway, pushed the throttle and started his takeoff run. Within seconds he had the girl airborne.

The minute the wheels left the runway, Merilee's left hand shot out and grabbed his thigh, her knuckles white.

Heat flashed straight to his groin and he inwardly groaned. A touch from the princess and his cock instantly hardened. This was an unpleasant development. All the bickering must have gotten his dick all riled up. Just what he didn't need.

He looked at her and her eyes were still closed, but she now had her bottom lip between her teeth. It was definitely the plane that had her so on edge. *Aw hell.* Even digging in deep for his inner ass wouldn't allow him to ignore this blatant cry for comfort. He placed his hand over hers, enveloping her fingers in his grasp. He gave a little squeeze.

Her head whipped toward him and she settled her gaze on his. She gave him a small smile of thanks before gently pulling her hand free, patting his thigh and twining her fingers together in her lap. His cock hardened all over again.

Aw, double hell

Other Available Books by Kendall Grace

Southern Exposure

Book One in the Southern Heat series

A quick trip to visit her hospitalized mother is lasting longer than Anna expected. About twelve *weeks* longer. It's not that she isn't used to taking care of her mom—Anna took over that job when her father died. But it's a little stressful vying for partnership in her New York law firm from the nowhere town of Liberty, Alabama. Fortunately the neighbor, a hot Southern charmer, is willing to keep her occupied.

Since Trey breached her defenses, he and Anna have been getting to know each other, in every way possible, all the while doing their level best to be discreet in this tiny, old-fashioned town. The woman he's coming to know is a far cry from the uptight lawyer he first met. And he likes the new Anna. A lot.

As her feelings for Trey deepen, Anna is torn between duty and desire. What she wants versus what she thinks she needs. Returning to New York, reverting to the formidable attorney her father molded, is the responsible thing to do.

Too bad that's not the woman Trey fell in love with…

Northern Exposure

Book Two in the Southern Heat series

Roslyn can't get to the nowhere town of Liberty, Alabama, where her good friend Anna lives fast enough. She screwed up big time at her law firm in New York. Disappearing in the Deep South seems like the perfect solution to clear her head and figure out where to go from here. A hot roll in the hay with a smoldering fellow out-of-towner is a welcome distraction. How was she to know he was the local preacher's son? Oops.

Wren has one objective—land the contract that will put him on the map as a business broker. So what if he has to kiss ass and portray himself as the perfect preacher's son to earn the trust of the business owner. He's survived worst in his past. But the temptress who seduces him is exactly who he doesn't need to be seen with if he wants to pull off this charade. Too bad he can't resist her.

Charlie Sierra Tango

Merilee Diego is desperate. With only days left to save her late father's charter company, she must seek aid from the one man who can help her. A man her father treated like a son. A man whose raw sex appeal never fails to send her pulse racing. Too bad he seems to hate her.

Lawson Manning isn't pleased to discover his final charter before branching out on his own is none other than his mentor's spoiled daughter. He's nothing if not professional, and decides to grin and bear it until he can rid himself of her in the Bahamas. His plan is thwarted when storms create an unwelcome detour to the hurricane-ravaged island of Walker's Cay.

Isolated, with only their tempers and simmering attraction between them, the two do their best not to kill each other. It isn't long before they discover a more creative, and hotter, outlet for their anger. But this detour creates a complication neither is prepared for.

Coming Soon

Innocent Exposure

Book Three in the Southern Heat Series

Abigail Dawson was always the perfect preacher's daughter. Pure of heart, body and soul. Until Johnny Williams broke her heart into a million pieces and she retaliated in the most stupid way possible. A mistake she can never take back—or face. Her only saving grace is that no one ever found out.

Johnny screwed up, big time, and lost the woman he loves in the process. Resigned to do anything to get her back, he puts himself front and center in her life. Not difficult to do in the tiny town of Liberty, Alabama. But just when he thinks he's making headway, she pulls back. Way back.

With time Abigail starts to forgive herself—and Johnny—and can see a future between them. But just as she's about to open her heart to him again, her mistake comes back to haunt her. With no place to hide in this little slice of the South, Abigail must own up to her transgression. Or walk away from Johnny forever.

Come Undone

New Adult

My sister became dependent on painkillers after a skiing accident left her leg broken in three places. I didn't understand and, yes, I judged her. After all, we were talking about her will. No one was forcing those pills down her throat. It seemed very cut-and-dried to me back then. But I know differently now.

The first time Stone touched her, Jane finally understood addiction...understood the aching need, the keen want for more...more of his hands...his mouth...his tongue. His complete mastery over her body. She knew the suffocation of crushing anxiety as she waited for her next hit, the flash of terrific pain when it didn't come.

Stone seems unwilling to give Jane what she needs; what she ultimately craves above all else. But addicts can't think beyond the fix. They'll resort to desperate measures to feed their need...even if they lose themselves in the process. Even if they come undone...

Playing for Keeps

New Adult

Pasts are best left behind, hidden deep in your memory—that is where I buried mine. The feel of his hands and mouth on my body, the way I lost myself in his touch. I fought so hard to forget. But just the sight of Christian brought it all back, forcing me to become consumed by him. Again.

Years before I had watched him, craved him—a guitarist in a band riding the wave to stardom—my brother's best friend. On the verge of womanhood, I never dared to reveal how I yearned. Until a cold New Year's Eve when I offered myself as the woman I'd become, bringing to fruition all I'd desired. As that night turned, so did my life. Devastatingly so. I never dreamed I'd become another of his one-night stands.

Can pasts can be exorcised if they come back to haunt you? And when a notorious playboy who broke your heart offers you his…how do you know if he's playing for keeps?

About the Author

Kendall Grace grew up in the Deep South, where she was taught to be all things Southern and proper. She always had a love for reading, but her passion for racy romance blossomed when she snuck a copy of *Forever* by Judy Blume past her mother at the bookstore. She's never strayed from that path.

She now resides in a large city in the South with her husband and two kids. When not performing the tasks of a Domestic Goddess and working the day job, she loves to sit down and write about steamy Southern men and the women who get caught up in their sexy drawls and chivalrous ways. She loves to hear from readers, so please visit her at www.authorkendallgrace.com

Visit Kendall's website for a complete booklist and other information:
www.authorkendallgrace.com

Follow Kendall on social media:

www.facebook.com/AuthorKendallGrace
www.twitter.com/writer_kendall

Email Kendall:
kendall@authorkendallgrace.com